LOVE'S WARM EMBRACE

LOVE'S WARM EMBRACE

Best Wishes!

[signature: Nancy Wolfe]

[signature: Mandi Carrigan]

NANCY WOLFE

with MANDI CARRIGAN

TATE PUBLISHING
AND ENTERPRISES, LLC

LOVE'S WARM EMBRACE

Best Wishes!
[signatures: Nancy Wolfe, Mandi Carrigan]

NANCY WOLFE
with MANDI CARRIGAN

TATE PUBLISHING
AND ENTERPRISES, LLC

Published by Tate Publishing & Enterprises, LLC
127 E. Trade Center Terrace | Mustang, Oklahoma 73064 USA
1.888.361.9473 | www.tatepublishing.com

Tate Publishing is committed to excellence in the publishing industry. The company reflects the philosophy established by the founders, based on Psalm 68:11,
"The Lord gave the word and great was the company of those who published it."

Book design copyright © 2013 by Tate Publishing, LLC. All rights reserved.
Cover design by Errol Villamante
Interior design by Honeylette Pino

Published in the United States of America

ISBN: 978-1-62746-874-9
1. Fiction / General
2. Fiction / Romance / General
13.08.14

This book is dedicated to our husbands.

Thank you for all your patience and support while we were working on this book. Without you, we could not have done it. With love!

And a special thanks to Kenny Hooker for helping me make my dream come true, and to Raimie and Tate Publishing for bringing everything to reality.

CHAPTER 1

Kansas, 1853

As I listened to the calming sound of the rain quietly hitting the windowpane, I wondered about my fate. What were those quiet sounding voices saying down in the main hall? I wondered if they were discussing whether or not I could finally be free. I didn't think I could handle this life much longer. My heart was beating so hard that it felt like it would pop out of my chest at any moment.

I remembered an earlier time when life was simple, happy, and loving. There were no worries at all. I was just enjoying life. I remembered the warm sun on my face, the gentle breeze flowing through my hair, and the sounds of nature entertaining my ears. I even went to school, which I loved.

Then my life changed almost in an instant, as I found myself locked up in a small room without even a window to enjoy the sites and sounds of the outdoors. There was no fresh air blowing softly through the open window. I was only allowed out to do some chores or whatever he wanted. By the time I was done with chores, I was too exhausted to worry about not having a window. I wasn't even allowed to go to school, but Kerry went for me; still I wished I could go. Then I thought that someday I would like to marry and have children of my own, yet that too, seems impossible.

I had tried to escape on several occasions only to be found and given a sound beating. *What have I ever done to deserve such misery? Will it ever stop? He has no right to treat me this way.*

"Come here, Cheyenne," he said. "Get my supper on the table. I'm as hungry as a bear." As I hurried to prepare his supper, he yelled again. "Cheyenne get some water on the stove to boil right now so I can soak my feet. Hurry up! Time's a-wasting." It was normal for him to interfere while I was cooking a meal, but still, it got on my nerves. *Oh, I must hurry with supper or the price I pay will be high.*

When supper was finally complete and served on the table, I decided to eat in my room. Once I finished, I would have other chores to do before I could go to sleep.

While his daughter, Kerry, and I cleaned the kitchen after supper, he bellowed out more orders for me to do.

When I finished all he wanted done, I would be locked up in my tiny room hoping he was not getting drunk. He was even meaner when he was drinking. At times, he was more drunk than sober, making my life miserable. Luckily though, he had a wife who would tend to his private needs. I thought I would just die if he made me bathe him like what she had to do.

After being locked up in that tiny room for years, I was moved several days later to a slightly bigger room upstairs. Why, I didn't know. The old worn furniture looked heavenly compared to what I was used to having. The room even had a window! It was a lovely view, and what a beautiful day to see it. I was excited to have such a room. Still, I wished I knew why he moved me upstairs.

When I turned to look at him, he simply said it was because I stopped trying to leave, but warned me what would happen if I ever tried to leave again. This time when he left, my door was not locked behind him. At first I wondered if he was beginning to trust me, or was it more likely that he knew that he was being true to his word and that I knew it too. In fact, I was sure it was the latter.

Quietly, someone knocked at my door, and when I opened it, Kerry was full of smiles. "I have wonderful news! We're going on an outing!" she said. "There's a circus in town and we can all go!"

"Thank you for the invitation, Kerry, but I better stay right here."

"Oh, but you can't! It's a family outing. All of us except Pa are going. You must come," she insisted.

"I know what you're saying, but if I leave this house, especially since he's not going, I could be in serious trouble. No, I'd better stay right here," I said. "You go and have a great time for me."

Kerry looked so disappointed, but she didn't press it any further. Kerry was a spirited young girl, who wore an adorable green dress with a white apron over it. She was very pretty with her blue eyes and blonde hair. She stood a little shorter than me. As she started to leave, she looked over her shoulder and whispered, "I'll bring back something for you."

"Thank you, that's very sweet of you, Kerry."

"You're welcome. See you soon," Kerry said as she slowly shut the door.

About three hours had gone by when suddenly I heard him yell, sounding viciously angry. "This time, Cheyenne, I'm going to knock some sense into you once and for all!"

"Yes, yes, I'm here!" I said, as I came running in as fast as my wobbly legs would take me. What did I do or not do? Then he saw me.

He stopped and turned to look at me with those angry dark eyes, and in a deep voice, he shouted, "Where have you been? I looked everywhere for you! You went with them, didn't you?" Quickly I shook my head, but he did not seem to believe me. "Do you expect me to believe that you never left this house? Well then, where were you?"

"I was in my room most of the time, except when I was doing my chores."

By this time, I was shaking severely as I realized what he meant to do. As I took a step back, he grabbed my arm. "Why not? Why didn't you go with them then?" It was almost as if he were hoping I went.

"Because you said I could not go anywhere." My voice was shaking when I answered.

He looked at me with his dark eyes. Then still holding on to my arm, he whisked me away. Once upstairs, he threw me into my room and slammed the door. I didn't have any idea what he was going to do next. Was he coming back or was he just going to leave me alone? He didn't lock the door behind him, which was a good thing. But I knew I couldn't leave my room until he called me or until it was time to make a meal.

Kerry, her mother, and her three brothers came through the front door about two hours later. All were screaming and laughing for all the fun they had, not realizing that their father was in a frightfully dark mood. They sounded like they had a great time. Still laughing and carrying on, they came up the steps and threw open my door. Needless to say, they startled me to death. They started to tell me all about their day "So she didn't go with you after all?" he asked.

Puzzled, the four siblings all chimed in, "No, no, she didn't come with us."

He glared at me with evil-looking eyes, then turned on his heel and stepped out the door just as quickly as he came in. With great relief, but still slightly trembling, I tried to relax and join in the conversation.

"What was that all about?" Kerry suddenly asked.

"He thought I went with you. He was very angry when he couldn't find me right away," I explained, "I told him I didn't go, but obviously he wasn't sure if I was telling the truth. So I'm very happy I didn't go with you."

"I guess you were right. I'm so sorry, Cheyenne."

"Thank you, Kerry, but don't be sorry, everything's just fine. I guess I better get supper started before he starts yelling again." Kerry nodded and left while the boys and I followed close behind.

While Kerry and I were cleaning up the kitchen mess from supper, he came in, slamming things around as he entered. "Who took my money clip?" he shouted.

His normally dark eyes looked as if they were burning with rage. Angry was certainly putting it mildly. Kerry right away ran as fast as she could out of the room. I, on the other hand, was trapped. I had been putting the clean pans away in the pantry when he came in.

"My children would never touch it, so that just leaves you! You took my money!" he screamed. "You're not supposed to be in my room as it is. Then you make it worse by stealing from me." He came at me as if ready to kill. I backed away, but there was nowhere to go. He grabbed me then and threw me onto the kitchen table with its delicate white table cloth. I knew what was coming, but all I could think about was getting away from this.

This huge person, smelling of tobacco and whiskey, was slightly taller than six feet and built like a lumberjack. I was a petite girl about five feet four inches tall and certainly no match for him. "I didn't touch it, I didn't!" I yelled.

As he swung, all I could do was pray that someday someone would come and get me out of here. He hit me with such force that I jerked.

"Where's my money?" he kept screaming.

"I never touched it! I swear I didn't," I screamed so he could hear me over his own ranting. Unfortunately, that angered him further. He also ignored what I said, as usual.

After what seemed to be an eternity, his wife Janet rushed into the kitchen. She heard him so clearly that she knew what he was yelling about. She was telling him that she was the guilty party. Although she too feared him, she hoped he would calm down when he heard where his money went.

"David," she shouted, "the banker came to the door wanting the payment we owe! Since you were not here, I gave him the payment!"

With hesitation, he stopped beating me to glare at Janet. He calmed a bit then and just scolded her. "Why didn't you tell me when you did it?" He looked back to me, took my hand, and then flew up the stairs. Then he practically threw me into my room just before he slammed the door.

"I must find a way out of here before he kills me. But how can I leave without getting caught?" I whispered as I stood by the window. Putting my head against the cold windowpane with tears in my eyes, all I could do was imagine the ability to freely walk down the road.

It was a miserable night. All I did was toss and turn, unable to get comfortable. Even though the beating did not last as long as usual, it was the hardest I had felt since the last time I attempted to escape. I hurt very much. It seemed that I hurt all over this morning. If I don't get moving soon before the sun would be up delivering a beautifully, colored sky, then I would be late for breakfast. I couldn't be late.

I got up to wash. It was going to be a very hot day today. I could tell already by how hot this room was. After dressing, I sat down for a moment feeling a bit odd. It was as if I knew something was going to happen, but what, I could not guess. *Oh, I'm just being silly.*

I stood and left the room as quietly as I could. When I got to the kitchen, Aunt Janet was already baking biscuits. She was about my height, wearing a white apron over her blue gingham dress, and with her long brown hair pulled up into a bun at the base of her head. She looked so much like my father. It was almost as if he were here. Unfortunately, Aunt Janet seemed to have withdrawn since the death of Uncle Ryan, her first husband.

Uncle Ryan was a real good man, unlike her current husband. Uncle Ryan built this beautiful, grand, two-story house. It was very similar to the one he lived in as a boy back East. It had a kitchen, a sitting room, a library, a dining area downstairs, and four bedrooms upstairs. Soon after Uncle Ryan's death, Aunt Janet married David Finch.

"Good morning, Aunt Janet," I said.

"Well, good morning to you, my dear. How are you this morning?" she replied as she was rolling the dough. But before I could answer, there was a very loud clap of thunder. It startled us. Within minutes everyone in the house was in the kitchen, all talking at once.

"Let's go, boys!" David commanded.

While David and the boys ran out to check on the house and barn, the ladies continued making breakfast. Suddenly the door flew open with David standing in the doorway. "Hurry up! We have a fire to put out!" He said the words so fast that we almost didn't make them out. Kerry and I ran out the door while Aunt Janet grabbed some blankets.

Everyone formed a line starting with me at the pump. After some time at the pump, I could not pump hard and fast enough. David came running with arms raised. Even after he saw I was struggling, he slapped me and pushed me out of the way. I lost my balance and fell. At the same time, he yelled for one of the boys to take over the pump. It didn't matter that I had been at the pump for quite a while.

I got up off the ground and hurried to get in line to pass buckets of water onto the fire. We worked as hard and fast as we could. The fire burned quickly, and the thick smoke made it very hard to breathe.

Aunt Janet's dress caught on fire. If not for the quick thinking of her eldest son Jeff, she would have been burned. She was near the fire throwing pails of water onto it when Jeff looked over at his mother to be sure she was all right. He saw the fire and rushed to throw water on her burning dress, putting the fire out.

We were praying we would put the fire out before it reached the house and barn. Prairie fires were very hard to put out quickly because of how fast they would burn. Sweat poured off of me as I frantically worked. *Will we make it? Will we put the fire out in time?*

CHAPTER 2

S ome time later, the fire was out. We all celebrated then, except for David. It helped that we had a little dirt surrounding most of the property near the house and barn. Evidently, the lightning started the fire. This was not too uncommon here in Kansas, especially when it was too dry. What a morning so far, and it was barely nine o'clock.

We were all tired and dirty with ashes and soot. No doubt, we all needed to bathe. Everyone took turns bathing, starting with the ladies. While I waited for my turn, I washed my hands and face in the kitchen before continuing with breakfast.

David came in the kitchen after washing outside at the table that Aunt Janet had set out for him to clean himself up before coming into the house. He then looked at me and said, "You can wash after breakfast is on the table and not before." I nodded as I continued to fix breakfast. A short time later, Aunt Janet and I had breakfast on the table.

As everyone else ate the biscuits and gravy, fried potatoes, and sausage, I decided to eat later so I could bathe now. I got water from outside at the pump for the tub. I put fresh water on the stove after draining the one that was previously in there. I carried it to the tub and poured it in. Two more pots should do it. After the third pot of water was added, it was warm enough for me to get in.

As I sat back trying to relax, all I could think about was how badly I missed my parents. Why did they have to die? Even to this day, it broke my heart in two just thinking about them and the way they died, especially how badly Papa had suffered before he died. They were such good and loving people. They didn't deserve to die that way. I could almost feel their loving, warm embraces. I missed helping Momma in the kitchen, making biscuits and apple pies. Before bed, Momma used to read to us.

An unexpected, loud voice suddenly brought me out of my thoughts. It was him again, always yelling at me! *Oh, what did I ever do to that man.*

"You better hurry out of that tub or I'm gonna come get you!" David shouted. With shock I quickly washed and got out of the tub. I certainly did not want him coming in here!

As I dressed, I thought I'd better eat something small to tide me over until dinnertime, which wouldn't be too long now. But when I went into the kitchen, David was there waiting for me. "You have chores to do before dinner so you'd better get moving."

"I haven't eaten yet," I said.

You can wait for dinner. Now get moving before I tan your backside!" I turned away, walking out of the kitchen to find out what Aunt Janet needed me to do.

We started making dinner a couple of hours later. Aunt Janet said David wanted biscuits, ham and beans with peaches, so I got to work. Just before I was ready to put dinner on the table, David walked in and said, "Aren't you ready yet? What do I need to do to hurry you along?"

"Nothing, it's ready now," I immediately said as I turned to put the food on the table. He just snarled at me and proceeded to eat his dinner. When everyone was served, I took my plate to my room to finally eat. I was hoping I could rest a little after dinner. But with David home today, that would be out of the question.

The next day, after I finished eating, I went to clean up the breakfast mess. Then I had to go ask David what he wanted me to do now until dinnertime. He was standing at the window when I stepped into the sitting room. He quickly turned to me and yelled, "Get to your room now!"

Just before I turned to go upstairs, I saw out of the window that someone was coming. I wasn't allowed near people, so I was ordered to my room anytime anyone came to visit. Luckily, however, that was rare.

"Get upstairs now, girl, if you know what's good for you." I ran up the stairs.

When I closed the door to my room, I leaned my ear against the door. I heard David loudly welcome a marshal. Then I heard my name mentioned by David again and again. I backed away from the door to sit by the window. It had started to rain heavily now. I wish I could hear better what was going on down there. *They're talking about me, but why* I hoped this wouldn't give David another excuse to hit me.

The rain was now coming down in buckets, sounding angry and at the same time revitalizing, giving me a calm, but exciting feeling. A loud crack of thunder rumbled in the sky nearby causing me to jump. I loved thunderstorms, but not the violent ones. There was a chill in the air now, so I grabbed a blanket off the bed and wrapped it around me.

Without warning, Kerry burst into my room. She was smiling, but with a tearstained face. I was puzzled. She was out of breath when she came up to me, most likely from running up the stairs. "The US marshal is here. He is talking to Pa about you." She managed to say between gulps of air.

"Slow down Kerry. Catch your breath so you can tell me what is going on."

"All right," she said. After a few minutes, she started talking again. "Marshal Hallowell found out how Pa has been treating you, and he said he was here to escort you out of here if you so choose."

We could hear David now arguing with the marshal. My mind was swirling so much that I couldn't think straight. As Kerry talked, I was trying to sort it all out. I then asked, "How? When did this happen? Who told the marshal? Why would he care? No one in town did. Every time I went to town with the family, it seemed like everyone avoided us as much as possible. I wasn't allowed to speak to anyone, and surely David and Aunt Janet wouldn't tell anyone."

Kerry shook her head. "I don't know all the details. I only know that Pa wants you downstairs now." She grabbed my hand and pulled me out the door and down the stairs. David was angry and he glared at me as if to say, "You'd better say the right things."

I looked at the marshal. He was so handsome. He had dark, black hair, and warm, blue eyes. He was over six feet tall, wearing tight fitting blue jeans and a blue western-cut shirt. His shoulders were wide and strong with powerful looking arms, and a slim waist. His smile was so enticing. I had never seen anyone more handsome. I immediately looked down to the floor. I could feel my face turning red.

"I am Marshal Hallowell, ma'am." He began to explain to me the reason for his visit today. I stood in amazement and was speechless.

David interrupted the marshal. "You can't just walk in here and take a member of my family away!"

"I'm afraid you're wrong about that," the marshal said. "She doesn't belong to you, Mr. Finch. After hearing how you have been treating Cheyenne, I did some investigating. You never took legal custody of her. Therefore, she does not belong to you. Cheyenne is free to leave if she so chooses."

When Marshal Hallowell was finished speaking, all eyes were on me. I first looked at Kerry, she was again tearing up. I glanced at the boys who stood quietly. When I looked at Aunt Janet, she smiled giving a slight nod of her head. Then she quickly glanced at her husband, hoping he didn't see. I didn't dare look at David for fear of what he might do. Oh, how badly I wanted out of here, but I was afraid. What if David tried to prevent the marshal from taking me away from here? What if he would follow us and try to take me then? Hopefully the marshal could handle it. If I went with the marshal, I would be free and not be beaten anymore.

Turning back to the marshal, I stepped a little closer to him, and with tears in my eyes and a shaky voice, I said, "Yes. I wish to leave."

David raised his hand as if he were going to backhand me. Immediately Marshal Hallowell was between David and me with his hand on his colt forty-five. The marshal's eyes dared David to try to hit me.

David slowly lowered his hand. "Go ahead and take her! She's useless anyway," he said, and then turned and stormed into the kitchen.

"You're serious about taking me away from here?" I asked the marshal.

"Yes, I'm serious. If you want to go pack we can leave now. I am prepared and will wait for you."

As I went up the stairs, Kerry was right behind me. I grabbed my suitcases and began to pack everything that belonged to me, with Kerry helping. "I will miss you. I'm glad that you're getting away from Pa, but you're my bestfriend, so I will miss you something awful." I held her a moment hoping that she wouldn't cry.

"I will miss everyone except your father.

When I continued packing, I wondered about this man wanting to take me away. I didn't even know him. Since he offered to help me, I figured he had to be better than the man I lived with now. I was excited, anxious, and nervous about leaving. I hoped that David wouldn't do anything foolish. It'd be horrible for me if David managed to keep me here. After the bags were packed, Kerry went to get her brothers, so they could help carry them down, and we could say good-bye.

"Marshal Hallowell, I'm ready to go," I said. Even with all the mixed feelings I had, my safety was the most important consideration for getting away from here as soon as we could.

CHAPTER 3

With everything loaded in the buckboard, we were ready to go. As we left the yard, I looked back to see everyone waving at me. David, however, was just looking out the window, steaming like an iron, I was sure. I hoped he wouldn't follow us to take me back.

As we rode, I started to relax more and more. Thinking of what I was leaving behind made me happy and sad at the same time. Sadly, I would miss everyone there except David. Getting no more beatings thrilled me the most. I took a slow, deep breath, realizing this was truly happening. I wasn't dreaming this time, but I pinched myself, anyway. I was free.

"Are you all right?" Marshal Hallowell asked.

"Oh, yes, I'm just relaxing for the first time in years."

"How long have you lived there?"

"Six years."

"If you don't mind me asking," he said, "What happened to your parents?"

"No not at all. They died in an unusual wagon accident. They were on their way home from town when they saw a rattlesnake on the road. When the snake started to rattle, it spooked the horses. The horses reared before they took off at their fastest speed causing the wagon to tip over, landing on my parents. Momma died right there, but Papa died the next day in town. Dr. Hampton said that Momma broke her neck, and Papa was bleeding inside. There was nothing he could do."

"I'm sorry you have gone through so much."

"Thank you. I also want to thank you for getting me out of there. I was so afraid that David was going to kill me one day," I said.

"It was my pleasure," he replied.

"I'm relieved that it finally stopped raining." I was so caught up with the events that transpired that I didn't even notice it had stopped raining and just in time too. "Oh, I am too. I didn't even notice until you mentioned it." We both laughed. It felt good to laugh, it had been a while.

"So how did you come to find out about me?" I asked.

"Well, I came to town one day about three weeks ago. While I was there, I overheard a conversation between two ladies in the mercantile. So I questioned them about it. After they were finished explaining how Finch treated you, I could only imagine things were much worse for you at home.

"I did some investigating to find out more. I then went to the court house I pulled some strings and got legal custody of you. This was all I needed to help get you away from Finch, legally."

"How? I mean, how did you get custody? David may be my step-uncle, but Janet is my blood aunt," I said.

"I took guardianship of you just yesterday. I had help from some friends I know. It was the only way to get you out of there," he said.

"Why would you do this when you didn't even know me?"

"It's simply because I don't approve of anyone being abused. No one should have to live like that. I was afraid he would take it too far one day. Besides, I knew your father. He was a good man. I met him when I first became a marshal," he said.

"Thank you again," I said quietly.

"You are very welcome."

"Where am I going to live? How will I survive?"

"I am putting you up in the boarding house, don't worry it's paid for," he said, "as for employment. We have a new seamstress in town that needs help. You can work for her if you want. I already spoke to her, and she is willing to hire you."

I was amazed! This man, whom I didn't even know, had done so much for me that I could never repay him. "I don't know what to say, or how I would ever repay you for your kindness."

"No need to worry about that now. You have more than enough to think about right now," he said.

"How long have you been a marshal?" I asked.

"For about seven and a half years."

"Do you enjoy it? Is it dangerous?"

"Yes, I like it, and yes, it is a little dangerous," he said with a chuckle.

"What is El Dorado like? I mean, I was never allowed to speak while in town. So, I don't know anyone. Is it a safe town?"

"Yes, it is a quiet town with very little trouble. For the most part, the people know each other and seem to get along fine. They would help anyone if they could. I can't believe you were not allowed to speak to anyone," he answered. "I don't know why he would even bring you to town."

"I don't have any idea on that one. I did have to help gather our supplies. I hope the people will be nice to me."

"Why on earth would you be worried about how the people will treat you?" he quickly asked.

"David was never afraid to hit me in front of anyone. If I even waved and smiled at someone, I would get hit. He would tell me to mind my own business. If I dropped something, he would hit me. If I wasn't fast enough, he would hit me. So I don't know how they will treat me after everything they saw."

"It wasn't your fault. I'm sure the town's people are smart enough to understand that. You'll be fine, I promise."

CHAPTER 4

As we rode through town, I looked around very closely as I never had been allowed to do before. El Dorado had a mill just inside the town, a blacksmith, two mercantiles, a bank, two hotels, two saloons, two restaurants, a small seamstress shop, the boarding house, and a school house.

We arrived at the boarding house. It looked like a very nice place. It was a huge house actually. It was decorated outside with flower bushes and a tree, with a porch around the house. Marshall Hallowell surprised me when he helped me down from the buckboard. He just looked at me with a smile, and I smiled back. This was a first for me. He was a true gentleman.

Once at the door of the house, a slightly big woman opened the door and invited us in. She had brown hair with a slight bit of gray, put in a bun at the back of her head. She had brown eyes and a nice smile. "Hello," she said, "and welcome, won't you come in. I'm Mrs. Taylor, and you are?"

"Hello," I said in a near whisper, "I am Cheyenne Wayne."

"Cheyenne, I welcome you to my boarding house and hope you enjoy your stay." she said.

"Well, Marshal Hallowell, I arranged everything for you. Your room is upstairs, the second door on the left. Visitors are only allowed in the sitting room and the dining room with notice of a supper guest." I nodded my head and smiled slightly. "It's all right, my dear. You have a safe place to stay and you can stay as long as you need. I am sure you'll be happy here."

I smiled and said, "Thank you."

"While the marshal brings your things inside, I will show you around," Mrs. Taylor said as she turned and walked into a room. I quietly followed her. It was a beautiful room. The flower wallpaper looked quite lovely. "This is the sitting room. It isn't real fancy, but it's comfortable," she said.

"Oh, no, it's beautiful!" I said right away.

"Thank you," Mrs. Taylor said with a smile.

As I looked around, there was a lovely blue settee and two blue armchairs sitting near a huge fireplace that covered one entire wall. There was a small desk in the corner opposite the fireplace. A large piano sat by the windows in the opposite corner of the desk. The sitting room gave me the feeling of being home, like when I was a small child. It is my new home for a while so I could be happy here and feel safe.

We then went across the hall to a large dining room with a huge, dark wood, stained table with ten chairs. It too, had lovely flowered wallpaper. It had a tea cart in one corner and a built-in cabinet on the wall opposite the tea cart. It was a very beautiful room.

"This is our dining area," Mrs. Taylor was saying. "Breakfast is at seven thirty, dinner is at twelve o'clock, and supper will be served at five o'clock every day. Well, let me show you to your room."

We walked upstairs to what will be my room. This room too, is very pretty. A large bed sat between the windows and on either side of it are small matching end tables, a small, marble top table in the far left corner, and a wardrobe with a changing screen in the opposite corner area on my left. There was a fireplace on the wall between an armchair that sat in the corner to my right and the wardrobe opposite the bed. The walls were plain, but the curtains made of a green satin type of material brightened up the room. The green bedspread and pillows matched the curtains too. With the windows open, there was a soft, cool breeze, which made the room smell fresh and clean.

"It's a beautiful room. I've never seen anything like it. It gives me a very homey feeling. Thank you for letting me stay," I told Mrs. Taylor.

"I'm glad you like it, Cheyenne," she replied with a smile. "Well, I will leave you now to settle in. Remember, supper is at five o'clock. After you're settled, you will probably have time for a nap before supper, so feel free to do so. If you need anything, just yell. I will send the marshal up with your things now."

"Thank you."

After a few moments, a knock came at the door. It was the marshal bringing some of my things. "I will bring up the rest now. I will be taking you to supper tonight so be ready to go at five o'clock," he said as a matter of fact.

"That's fine, but you need to tell Mrs. Taylor now so she won't expect me."

"All right, I will do that now," he said, "see you at five."

I began unpacking. I didn't own much, so there wasn't much to put away. As soon as I got some money, I would buy material for dresses and personal things. I sat on the beautiful bed and thought about the day and how exciting it would be to go outside and not be hit. In fact, I would never be hit again.

It was so nice of the marshal to take me to supper, that even though it wasn't proper, I still intended to go. I still couldn't believe how things had changed for me.

Oh, look at the time! I must hurry Marshal Hallowell will be here any minute now. I washed up and put on a clean blue dress and pinned my hair at the sides. "There, I'm ready to go," I said out loud. I was so nervous, I had never been out to eat, and certainly not with a man.

Just as I got to the bottom of the stairs, Marshal Hallowell walked in. He looked at me, smiled and said, "Looks like we have good timing."

I wasn't sure I should go. I had never been out to supper alone with anyone before, especially with a man.

"It's all right. Shall we go?" he asked, and I nodded.

We went to Joann's Restaurant just down the street. It was a nice place, but a little crowded. There were many tables, each decorated with white table cloths and a flower in a small vase. We found a table by the window.

"This is new to me. I've never been to a restaurant."

"It's all right, I will assist you. Look at the menu and pick what you want to eat and drink. I will pay the bill so don't worry about that. That's all there is to it. Just relax, Cheyenne, you will enjoy yourself. The food here is very good and the owner is real nice. You'll like her."

"Oh, thank you," I replied.

Everything looked so good that it was hard to decide which to choose. After several minutes, I finally ordered a pork dinner, and the marshal ordered the steak dinner.

"Have you thought about working in the seamstress shop?" the marshall asked.

"Yes, I think it would be fun."

"Good, we can stop by her shop after we eat to see when you can start."

"All right," I said. I looked around and saw several people looking at us. I then looked at the marshal and asked, "Why are they all looking at us like that?"

"Most likely it's because they're not used to you being out without Finch," the marshal responded. "Don't pay them any mind, they will soon get used to it and go about their business."

"I'm not used to being out of the house without him around either," I replied.

"I suppose you'd better get used to it because you are independent now, and he can't bother you anymore."

I thought about this day, but never believed it would happen. Yet, I was a little afraid still that David may do something. "Are you sure he can't bother me again? What about when he comes to town?"

"Don't worry too much about him. I have already talked to the sheriff. He will be keeping an eye on you while I'm away. He knows I'm your guardian so it would be unwise of David to do anything to you." The marshal reassured me. Our food arrived then, so we ate. We talked a little more and finished our coffee and dessert.

We were on the way back to the boarding house, after leaving the seamstress shop, when the marshal said, "I have to be out of town for a while, but I'll be back as quick as I can. Mrs. Taylor will take good care of you, and of course, so will the sheriff. Since Mrs. Carey wants you to start tomorrow at the shop, you may be too busy to notice that I'm gone."

I looked up at him and smiled. "Thank you for everything you're doing for me. I can't begin to thank you enough. Yes, working with Mrs. Carey will pass the time quickly. She's very nice. I think I'll enjoy it very much. With the pay she gives me, I'll be able to support myself and still buy things I need."

"That's what I'm hoping for," he said with a smile. "Well I'd better get you to the boarding house, it's getting dark and you don't have your shawl with you."

"Oh, I don't have a shawl, never needed one. I wasn't allowed outside very often and when I was, it was for a short time and never alone."

He stopped, turned to look at me and said, "You're not serious?" His voice rose slightly.

"Yes, I'm afraid so." I looked into his eyes, and I can see the anger building in him. He took a few deep breaths, and then it took him only a few minutes to calm down again. Then we continued our walk to the boarding house.

Once there, he reassured me that everything would be fine, and that he would be back as soon as he could. Then suddenly, he leaned down, put his finger under my chin, and looked into my eyes. "Don't worry too much, all right? Everything will be just fine. I doubt Finch will try anything since he'd be interfering with the law. The sheriff will keep a good eye on you. Remember that," he said.

I smiled and nodded. He kissed me on my cheek, then turned and walked away. I stood there stunned for a moment that he kissed my cheek. I then turned and went inside. I went straight upstairs to my room and sat down on the bed. "I never had such a lovely, big room," I whispered.

I was still amazed at the turn of events. Then when he kissed me on the cheek, I was stunned, it was so unexpected. The only male that ever kissed me was my father when I was little. This new way of life was really going to take a lot of getting used to. I was, however, excited about earning my own money. Money to buy what I needed and what I desired.

I had been working for Mrs. Carey for eight days now. It was working out beautifully. Luckily my mother taught me at an early age how to sew. Then of course, Aunt Janet showed me more, so it wasn't hard to learn the different details Mrs. Carey had to show me. I enjoyed it so much that the time just flew by. I did not only enjoy working here, but I also liked having my own money. That was something I never had in all my life. Well, it was four-thirty, time for me to leave, so I got up and said, "Thank you, Mrs. Carey, I'll see you tomorrow."

When I arrived at the boarding house, Mrs. Taylor asked me if I would mind going to the mercantile for her. She needed some butter for supper, so I turned around and went back out the door. I needed to hurry since it was almost suppertime.

After getting the butter, I thanked Mr. Armfeld and left the shop. I was on the way back from the mercantile with the butter when suddenly someone grabbed me putting their hand over my mouth and pulling me behind a saloon.

Once in the back, he turned me around. My eyes widened, and I froze. It was David, and he was starting to backhand me several times. He then turned me around and threw me on the ground, causing the butter to fall to the ground as well. Using his belt, he began beating me. I wanted to scream, but nothing would come out. He was yelling at me saying I had no business leaving, that I belonged to him.

After what seemed like an eternity, he dragged me to his horse in the front of the saloon. He threw me face down over the horse.

Just as he climbed into the saddle, the sheriff saw us and yelled. But David paid no attention. He kicked his horse and rode as fast as he could out of town.

CHAPTER 5

I hurt more than ever before, including my ribs as they were getting beat up traveling on this horse in this position. When I tried to readjust, David would hit me. I guess he thought I was trying to get down off the horse. I wondered very much why this man hated me so much. I never did anything to him. Why did he want me so badly, yet wanted to hurt me every chance he got?

I couldn't keep the tears from falling. I wasn't sure if it was from the physical pain or the emotional. I wish I could stop, however. I didn't want him to see me cry.

About halfway to David's farm, a man on horseback caught up to us. It was the sheriff! Sheriff Mason reached for David's horse's reins and pulled us to a halt and tied them to his horse's saddle. Before David could react, the sheriff already had his gun drawn.

"Finch, put your hands behind your back, or you're a dead man," the sheriff said to David. David snarled, but did as he was told.

The sheriff, still on his horse, tied the rope around David's wrists. As Sheriff Mason slipped off his horse, he grabbed David's left leg. He managed to tie David's legs under his horse's belly. Sheriff Mason also gently helped me off David's horse. It was then he saw what David had done to me. He gently picked me up and put me onto his horse. "Are you all right?" he asked.

"Yes, I'll be fine," I whispered.

Then he climbed onto the saddle. He held me in front of him as he grabbed the reins of both horses, and we headed toward town. I didn't know which was worse, being put on my belly or trying to sit while riding.

The sheriff was a tall man, about as tall as the marshal. He had wide shoulders and a slim waist. He held me with strong, muscular arms. His legs were lean and long. He had black hair and almost black eyes, since they were so dark. I could feel his strong, yet gentle arms around me. He was as handsome as the marshal and was very kind. He was able to save me from a situation that could have cost me my life.

Once in town, we headed straight to the boarding house.

"I need to get you some medical care. Mrs. Taylor can help you until the doctor arrives," he said. I nodded my head and whispered a thank you. "Aw, no need to thank me, little lady. I'm only sorry I couldn't have prevented it. I didn't even know he was in town. Well, you won't have to worry about him hurting you again. He is going to jail for a long time."

"He's really going to jail for a good while?"

"Yes, he is." We were almost to the boarding house when the sheriff said, "By the way, my name is John Mason. Yours is Cheyenne, correct?"

"Yes, that's right."

We finally reached the boarding house. The sheriff got down first, and then put his hands around my waist to help me get down. I could barely walk, so he picked me up and carried me into the house. Mrs. Taylor came out of the dining room. With a shocked look on her face, she asked, "What on earth happened?"

"I need to go get Doctor Comings, and put this animal behind bars. Where is her room?" Sheriff Mason asked Mrs. Taylor after explaining everything.

Mrs. Taylor began to cry. "It's my fault. I never should have sent her to the mercantile. Oh, my, I am so sorry!" she said as she guided him to my room. Mason put me down on the bed and asked Mrs. Taylor to look after me until he came back with the doctor. "Oh, of course, I will!" she exclaimed, still teary-eyed.

The sheriff left, and Mrs. Taylor gathered supplies to tend to my wounds. "I'm not going to help you undress just yet, my dear, not until we are sure you have no broken bones. I wouldn't want to make things worse. How did this happen?" she asked.

"Thank you for your help. I was on my way home with the butter when David grabbed me. He beat me for leaving and tried to ride us out of town. Luckily, the sheriff saw us and he rescued me."

>><<<

Outside, as I climbed into the saddle, Miss Anderson came over to me. "Hello, sheriff," she said.

"Miss Anderson," I said as I touched my hat.

"Is Cheyenne going to be all right?"

"I hope so, I'm sorry, but I must hurry." I tipped my hat.

I turned my horse around and rode over to the doctor's office. I didn't dismount, instead, I just hollered for the doctor. I gave the doctor a brief explanation of what happened when he came out of his office. I then turned the horse and rode to my own office.

After I dismounted, I pulled David off the horse and pushed him inside and into a cell. Locking the door, I said, "You are going away for a long time for this. You are under arrest for kidnapping and attempted murder."

"Attempted murder! I didn't try to kill her. She's my niece and how I choose to discipline her is my business. You can't arrest me for kidnapping my own family!"

"She's not yours, she now belongs to Marshal Hallowell, all legal like," I shouted.

"He's not family! We are her family and all she has left!"

Before David took his next breath, I gritted my teeth and told him, "Shut up or I will string you up myself!" Just as I was locking the second cell door, the deputy walked into the office. I told Deputy Jackson what was going on and then said, "I need to go check on Cheyenne." Deputy Jackson said it was fine and sat behind the desk.

"Keep me posted, will you?" the deputy asked. I agreed and headed back to the boarding house.

>>><<<

Sheriff Mason knocked on the door, and Mrs. Taylor told him to come in.

"How is she?" Mason asked.

"She is badly beaten, but she will recover just fine," Mrs. Taylor said.

Then Doctor Comings said, "She does have a few badly bruised ribs, her backside from top to bottom is a mess. Cuts and welts all over. Luckily nothing is broken. Now keep these bandages on, keep her warm, and give her liquids. I will be back tomorrow. Send someone if you need me sooner." He had also treated my wounds and covered them with bandages.

"What do I owe you, doc?" Sheriff Mason asked.

"Don't worry about it, sheriff," Doctor Comings said. "You can just buy me supper."

Doctor Comings was an older gentleman, maybe in his late fifties to early sixties. He was a little short though, maybe five and a half feet tall. He had a black mustache that hung to his chin. His black hair and eyes were a warm brown. He was not at all thin. He looked like he had a hearty appetite, though he didn't seem heavy. He was wearing a long black coat and pants with a white shirt and a string tie, making him more attractive. He was a kind and gentle man. He probably would make a good husband for a special lady one day. Why he wasn't already married, I couldn't guess.

Mrs. Taylor then chased them both out of the room. "I have to get Cheyenne something to eat and then have her ready for bed," She said. She thanked them both and invited them to supper downstairs. They both accepted and together they went down the stairs to the dining room.

After Mrs. Taylor got them each a plate, she took one up to me. "Here, honey, do you think you can eat something?" she asked.

"I think I can manage. I'm very hungry, thank you very much."

"After you eat, just leave your plate and I'll get it later. Then you should lie down and rest."

The next morning, there was a soft knock at the door. I invited Mrs. Taylor in. "How are you feeling this morning, my dear?" she asked.

"Not too good I'm afraid," I replied.

"I brought you some breakfast, are you up to eating?" she asked as she came closer with the tray.

"Yes, thank you, I'm hungry." I had difficulty sitting up, but I managed with Mrs. Taylor's help. "I'm not used to eating something I didn't cook and in bed no less," I said.

Mrs. Taylor smiled as she replied, "Well then, it should taste extra special, don't you think?" I laughed, although it hurt. I nodded my head and started eating, and Mrs. Taylor stepped out of the room. "I'll be back in a bit."

When I finished eating, I started to get up so I could dress, but it was difficult. I sat there for several minutes when someone knocked at the door. "Come in."

Mrs. Taylor opened the door, and as she entered, she ran to my side saying, "No, no, you mustn't get up! Just lie back down and rest for today. Give yourself time to heal a little before you try to get up." Reluctantly, I did as she said. "You'll have plenty of time to get back to normal. There is nothing pressing for you to do." She fluffed up my pillows as she spoke to make sure I was comfortable.

"I'm supposed to work today."

"I already sent a note to Mrs. Carey explaining why you can't be there," she said.

"Oh, thank you."

Just then, there was some commotion downstairs, and Mrs. Taylor went to see what was going on. She was standing at the top of the stairs.

"What is going on down there?" she asked.

"This man is trying to come up there to see Miss Cheyenne, but I keep telling him he can't go up there," Miss Marcus, another tenant, said.

"I'm Marshal Hallowell and I'm here to see Cheyenne. She is my ward," he told Miss Marcus.

"Just a minute," Miss Marcus insisted. She yelled up the stairs to Mrs. Taylor and told her that it was Marshall Hallowell.

"Send him up. It's all right, Tami." Mrs. Taylor said, so Miss Marcus turned to allow the marshal up.

Miss Marcus, who was also fondly called Tami, was a very nice lady. She was rather tiny though. She may be five feet tall with a small build. She had a tiny waist and short legs. She had large light green eyes and blonde hair, which she wears in a bun on top of her head. She was very lovely indeed.

Mrs. Taylor stopped him at the top of the stairs to let him know what had happened to me. When she finished, the marshal answered, "Yes, I heard, thank you." She then let him in.

"Are you all right, Cheyenne?" he asked with a concerned look. He seemed strange somehow.

"Yes, I'm fine. I will heal," I told him.

The marshal though became a little angry, and at the same time concerned, when he saw me. "Are you sure you're all right?"

"Yes, the doctor said I only have bruised ribs and nothing is broken, what a relief!" He didn't seem to believe that, but he let it go. He told me about his trip, and we talked a little about other things.

"David is in jail, the sheriff told me. How long will he stay there?" I said, looking at him.

"As soon as the circuit judge arrives, there will be a hearing, then most likely he'll be sent to prison, if he ever lives that long." I was surprised by his statement, but didn't reply. He then stood up. "Get some rest, and I'll see you later," he said as he left.

At the end of the day, around suppertime, Marshal Hallowell came by with supper for both of us. The food he brought from the café was excellent. "The circuit judge will be here the day after tomorrow. Are you up for it?" he asked.

Reluctantly and quietly, I said, "Yes, I guess so, or at least I hope so."

"Listen to me, Cheyenne, don't be afraid of him. He can't hurt you again. He will be well-guarded and restrained. He can't get near you. If you get nervous, just look at me or the attorneys and no one else. You'll do just fine."

"All right," I replied with an uncertain smile.

"Okay, it's time for me to go now. You get some rest, and I'll see you tomorrow."

I looked up at him and smiled. "I'll see you tomorrow, and thank you for supper."

On the next day, the hearing took place, and as far as I could tell, it went well. I chose my best blue dress to wear and pulled my hair up on the sides. I wore the only hat I had, it was worn, but it matched the dress well. I was a little nervous when I gave my testimony, but I just told the truth. Not only did they ask me about the night David beat me, but also about the past relationship with David and how he treated me. The bruises still apparent on my face helped, I was sure. After a few more questions, I was finished.

Mrs. Taylor had come, as well as Marshal Hallowell. "I'm so glad it's over." I told them. "I can't believe the judge found him guilty and sentenced him to twenty years in jail. Twenty years, that's a long time."

"Maybe you can relax now knowing he won't be hurting you anymore," Mrs. Taylor said. I just smiled and nodded.

I saw Aunt Janet then, she was expressionless. I went to her and gave her a hug and said, "I'm so sorry."

"It's not your fault, Cheyenne. He never should have tried to kidnap you and beat you again, and so badly too. We'll be fine. The farm is paid in full, so I won't lose my home."

"That's good to hear. How are the kids, especially Kerry?"

"They're fine. They know it's going to be rough without their father, but they will manage, I'm sure."

"I miss Kerry so much, Aunt Janet. I wish she were here right now."

"I know, Cheyenne, she misses you too."

"Would you please give her this note I wrote? It just explains things, and how I'm doing."

"I will," she said. Then we both said good-bye and hugged once more.

After that, Mrs. Taylor and I left. As we walked home together, Marshal Hallowell caught up to us. "Good morning, ladies! You did really well, Cheyenne. How do you feel?"

"Oh, I feel—"

I was interrupted when David yelled, "This isn't over yet missy, you're going to pay for this!" We turned just in time to see the deputy hit him in his middle, telling him to shut his mouth.

Marshal Hallowell put his hand at my waist and turned me around saying, "Don't pay him any mind. He can't hurt you. He's just trying to scare you. He's being escorted by the deputy and two others. He's also shackled. He will be taken to the prison under guard in a few days, so no more worries. Let's get you home, and maybe something to eat too."

"Well, I'd feel better if he would be gone already. But I will try," I said.

A few days later, the marshal and I sat in the sitting room of the boarding house, just talking and enjoying each other's company. It was a very lovely day outside. The sun was shining brightly, birds were singing, and the beautiful, blue sky had very few clouds, making the day warmer. The windows of the sitting room were open, allowing a cool, fresh smelling breeze to enter the room. We could smell the sweet aroma of the lilac bushes, and they were heavenly.

By mid-afternoon, the sky became cloudy, dark clouds followed behind. A storm was brewing. "It looks like it's going to be a bad one," Hallowell said.

Mrs. Taylor came into the sitting room carrying the cups of coffee and mentioned the storm as well, and several minutes later, it hit. The wind blew hard and strong, and the rain came down fast and furious, which was now coming in through the windows. We raced to close them. Just in time too, suddenly it began to hail. The hail balls were large, about the size of a plum pounding on the house quite loudly, making it sound like there were horses running on the roof. The hail crashed into the windows and began breaking them. We could also hear the windows breaking upstairs.

We were worried about what might happen next. With hail as large as this, we would most likely see a twister. There was little doubt what we needed to do. We gathered everyone who was here and went into the hallway, since there were no windows. Without windows, we could avoid being hit by flying glass when they broke. I thought it was real eerie out there. We were not there too long when we heard it. That scary sound made everyone worry. *That roar! A twister! Oh, no, it's a twister!*

More windows started breaking, blowing out everywhere. The front door was ripped from its hinges. There were glass and debris flying everywhere. We huddled more closely to one another. The sound was deafening as it grew stronger, we could hardly hear each other speaking. Miss Marcus started to scream. *Was the house going to fall in on top of us?*

All of sudden a tree blew through the front doorway. All the ladies screamed at the sudden sound and movement of the tree. *Is it going to keep coming toward us?* We moved closer to the kitchen then. The sounds were so loud now that it seemed to be right on top of us; my ears kept popping. The house felt as if it were moving. All we could do is hold on to each other and pray.

CHAPTER 6

After what seemed to have been hours, the horrible roar was finally dying down. "Is it over? I don't seem to hear it anymore, it must be over," I said.

"Is everyone all right?" Marshal Hallowell asked. Everyone said that they were fine. "We need to check to see if it is safe to go outside, so we can check on the town's people and the damage of the house," the marshal said.

We all started to look around the house for damage. All the windows were broken. There was some roof damage, and of course, the front door too where a tree now rested instead. Luckily that seemed to be all that was wrong with the house. As loud as it was, I was surprised there wasn't any more damage. It missed us, but it hit the house two doors down.

The town, on the other hand, had a lot more damage. Trees were down everywhere. Several houses and one of the saloon were completely destroyed. Others had roof damage, broken windows, pieces of wood stuck in walls of houses and shops, and so many things thrown around the town. There were wagons and buckboards that were busted up, and some you could barely tell what they were. The sheriff, marshal, and deputy were going to have their hands full.

A lot of the town's people were out checking on each other and the damage. We helped the injured and the men carried out the dead.

The marshal began running back. "Are you sure everyone is all right? Cheyenne are you all right?" he asked as he touched my arm.

"Yes, we're all okay. How about you? There's blood on your shoulder, let me take a look," Mrs. Taylor said. The marshal and

I just looked at them as Mrs. Taylor looked at the marshal's shoulder. "Yes, you have a large cut on your shoulder. You might want to get to the doctor," she said.

"No, it'll be all right. I have too much to do right now. I'll see him later," the marshal said.

"You better, you don't want to get an infection," Mrs. Taylor told him.

He tipped his hat then, smiled and said, "Ladies." I smiled and waved good-bye as he left to help the town folks.

The whole town, including the women and children, worked together to get the town cleaned up. For the most part, it didn't take too long to fix some things. Rebuilding the houses and the saloon would take longer.

"It could have been worse. So we have a lot to be grateful for," Miss Anderson said.

"Yes, it could have been worse and unfortunately, we lost five people. Although I am saddened by the loss of those people, I'm grateful we didn't lose more," I said.

The marshal checked on me often but couldn't stay long. There was just too much to do. He either came to supper or took me out to eat. Luckily the restaurant wasn't damaged. I had asked him once, "Shouldn't you be doing your job as marshal?"

"I took some time off. I needed a break," he replied. We left it at that.

I was beginning to get used to Marshal Hallowell being around. Every day I relaxed more and more, knowing now that I was safe. I was feeling strange these days, however, feelings I had never known before. I didn't understand or know where it was coming from. Maybe I should ask Mrs. Taylor. I was sure she would know what was wrong. I just hoped it was nothing serious.

Mrs. Taylor was in the sitting room reading when I came in. "Hello, Mrs. Taylor."

She looked up. "Hello, dear. How are you this fine day?"

"I'm all right, I think."

"What do you mean *you think*?" she asked.

"Well, I'm not feeling right. I don't know what's wrong. I'm having strange feelings. I don't know what's causing them, but I hope it's nothing serious."

"What kind of feelings?" Mrs. Taylor was smiling.

"I don't know exactly. I have a giddy feeling, I get chills, and I feel warm at the same time. My heart is thumping quickly and I feel anxious. Oh, I don't know how to describe it. Sometimes I feel nervous, but I don't know why." Mrs. Taylor giggled and suggested we go to my room. As we walked up the stairs, I said, "Please tell me it's not serious."

"It's all right, dear," she said.

Once we reached my room, I closed the door behind us. "Come sit down, dear," Mrs. Taylor said. So I did as she suggested, sitting across from her, with my hands in my lap. "When did you start having these feelings?" she asked.

"Well, I'm not sure exactly. I do, however, notice it more when the marshal is around or if I think about him."

She smiled and said, "Well, dear, it seems that you're having special feelings for our marshal. You care about him deeply."

"Of course, I care about him. We have come to know each other quite well. But what does that have to do with this funny feeling?" I asked with curiosity.

"I do believe, my dear, you are falling in love with Marshal Hallowell," she said.

"I am?" I shook my head. "How do you know?"

With another giggle, she declared, "I had them too for my husband, dear. I still do when I think of him."

Then I giggled. "Oh, my, I'm falling in love? The only people I ever loved were my parents. But I didn't feel this way about them," I said.

"This is a different kind of love. You do feel a warmth come over your heart when you think of him, true?"

"Yes, as a matter of fact." I sure was glad that I was sitting down. If I weren't, I'd probably have ended up on the floor. "What do I do about it?"

"Nothing," she said. "I suggest you wait until you get closer to one another. If he doesn't feel the same, I'd hate to see you get hurt."

I nodded my head and frowned a little. "What if I fall in love with him, but he doesn't fall in love with me?"

"Well, we'll just have to wait and see. Sometimes it takes time, a long time to know you're in love. Take one day at a time. You'll know one way or the other in due time. Maybe sooner than later," she said. Then she hugged me and said she needed to get supper going. I offered my help, but she declined.

"Thank you," I said as she left the room.

"You're welcome, dear."

I leaned back against my pillows, trying to let all of it sink in. *Is this what love feels like? Oh, what if this is true! If it is, I hope he will love me too. Oh, my, that feeling is coming back.* I was feeling a bit anxious, since I was looking forward to seeing him again. *I can't get my hopes up. He may not feel the same way for me as I do him. I must remember what Mrs. Taylor said. I need to go slow, take one day at a time. I don't even know his first name. I guess I should ask him. Well, maybe not. I should wait for him to offer it. It wouldn't be ladylike if I asked him. I will have to wait and see. Well, it's time for supper, I better get down there.*

By the time I got downstairs, Marshal Hallowell came walking in. "Hello, Marshal."

"Hello, Cheyenne how are you this fine evening?" he asked.

"Just fine, thank you. And yourself?" I responded.

"I'm good. Shall we?" He put his arm out for me to take, which I did.

After supper, Marshal Hallowell asked if I would like to take a short walk. I said yes. As we walked, we talked about our day. I told him that Mrs. Carey was expecting a baby. He told me that

Deputy Haskell was getting married next month. There was lots of good news today.

It was wonderful to be walking with him. He was so charming and a real gentleman. I never thought I would be in such good company. I thought it would never be possible. Maybe Mrs. Taylor was right, I was falling in love with him. I loved spending time with him and I thought this was very romantic. I didn't want the night to end.

"Well, here we are back at the boarding house. It's been a very nice evening," Marshal Hallowell said.

"Yes, it's been a lovely evening, thank you," I replied as he leaned down to kiss my cheek. "Good night, Marshal." He said good night and left.

It had been three months since the twister. The town was really on its way to recovery. Roofs and windows had been repaired. The houses and saloon were coming along nicely. The trees had been cleared away and cut up for firewood.

Except for a week when Marshal Hallowell had to be away, we spent every night together. We laughed, talked, walked, and took carriage rides. Our evenings together had been very special to me. My feelings for him were growing. I didn't know whether or not he had feelings for me. He hadn't given me any signs. Mrs. Taylor though thought he must have feelings for me by how much time he had spent with me. Oh, how I hoped she was right.

I had asked Mrs. Taylor what, if anything, I should watch for to see if he liked me more than a friend. She told me, spending every night together was a good start. We both giggled. Also, if he held my hand, if he hugged me, or if he tried to kiss me, that would do for a sign too. So far he hadn't done any of those things, except kiss my cheek. He put his hand on my waist often but I guessed that didn't mean anything. I saw him do that to Mrs. Taylor a few times too.

We went for a buggy ride the other night, and he held my hand to get up or down, but that was expected of any gentleman,

Mrs. Taylor told me. *Well, let's see what tonight brings. He is taking me to supper at the hotel, no less. In fact, he should be arriving soon.*

An hour later, Marshal Hallowell walked into the boarding house. "Hello, Mrs. Taylor, how are you this evening?"

"Oh, just fine, thank you. And you?"

"I'm good, thank you."

At that moment, I came down the stairs. The marshal looked up and said, "Hello, Cheyenne."

"Good evening, marshal," I said.

"Are you ready?" he asked.

"Yes," I replied as I turned to look at Mrs. Taylor, "see you later."

"See you later," she said. At that, the marshal put his hand on the small of my waist and led me out the door.

While we sat in the hotel dining room waiting for our food, we talked as usual, except he seemed a little distant. When I couldn't figure out why, I asked, "What's wrong, Marshal? Is everything all right? You're not ill or anything, are you? Listen to me asking you all these questions, it's just that you seem miles away."

He smiled and said, "Don't you think it's time for you to call me by my first name? We've been seeing each other for a while now. I think it's time."

I was surprised. "I can't, I don't know your first name," I said, and we both laughed then.

"I'm sorry, Cheyenne, I thought I told you. It's Michael," he said.

"Apology accepted, Michael. That's a very nice name."

"Thank you."

"So, Michael, what's wrong?" I asked.

"Well," he began. "I have to leave for a little while again. But I won't be gone as long this time."

"Oh, I will miss you."

"When is your birthday, Cheyenne?"

"My birthday is August tenth," I told him.

"That's a nice month for a birthday, and it's right around the corner."

I giggled and said, "Thank you. Why do you ask?"

"I just wondered what you would like for your birthday."

"Well, I don't know, I haven't given it much thought. I haven't celebrated it in years, and no one has given me anything for my birthday either. It's always been just another day," I replied.

Michael looked very surprised. "You're not serious! Even your aunt wouldn't give you anything, not even a cake?" He couldn't believe it.

"No, David wouldn't let her," I said.

"Well, you will this year," he said. "I will be leaving early tomorrow. I want to get back here quickly,"

"Why is that?" I asked.

"I have some business to attend to."

"Oh, so you will need to go to bed early then."

"Yes."

"That's all right, I understand."

He smiled. "I knew you would. Oh, our supper has arrived. Shall we?"

"Yes," I said, smiling back.

Supper ended all too soon. We decided to sit on the swing on the porch of the boarding house to enjoy the rest of the evening. It was a beautiful evening. The sky was clear, and with the stars and the moon shining so brightly, it gave plenty of light to see. You could still hear dogs barking and howling. Otherwise, it was peaceful.

"Isn't it a lovely evening?" I asked Michael.

"Yes it is," he said.

"I will miss this when the cold weather comes."

He nodded his head in agreement. Then he said, "I will miss you while I'm gone. I want you to take good care of yourself until I get back."

"I will. Do you know how long you will be gone?"

"If all goes well, just a couple of days. I will have Sheriff Mason look in on you while I'm gone," he said.

"Oh, Michael, that's not necessary, I have Mrs. Taylor and Mrs. Carey to keep me company until you get back. And David is in jail, so he's no longer a threat to me."

"No, I insist. I want to know that you're safe, even though I don't think anything will happen," he said. I was a little surprised at his tone, but I agreed.

We talked a little bit longer then said good night. "Now remember, Sheriff Mason will be by to check on you. If you need anything, just ask him. He will be there for you for anything. If you need anything from the mercantile, just put it on my account, understand? I already spoke to Mr. Hansen, and he put you on my account."

"Yes," I said quietly. He then kissed me on the cheek.

"Good night, Cheyenne take care of yourself for me," he said. Then he turned and left.

I stood there for a moment before going in, just watching him walk away. It was puzzling to me that he wanted the sheriff to keep an eye on me so badly. I felt safe here now. With Michael having custody, what could David do about it? Besides, David was in jail so he wouldn't able to harm me again. I wished I knew why Michael was so worried that he needed the sheriff to look after me. I turned and went inside.

CHAPTER 7

I t was about four o'clock when Mrs. Carey decided that we would call it a day. I was just about ready to walk out the door when I heard the door open. I turned to find that it was Michael.

"Michael!" I said with enthusiasm. I was so pleased to see him. I went up to him, and he kissed me on the cheek. Then he leaned down and gave me a hug. I was shocked. I was pleased, of course, but shocked nonetheless. He whispered in my ear that he missed me, and I said the same.

He pushed me away slightly and said, "Are you ready to go?"

"Yes," I said.

"Good, I'm starved. I just got back, cleaned up, and then came straight here."

"Oh, my, well, in that case, let's go to supper."

While we ate, Michael told me a little about his trip. Mostly he wanted to know how things went with me. "You did allow the sheriff to check on you, right?"

"Yes, just like I said I would."

"Good. We are going to have a special supper tomorrow evening, so plan for it."

"All right."

We talked more while we ate.

"Where are you from?" I asked.

"Originally, I lived in Oklahoma territory. My father has a large horse ranch there. Then I went to Texas."

"Really? Why did you go to Texas?"

"I wanted to be a US Marshall, and that is where they wanted me. I go to other states as well, like here in Kansas, but mostly I stay around Texas."

"How long have you been a marshal?"

"I joined when I was eighteen, so that is about seven and a half years now."

"Do you plan on being a marshal forever?"

"Probably not, I would like to have a family one day, and I wouldn't want to be a marshal then. I'd want to be with my family."

"Well, that makes sense. I guess it would be hard having a family while being a marshal who is gone all the time." After a while, I said, "Well, it's getting late." We left to go home.

As I lay in bed that night, I wondered why he said a "special" supper. There was no special occasion that I was aware of. I was getting that giddy feeling again. I must be anxious about tomorrow evening.

Michael was such a wonderful man. He treated me better than anyone ever had. My heart just melted thinking about him. I hoped I wasn't getting my hopes up about him, however. I would hate to have my heart broken. I couldn't let myself get so wrapped up with him, especially if he didn't feel the same. Yet, he did give me a hug today. Mrs. Taylor said to watch out for that kind of thing. Maybe, just maybe, he liked me more than as a ward or a friend.

Still, I was on my own now and I needed to accept that. For the first time in my life, I was the only person I had to listen to. Not getting beat is the best thing out of all of this. I didn't have to live in fear anymore. I couldn't help it, I was so happy that Michael was back. I then went to sleep feeling good about my new life.

I was getting dressed for our special dinner, when Mrs. Taylor came up. "You're looking very nice, my dear. Would you like me to do your hair?" she asked.

"Oh, that would be lovely, thank you." As she worked on my hair, we talked. Earlier today I told her about this special dinner. She was just as curious as I was. "I know I'm anxious about tonight, I'm nervous," I told her.

"I'll bet you are, dear," she said. "I would be too. There, we're all done. You better get finished now he will be here any minute."

"Yes, I will, and thank you."

Not more than five minutes after she left, I was ready. When I came down the stairs, Michael was already waiting for me. "You look beautiful tonight," he said with a grin.

"Why, thank you, kind sir," I giggled.

"Shall we go?"

"Yes, good-bye Mrs. Taylor, and thank you."

The motel dining room was a very elegant room. Beautiful chandeliers hung from the ceiling, which set off romantic candle lighting. There were many tables all decorated with white-laced tablecloths and flower vases in the center. The summer flowers were simply gorgeous too.

As soon as we finished eating our dinner, our cake and coffee came. We were talking, so we didn't notice at first. I was taking two bites of my cake when I bit into something hard. I pulled it out of my mouth, then looked at Michael. He had a big grin on his face. I looked at it again, I couldn't believe my eyes! It was a ring! I looked at Michael with tears in my eyes, and right away he said, "Will you do me the honor of becoming my wife?"

I flew at him almost knocking us to the floor. "Yes, oh, yes!" I said. After he put the ring on my finger, he suggested that we take a walk, leaving our cake and coffee unfinished.

During our walk, Michael told me, "I'm resigning as a marshal. I want to be with my wife and have children. I do, however, want to be a sheriff in another town."

I was speechless. I didn't know that many people here, but I would miss the ones I had come to know. I'd miss working in the seamstress shop as well. "Do you have one in mind?" I finally said.

"Yes, but we could discuss all of this tomorrow. I just wanted you to know I no longer want to be a marshal. Also, I want to wed shortly after your birthday. I know its short notice, but I can't go too long without working."

When we arrived at the boarding house, he said good night and that he would see me tomorrow. He kissed me and said, "I love you". I was breathless when the kiss ended.

"I love you, Michael. This was an amazing evening. I'll see you tomorrow."

"I'll see you tomorrow."

I stood by the door for a minute to catch my breath. I didn't notice Mrs. Taylor until she asked when she saw me, "Are you all right?"

"Oh, yes, I'm wonderful!"

"Well, if I may say, you're in a happy mood. Did something happen to put you in such a mood?"

"He asked me to marry him!" I exclaimed as I burst into tears.

Mrs. Taylor was so excited that she hugged me so tight I felt as if I could no longer breathe. We went and sat down in the sitting room, and she had me tell her everything.

"Well, I took a bite of a piece of cake when I bit into something hard. It was such a surprise, I was speechless. Then I jumped up and flew at him almost knocking us to the floor!" We both laughed then.

"Well, when is the wedding?"

"I'm not sure yet, I only know he wants to marry soon after my birthday, which is next week,"

"Oh, my! That soon! Why so soon?"

"Yes, that soon, and I'm not sure why he wants to marry me so soon. It may have to do with the part that he resigned from being a marshall and he wants to be a sheriff in another town, so he can be with his wife. No matter, it's fine with me," I said.

We started talking a little about the wedding plans. Even though the date wasn't set yet, there were things we could do. We had lists to make, things needed to buy and make, the menu, and that sort of thing.

Then she ushered me up the stairs, telling me, "You need to get some sleep. We have a lot to do tomorrow."

Surprised by her reaction, I said, "Good night, Mrs. Taylor," and I went to my room.

I woke up to a soft knock at my door. "Come in," I said, still sleepy. Mrs. Taylor then walked into the room holding a tray, with a flower on it. I sat up and asked, "What's this?"

She smiled. "It's breakfast. I thought today would be a good day to bring you some."

"Oh, thank you. This is very nice of you, but what's the special occasion?"

"Surely you must know that." She said with a giggle.

I thought for a minute, and then I remembered. "My birthday! I didn't realize, I totally forgot."

"Well, Happy Birthday! Enjoy your breakfast, dear," she said as she walked out the door.

After finishing with breakfast, I quickly washed and dressed. I wore my nice blue dress and pulled my hair up at the sides as I usually did. I saw Mrs. Taylor in the sitting room as I came down the stairs and thought I would join her. To my surprise, Michael was sitting in the room as well, with a package.

"Good morning," I said. They both responded in kind. I sat down in the chair next to Michael. He leaned over and kissed my cheek.

"I have something for you," he said and gave me the box.

"For me? Thank you. What is it?"

"Open it," he said with enthusiasm. So I did.

"Oh, Michael, it's beautiful, I love it! Thank you!"

"Try it on," he said. I stood up and put on the most beautiful shawl I had ever seen. It was made of white silk and had fringe all around it.

"You look beautiful in it, I must say," Mrs. Taylor said.

"I think so too, Mrs. Taylor," Michael said.

"Where did you get something so utterly beautiful?" I said.

"I had to special order it from Mrs. Carey," he said with a smile.

I laughed and said, "I can't believe you did that right under my nose." Then everyone laughed.

"What a lovely thing to do, Marshal," Mrs. Taylor said.

"I will cherish it always," I said as I leaned down to kiss Michael on the cheek.

I started to take the shawl off when Michael stopped me. "Don't take it off yet, there's a nip in the air and I want to take you for a walk." I looked at Mrs. Taylor for a moment then back at Michael.

"I would be happy to go for a walk."

"Here, dear, it isn't much, but Happy Birthday," Mrs. Taylor said, and I opened the small box she handed me to find a small handbag and two beautiful handkerchiefs inside it.

"They're lovely, thank you so much," I said as I gave her a hug.

Michael said then, "Shall we go?"

"Thank you, Mrs. Taylor. See you later," I said as I stood up, and Michael and I left.

"I think we need to agree to a wedding date, don't you?" Michael asked as we were walking.

"Yes, that would be a good idea. Do you have a date in mind?"

"I was thinking about in two weeks from Saturday," he suggested.

"Oh, that soon."

"Is that too soon?"

"No, I think I can manage," I said with a giggle.

"Then the date is set."

"What about the custody?" I asked.

"Oh, that was just temporary to get you away from that monster, Finch. It ended when you turned eighteen. You are independent, for now," he replied.

I giggled. I liked how he said "for now." It made a girl feel wanted. I loved him more when he made me feel wanted. In just a short time, I would be Mrs. Michael Hallowell. So much was happening to me so fast, it was hard to keep myself focused.

"Now all we have to do," Michael said, "is plan our move. Well, besides the wedding, of course." He chuckled at the surprised look on my face. He must have known what I was thinking since he made the comment about the wedding. "We can discuss the move this evening. I will let you take care of most of the wedding details. I will arrange for my best man and the honeymoon," he said with a grin. I smiled, not exactly sure of what he meant.

"All right, I'll plan the rest, but don't be surprised if I ask for your opinion on some things," I answered in agreement.

"It's a deal then." He picked me up and hugged me. "I can't wait until you are Mrs. Michael Hallowell," he said with a laugh.

"I bet you can't," I said and laughed with him.

After saying good-bye to Michael, I sat down with Mrs. Taylor to discuss the wedding. She jumped to her feet when I told her the wedding date that Michael and I had agreed upon, August twenty-fourth, which is in two weeks.

"Two weeks!" she exclaimed. "We need to get over to Mrs. Carey right away. That's not much time to make a wedding dress." She pulled me by the hand and led me out of the room as she spoke. "We have much to do to prepare. We need to get your dress, let everyone know, and get someone to make a cake. We have a few people in town who play music, so they may want to get together and practice some before the big day. Where are the lists? We have shopping to do too, so we need to go."

I didn't realize there was so much involved in preparing for a wedding. I needed to go to several fittings for the dress, and it was going to be a beautiful gown. Mrs. Taylor took over the invitation list. She invited everyone very quickly. Making up the food menu was easy; making all the food on the other hand, would have been a real challenge, until most of the women said they would bring some of the food for the reception. I thought we would have everything ready on time.

I was getting so anxious. I had that flutter in my belly again, worse than I ever had. I thought I had it bad when I first found out I was falling in love with Michael. I was nervous too, and it was going to be a very busy day.

I hoped nothing goes wrong that day. I didn't want my wedding day to be ruined. I hoped the weather would be nice as well. I needed to stop worrying. The most important thing was that I would be marrying Michael. I couldn't believe this was happening. My life turned around so quickly that it was hard to imagine this would happen. It was like a dream where I would wake up eventually to realize it wasn't real. Only it was real. I was getting married to a wonderful, caring man.

CHAPTER 8

The wedding went without any problems. The day couldn't have been more beautiful. The sunny sky had no clouds to speak of, and a gentle breeze came in from the south, just enough to keep it from being too hot. The whole town was in attendance, and it made a gorgeous scene for a wedding day.

My gown was a white satin with lace trim, the satin train stretched nearly three feet behind me and had a white lace veil. Mrs. Taylor had surprised me the night before with a new satin bag to match my dress and a sapphire necklace that she told me her husband had given it to her on the eve of their wedding. She wanted me to have it since I was as close to a daughter as she would have. Since, I didn't have my mom to support me on the most important day of my life, she will step in for her. Now that I have something old, something new, and something blue, all I need is something borrowed. Mrs. Carey loaned me her beautiful diamond and sapphire earrings. She had seen the necklace from Mrs. Taylor, and she was enthusiastic because she had earrings to match. I carried a small bouquet of wild flowers made up of Blue Stars, Blue False Indigo, blue-purple Asters, and a touch of Red Cardinals. Mrs. Taylor fixed my hair beautifully it was an upswept style with short tight curls framing my face.

Michael wore a magnificent black suit with a white shirt. He wore the new bolo tie I gave him for a wedding gift. He laughed at first when he saw it because of it having a horse on it with a blue background. I hoped he would like it. Michael arranged for Mr. and Mrs. James' four-year-old son, Anthony, to hold the rings, which he tried several times during the ceremony to hand them to Michael. Jack and Missy's five-year-old twin daughters,

Marlene and Kathryn, were flower girls, and they managed to throw petals everywhere, including on the guests.

The ceremony was short but it was wonderful. The judge that performed the ceremony looked dashing himself in his black suit. He made a small speech then went into the vows. We put rings on each other to make it complete, then the judge introduced us for the first time as Mr. and Mrs. Michael Hallowell.

The reception was marvelous; there were all kinds of food and desserts that the neighbors brought. Children played while parents talked. Many of our guests danced to outstanding music being played on fiddles, a guitar, and a clarinet. Everyone was enjoying themselves tremendously.

Before the reception could wind down, I threw the bouquet, which Carol caught, and Michael and I sliced the cake for our first bite together. Then Michael and I climbed into our carriage to go to the hotel, leaving everyone there to enjoy the rest of the day.

"Here we are, Mrs. Hallowell," Michael said, bringing me out of my thoughts.

"Oh, I'm sorry, I was just thinking about our day. It was a beautiful day wasn't it?"

"Yes, it was, but it's not over yet," he said, coming around the carriage with a grin. He helped me down, and we walked into the hotel. "Are you hungry?" Michael asked.

"Yes, I am famished! I was so busy with all of our guests that I didn't get a chance to eat."

"I didn't eat much, either, so how about we stop in the hotel dinning room and get supper before we go up to our room?"

"Oh, that sounds devine, my love!" My belly rumbled, and I blushed when Michael looked at me, but he just kissed my forehead. He is such a gentleman that he ignored my belly noise. I am sure he heard it, however.

We walked into the dinning area and took a seat near a window. A pretty, young girl came to take our order. When I looked up, she was staring at Michael; but when she saw I was looking at her, she had blushed and asked me for my order first. We both ordered steak and potatoes with sweet rolls. Since we were still in our wedding clothes, the hotel manager gave us cake for dessert on the house.

We then went straight upstairs to our room. Michael had paid for the room two weeks ago, so we wouldn't have to worry about all the rooms being occupied. The bell boy had already taken the bags upstairs. Once we got to the door, Michael suddenly lifted me up into his arms. I took in a sudden inhale of breath, and we both laughed. Then he carried me inside.

Michael set me down on my feet, as I looked around the room. It was simply breathtaking. I had never seen anything so fancy. It had a big bed with a lovely blue quilt and a night table, and two plush chairs on either side of the fireplace. The curtains on the windows matched the quilt in color, and a small table with a beautiful wash basin and pitcher on it stood in one corner. In another corner, a small wooden table also sat with a bucket containing a bottle of wine and the two glasses sitting in front of it.

Michael walked over to the table and opened the bottle, filling both glasses half-full of the liquid. "What is that?" I asked.

"It's champagne," he said as he handed me a glass. "Just sips now."

I took a sip and giggled. "It tickled my nose."

"Yes, it does," Michael said as he laughed.

Michael came to me, took my glass and set it back on the table, then took me into his arms. "Hello, Mrs. Hallowell," he said.

"Hello, Mr. Hallowell." I replied with a giggle.

"Dance with me, Mrs. Hallowell."

"What? Michael, there is no music."

"We can make our own, honey."

He then took me in his arms, and he twirled me around the room until I was dizzy from the champagne and laughing. It is so amazing just to be with him and no one else, but I am also a little nervous about tonight. So, I went over to the table and took another drink of champagne as my mouth was suddenly very dry. I know what happens between animals so I can only imagine what happens between husbands and wives. But, even if it is painful, it's worth a lifetime with Michael. I'm not going to think of that right now. I want to enjoy this time with my husband. Unfortunately, he noticed me waver a little and asked me what is wrong.

"I guess I'm not used to drinking champage, my love." He just smiled at me then held me a little tighter to his chest and kissed me on my forehead then on my cheeks, nose, and finally a soft, tender kiss on my lips.

"Just drink slowly." He took the glass from my hand.

My heart was racing so fast, I was getting lightheaded, or was it the champagne? My body was like pudding when he would kiss me like that; it was like I was made of jelly instead of bone.

He then bent down and kissed me. It was a warm, sweet, loving kiss. Then it grew stronger—more intense. When he released me, I was breathless. I didn't even realize that he had unfastened my gown until then. Then he did things to my body I've never experienced before. His caresses were gentle. Passion grew between us. He turned my blood to liquid fire until I shook with intense pleasure. Then Michael joined me. Unbelievably, the passion increased more than before. I climbed into a world I have never experience in my life. Before I knew it, we both exploded into a wonderous world of extreme exhilaration.

Making love is indescribable. What wondrous feelings came with it. As we lay snuggling, I asked Michael, "Will we do this again? Will it be like that all the time?"

He replied slighly, "Let's find out, honey." I giggled.

My answer came: yes.

CHAPTER 9

I woke the next morning to find that I was alone. What a wonderful night we had. I never thought anything like that existed, so much passion, and so exhilarating. I covered myself with the blanket, still a little embarrassed. I did feel wonderful, however. Michael made me feel things I never knew existed. He was so gentle and understanding last night. I was truly grateful to have such an understanding and patient husband.

At first I was so frightened because I didn't know this expirence was part of married life. Not having a mother to tell me about this is probably why I was so scared and resisted. Eventhough I was scared and embarrassed I did as Michael asked because I trusted him. After a while I came to enjoy the wonderous sensations my body gave me in response to Michael's touch. My love for him grew even more.

All of a sudden, the door opened. Michael walked in carrying a tray of food. "Morning," he said, gently kicking the door shut. "Are you hungry?"

"Oh, yes, I'm famished," I told him.

"How do you feel this morning?"

"I feel wonderful! And you?"

"I'm great, I didn't hurt you too bad, did I?" he asked as he set the tray down in front of me.

"No, I'm fine, a little sore, but fine," I replied with a smile. Michael smiled back then leaned down and kissed me. What a wonderful kiss that was. It was so loving, and I felt so alive and loved when he kissed me. "What are we going to do today?" I asked him.

"I thought that after breakfast and dessert," he said as he smiled and winked at me. "We would get a picnic dinner and go for a buggy ride."

"Ooh, sounds lovely," I replied with a giggle.

It was early afternoon by the time we got into a carriage. It was a lovely day, however. I saw some clouds in the far distance, which could bring rain. I pointed that out to Michael, and he just shrugged and said, "Well, we had better eat our dinner quickly and get back to our room before the rain comes."

"Michael!" I said in astonishment. "You're a rascal, aren't you?"

"You better believe it, honey!" he said in response, and we both laughed.

We rode to just outside the end of town and picked a nice grassy place to set up our picnic. It was a nice day for a picnic; the birds were singing, it wasn't too hot, and the cool breeze was light and sweet-smelling. The dark clouds seemed to be moving slowly, so it looked like we wouldn't have to rush too much.

We spread the blanket out on the cool grass and sat down. We pulled out our dinner of cold chicken, potatoes, and two pieces of apple pie.

"What a wonderful dinner, Michael," I said.

As we enjoyed our dinner, Michael suddenly said, "I've been thinking again about not continuing as a marshal—"

"But why?" I interrupted.

"It's because I don't want to be away from you all the time, honey. I want to start a family, and I can't do that if I'm gone all the time."

"What are we going to do?"

"Well," he said. "I want to be a sheriff up in Auburn. It's a nice town that is growing fairly quickly. I can make a decent living as sheriff. Plus, Auburn is not too far from Topeka."

"It sounds like you did your homework on Auburn."

"Yes, well, sometimes I had to go up there on marshal business. How does that sound to you?"

"I'll miss my new friends, but I could make more new friends. I would follow you to the ends of the earth, my love" I said softly.

"Really! That's wonderful, honey! I think we need to start making plans now." He seemed so excited about this, and that was a good thing. "We don't really have a place to live yet. I have some money enough to buy us a place. We need to move within the week."

"Oh, my, that soon?"

"Yes, honey, we can't stay in the hotel too long. I also found out that Auburn needs a sheriff now."

"I don't have much to pack, so it won't take me long. Will we buy our supplies there for our house?" I asked.

"Yes, whatever we need. We will stay at the hotel for two more days, and then we should be on our way, all right?" Michael replied.

"All right, my love." I said softly. We sat talking for a little while, then packed up and headed back to town.

Once we got into town, there was some commotion. Michael and I stopped the carriage and went to see if something was wrong. The town was in an uproar, people were yelling, and some of the men were holding rifles. Michael and I just looked at each other for a moment. Michael went up to the sheriff and asked, "What's going on?" "Rustlers!" the sheriff said.

"All right, let me get my wife settled and you start getting a posse together, if you can calm them down long enough. Whose herd was hit?" Michael asked.

"The Cannon place, rustlers have taken half the herd!" Sheriff Mason said.

Michael took me to the boarding house to stay with Mrs. Taylor. "Why are you bringing me here?" I asked.

"You'll be safe. You can gather up your things. Have them ready to go when I get back."

"What's going on?" I asked. He told me about the rustlers and Mr. Cannon. "I heard that, darling. What are you going to do?"

"Go after them with a posse," he said. Then he kissed me, left the carriage, and ran down the street.

I walked into the house to find Mrs. Taylor coming down the stairs. "What are you doing here, dear? Aren't you supposed to be on your honeymoon? Where's Michael?"

"I guess it's put on hold, there are rustlers that took almost half of Mr. Cannon's herd," I told her.

"Shall we sit? Would you like something to drink?" Mrs. Taylor asked.

"Not now, thank you."

We went into the sitting room. She asked if I was all right and I said, "Yes, I'm fine. How are you today?"

"I'm good, thank you," she said.

"I have some unexpected news." I began as she sat waiting patiently. "Michael wants to move to Auburn to become a sheriff. He doesn't want to be a marshal anymore. He wants to be near me and start a family, and he said he can't do that and be gone all the time. I'm going to miss you so much, Mrs. Taylor."

"I will miss you too, dear," she said sadly.

"Michael wants me to pack up my things, so we'll be ready when he returns."

"Well, we can do that in a little while. Would you like some coffee or tea perhaps?" she asked me.

"I think some tea would be very nice, thank you."

Mrs. Taylor left briefly to get some tea for us. We talked, and I asked her, "Why didn't you tell me? Is that the only way to have babies?"

She smiled and said, "Yes, dear, that's the only way to have babies. I didn't know how to tell you, dear. It's a very sensitive subject. I'm sorry."

"Making love is shocking yet exciting. Is this normal?"

"Yes, dear, it is normal."

"Thank you," I told her. We talked about many things, enjoying our time together, little as it is. "You will visit, won't you?" I asked.

"Yes, you will too?" she replied.

"Oh, yes, as often as I can. Thank you for being there for me. You have been like a mother to me, and I'm going to miss you terribly."

"It was my pleasure, dear. I will always be there for you. I will miss you too," Mrs. Taylor replied.

>>><<<

Sheriff Mason was organizing the posse when he saw me coming. "Hello, John are we ready?" I asked.

"Hello, Mike, we're almost ready. Everyone wanted to come but we could only pick some. I asked the others to watch the town instead," Mason said.

We were almost to the Cannon place when I asked Sheriff Mason, "Does anyone know the direction they took?"

"Yes, they headed west."

"Well, John, let's get a move on," I said. We rode fast and hard. My adrenaline was pumping, anxious to find these scumbags and get back to Cheyenne.

After about two hours, we caught up with them. We were far enough back that they couldn't see us coming. They couldn't travel very fast with such a large herd, so it wasn't that hard to find them. We took cover in the trees until we could see how many there were. Luckily for us, it didn't take very long; we were ready for the ambush. We sent half of the posse up ahead to take care of those men up in front. Sheriff Mason took the lead.

When everyone was set, we went in with guns blazing. The rustlers were caught off guard, but managed to start firing soon after we did. Sheriff Mason managed to get one down. I could hear the swish sounds of bullets flying past me. Keeping my head down as much as possible, I rode a little closer. With my target in sight, I fired. He went down. All of a sudden, I felt this searing, burning pain in my back. I leaned over my horse but kept firing. All I could think about was getting these rustlers and getting back to my Cheyenne. *Oh, how I love that girl.*

After what seemed to be an eternity, the gunfire ceased. We managed to kill three of them. We had one in custody and another got away. About then, I fell from my horse.

>>><<<

Mrs. Taylor and I drank our tea and crackers as we talked. I knew that soon I would have to start packing my things.

"Cheyenne, dear," Mrs. Taylor said, "you were lost in thought."

"Oh, I'm sorry," I apologized. "I was thinking about this move, I'm not sure about it."

"What do you mean, dear?"

"I don't know if I'm ready to leave here."

"Well, dear," she began. "It's new, you were just getting settled here so this move comes as a shock. When you go with your husband, look at it as an adventure. Before you know it, you will be settled, making new friends, and taking care of your husband. Don't forget you will be writing to me as well." She snickered. "You won't have time to worry."

"I suppose you're right. I'm just being silly."

"Would you like to come help me start dinner?" Mrs. Taylor asked.

"Yes, I'd be happy to help. Thank you again," I said.

We almost had supper ready when the door burst open. It was so loud it startled both of us. We went to see what was happening. Sheriff Mason and his deputy, Bob, were carrying Michael. I started to panic and then realized that would not help him right now. *I have to keep calm. I can panic later.* Mrs. Taylor told them to take him to my room.

Once he was on the bed, I removed his boots and his shirt. Michael moaned. The sheriff said he would be back with the doctor. I looked at Mrs. Taylor, and she looked at me.

"Where is his wound?" I asked her.

"Maybe on his back, but we shouldn't move him without the doctor," she said.

"I'm so worried, Mrs. Taylor. He can't die on me, he just can't!" I said, almost in tears.

"Don't worry yourself over that, dear, I'm sure he will be just fine."

At that moment, a knock came at the door. Mrs. Taylor said to come in. It was the doctor. "Oh, Doctor Comings, thank you for coming here. It doesn't look good. I think he was hurt pretty badly because he won't wake up," I said.

"Don't worry, dear, we will take care of him," Doctor Comings said as he looked him over. "We must roll him over. The wound is on Michael's back." After rolling him over, Doctor Comings took a good look. "The bullet is still in him, I must get it out right away. Hopefully it didn't hit any major organs," he said.

"Is he going to be all right, Doctor?" I asked with fear.

"I hope so. Mrs. Taylor, I need some bath sheets and hot water, and if you will assist me, I would appreciate it. Mrs. Hallowell, why don't you wait downstairs?"

"I'm staying here with my husband. I will help you."

Doctor Comings went to work then. He cleaned the wound, got out some instruments and began to retrieve the bullet from my husband's body. I helped soak up the blood as he worked.

It took quite some time to get the bullet out, but it was successful. "Getting the bullet out is only part of the problem," the doctor explained. "The bullet was lodged between the ribs, but didn't hit the lung. It appears to have cracked the two ribs though. He can't be moved until we are sure the ribs won't break and puncture the lung. If that happens, we could lose him. Once we close him up, we have to watch out for infection too. It may take a while before we know."

When Doctor Comings finished his work he said, "All we can do now is wait. I will be by tomorrow. If he gets an infection, send someone to get me right away. Watch out for redness, swelling, or increased pain. Call on me immediately if he develops a fever. I will be by early tomorrow morning."

"All right, thank you very much, Doctor Comings," I said.

"You're welcome," he said while getting his supplies together.

Staying with Michael all night was uneventful. He slept fairly calmly. I could tell he was in pain, however. So far, thank God, he hadn't developed a fever. I prayed and cried throughout the night hoping he would not get an infection. I played our wedding day, and night, over in my head half a dozen times just to keep my mind busy instead of worrying.

I walked over to Michael. I put my hand on his shoulder, first watching it move gently, then I leaned over and whispered, "Please be all right, my love. I don't want to lose you. I love you so much and I hate seeing you like this."

Just then, he reached for my hand. Opening his eyes, he said, "Oh, honey, I'm not going anywhere." He tried to get up, but I gently pushed him back down.

"Doctor Comings says you can't move for a few days. You have a couple of ribs that are cracked, and he doesn't want them to break. So please be still." With reluctance, he did as I asked. "If you don't develop an infection, you will be up and around in no time."

"What happened?" he asked.

"You were shot in the back. Doctor Comings removed the bullet." He started getting sleepy again. "Rest now, my love. We can talk more later." Then I gave him a kiss and let him rest.

Sheriff Mason came by to check on Michael. "How's he doing?" he asked.

"He seems better. He was awake earlier and talking a little."

At that moment, Michael suddenly said, "I'm awake, let Sheriff Mason come in, honey."

"Hello, Mike, how are you feeling?" asked the sheriff.

"I'm fine John," Michael began, "tell me about the rustlers. Did we get them all?"

"Well, we got all but one, three are dead, and one is in jail," the sheriff answered, "don't you remember?"

"I suppose I forgot. Did you manage to get the name of the one who got away?" Michael said.

"Yes, the men are out looking for him now," he said.

"Good. Do you know who shot me?"

"No, we are trying to figure that out." said the sheriff.

A short time later, Michael went back to sleep.

"He needs his rest now Sheriff Mason, thank you for coming by," I said.

"See you later Cheyenne," he said as he walked to the door.

I hope Michael isn't over doing things by talking so much right now. I love him so and hate seeing him like this. I wish there was more I could do for him. I feel so useless. "Oh, my love, get better soon please," I said as I rubbed his hair.

By supper time, Michael developed a fever. He was moaning more in his sleep and hadn't woken up since the sheriff was here. I shouted for Mrs. Taylor to get the doctor. She sent Carol Anderson, to get Doctor Comings. "Oh, I pray he will be all right!" I said with tears streaming down my face. Mrs. Taylor came running upstairs.

CHAPTER 10

Doctor Comings came in to assess the situation. He checked Michael's forehead then his wound. He could see red around the wound with swelling. He ordered a pot of hot water, a pot of cold water, and bath sheets. He told us to keep him warm, keep brushing his brow with the cool water, keep hot bath sheets on his wound, and give him water. Then he left saying, "I'll be back in a few hours. There's nothing more that we can do."

By the next morning, Michael's fever was worse. He started thrashing around, moaning. He was getting delirious, saying all kind of things I didn't understand. But when he called out my name, I was at his side in a heart beat. "I'm here darling, I'm right here," I said. "We did everything the doctor told us. Yet, Michael seemed to be getting worse. I can't loose him, I just can't!" I cried. Mrs. Taylor offered to sit with Michael for a while so I could rest. "I don't want to leave him," I said with tears in my eyes. She came to me and hugged me.

"Shhh, he will be okay, I promise. He's a fighter and he loves you. He don't want to leave you either. Why don't you rest in that arm chair and I will sit with him a while."

"All right," I replied, "as long as you wake me if anything happens."

"I will, now get some rest now," she said.

When I woke, I could smell something cooking. Mrs. Taylor was sitting beside Michael. "Hello Mrs. Taylor, who is cooking supper?"

"Hello Cheyenne, Carol Anderson is. She volunteered when she saw I was preoccupied," Mrs. Taylor said.

"How is he?" I asked.

"The same," she replied, "Mrs. Jennings sent her son, Kyle over to help tote water for us, and help in anyway we needed."

I smiled slightly and said, "That was very nice of her. Remind me to thank her later." Mrs. Taylor just nodded.

Kyle was a nice looking boy. He was eleven years old with blonde hair and green eyes. He was a bit thin but has potential of filling out, judging by his wide shoulders. He was very polite and very helpful. I don't know how we could manage without him. He went up and down the stairs numerous times to help us out. I made the comment that I didn't know how I could repay him. Then, he smiled and said, "A piece of pie would be nice." I smiled and looked at Mrs. Taylor.

"Go down and get a piece. Tell Miss Anderson I said it was all right," said Mrs. Taylor.

With a big grin on his face, he started heading out of the room then he looked over his shoulder and said, "Thank you!" Before sprinting down to the kitchen.

As I checked on Michael, Miss Anderson brought up a tray of food. "Here Mrs. Hallowell, I brought you some supper," she said.

"Please call me Cheyenne," I said.

"You can call me Carol. Here's some supper Cheyenne."

"Oh, dear, I don't think I can eat anything, but thank you," I said.

"Listen, Cheyenne," Mrs. Taylor said. "You must eat something. You haven't eaten since yesterday afternoon. You must keep up your strength. I don't think your husband would like it if he found out you're not eating." That was the ticket, it was all I needed to hear to sit down and eat.

"All right, I'll eat. Would you care to join me? I don't want to be alone." So Mrs. Taylor asked Carol to bring in some food for her, and Carol was more than willing.

Carol Anderson was a beautiful young woman. She was about my height and weight with big sky blue eyes and long brown hair, which she wore in a bun at the nape of her neck. She was a little shy but a very pleasant woman. She helped Mrs. Taylor quite often.

Just after we finished eating, Doctor Comings came in. "How's he doing this evening?" he asked.

"The same," Mrs. Taylor said before I could get the words out. Doctor Comings then checked Michael's wound then his forehead.

"How much longer before he gets better?" I asked.

"I'm not sure, Mrs. Hallowell. Let's give it another day or two. Once the fever breaks, we'll be on the road to recovery," he said. "I'll be back in the morning, but if you need me just send someone to get me."

"Thank you again, Doctor Comings."

Two days had passed, and his fever seemed to be coming down; he was no longer as hot. Then I noticed he was no longer thrashing around or talking strangely too. My hopes started to rise. *He is going to get better!* I gave him some water, and he took it without me having to shove it down his throat.

After dinner, I dozed in the chair near the bed. We had done everything we could for now. I was exhausted but didn't want to leave Michael. Off in the distance, I could hear a sound, a quiet sound, I could barely make it out. Then I heard it again, but this time it was a little louder. It sounded like water. *Water!* I opened my eyes and jumped up.

"Water," Michael said. I hurried to him and gave him some water. He opened his eyes.

I cried and then I hugged him. "You're awake! You're alive! I'm so relieved!"

"Yes, I'm awake. What's wrong?" he asked.

"You've been very ill. You had a high fever and were delirious. How do you feel?"

"I hurt and I'm thirsty," he told me.

"Here drink some more," I said as I gave him the water.

"How long have I been out?" he asked.

"A couple of days," I said, "I have missed you my love." He reached for me, so I gave him another hug. He just held me for a few moments.

I yelled for Mrs. Taylor to give her the good news. She sent Kyle to get Doctor Comings. "Oh, I'm so happy you are better, Mr. Hallowell," she said.

"Thank you. Me too, from the sounds of it," Michael said. "And it's Michael, if you don't mind."

"Not at all, Michael."

At that moment, he tried sitting up, but Mrs. Taylor said, "Just wait for the doctor."

"Yes, my love, please wait for the doctor," I said. He growled and lay back down.

Doctor Comings came in a short time later. "I see you're feeling some better," he said.

"Yes, I'm much better, thank you," Michael said.

"Good, now let me take a look." He examined Michael's back and checked his forehead. "How does your back feel?"

"It hurts some."

"Well, it's looking better, and your fever is almost gone," Doctor Comings said. "Your ribs are on the mend, but you still need to take it easy and get a lot of rest. No lifting heavy things. Don't push it, you've been through quite an ordeal."

"All right, doc."

"If you need anything or your back starts to hurt more, come get me," Doctor Comings said as he was leaving.

"Will do, Doc, thanks," Michael said.

"I'll walk you out, Doctor Comings," I said. "Thank you so much. Are you sure he's all right? He's out of the woods, right? He won't regress?"

"No, he won't regress. He's going to be fine. Don't worry," Doctor Comings said.

"Thank you, Doctor."

Going back upstairs, I asked Michael if he wanted to eat something. "Yes, I'm hungry," he said. Mrs. Taylor said she would go downstairs to fix him a plate of food.

"Thank you, Mrs. Taylor," I said, and she just waved. Then I looked back at Michael. "Oh, Michael, I was never so scared. Please don't scare me like that again," I said as I went to him.

He chuckled and said, "I won't honey."

The next morning, during breakfast, we talked more about moving. "I think we need to move in the next few days," Michael said.

"That soon? Are you really ready for that? The doctor said you have to take it easy and no lifting," I said.

"I feel pretty good, honey. No need to sit around here looking at the four walls,"

"I realize you are bored, my love, but the doctor knows best about healing. You may feel better, but that doesn't mean you are better. Your ribs are most likely still cracked. The doctor's biggest worry is that one of your ribs may enter a lung, and that will be a big problem. Maybe even kill you."

"Well then, I guess we can wait a few more days. I'll talk to the doctor. Will that make you feel better?" he asked.

"Yes, my love, it will," I said.

"We'll need to move soon or I won't have that job as sheriff, which reminds me, will you check the telegraph office see if anything was sent to me?"

"All right, my love, we'll move soon. I will go to the telegraph office after breakfast. Now, finish breakfast so you can get some rest. By the way, will we have a house waiting for us when we get there?"

"Yes, I will ask Mason to check on things for me about that and the furniture, thank you for reminding me," he said as he chuckled.

"I need to get a few things from the mercantile, do you need anything?" I asked.

"Yes, I need some soap and something to read. And oh, put it on our account," he said.

"Our account?"

"Yes, honey, our account."

"Well, it's definitely going to take me time to get used to that. I'll be back shortly." I leaned over and kissed him, then left the room.

CHAPTER 11

"A re you all packed up, honey?" Michael asked.

"Yes, are we going to pick up some supplies to take with us?"

"Yes, just a little. We can't fit too much in the carriage I bought."

"All right, it's a lovely carriage, by the way, and fancy. A double-seated carriage," I told him.

"I thought you would like it. It's nicer than the one we rented."

"Is the house already furnished or do we need to buy furniture? Did you ask Sheriff Mason about it?"

He chuckled and said, "Mason said he believes it's furnished. If not, we'll need to get the basics, at least, for now. Since I bought the house outright for such a low price, we have extra money to get things we need."

"All right, I'd better go say my good-byes then."

I went downstairs to find Mrs. Taylor in the kitchen, along with Carol Anderson and Tami Marcus. "Hello, ladies," I said. They each said hello. "Well, we're all packed and ready to go," I said with tears in my eyes. "I came to say. Good-bye. I'm going to miss all of you very much."

Mrs. Taylor came over to me and said, "So soon?"

"I'm afraid so," I replied.

"Let's all go to the sitting room, shall we?" Mrs. Taylor said.

In a single file, we all walked to the sitting room. There were a few ladies from town sitting in there. We all said our pleasantries, and everyone began talking. Mrs. Taylor came to me and said, "This is a going-away party, dear. We have cake and gifts."

"For me?" I asked with tears in my eyes.

"Yes," Mrs. Taylor said with a giggle.

"It's very sweet, thank you, everyone!" I said, crying.

We talked for a short time and then we had some coffee and cake. After that, they all handed me gifts to open. I got some pots, silverware, cooking spoons, a dish set, sheets, and bath sheets. The women in town had pitched in to help pay for everything they gave me. "I'm so grateful. I can't begin to tell you. Thank you all so much."

Then I began the hard task of saying good-bye, saving Mrs. Taylor for last. "I'll never forget you no matter where we go. We'll come back for a visit from time to time, I promise. Thank you for everything!" I told her.

Mrs. Taylor began to cry as she held me. "You better come and visit. I will miss you."

"And I'll miss you too."

"Well, it seems that I have some work to do, huh?" a voice sounded.

I giggled and said, "Yes, Michael, you do."

"Well, ladies, it's been a pleasure. I better get all of this stuff loaded. Thank you all for everything. Take care," he said as he started picking things up.

"Well, I'd better help him," I said. The ladies began picking up the gifts and followed us outside.

After loading up the carriage, I hugged Mrs. Taylor again and said good-bye to everyone once more. Michael helped me up into the carriage then climbed in himself. We were on our way to our new home. I only prayed it was as nice as it was here. In a way, I would be glad to be away from here. The farther away I was from where David lived, the better. I was still not comfortable, even knowing that he was in jail.

"How long before we get there do you imagine?" I asked.

"About a day and a half or so," Michael said. "Are you anxious to see the new house?"

"Yes, do we have what we need to sleep under the stars tonight?" I asked.

"Of course, honey. Can't have my wife sleeping without a pillow and blanket, now can I?"

I giggled and said, "No, I guess not."

"I know you will miss everyone, but you'll make some new friends. And you can always write to your old friends. We'll come back to visit them, I promise honey," Michael said.

"I know, my love. I guess I'm just real nervous."

"I know you are. It will be just fine, honey. Did you like the gifts the ladies got for you?"

"Oh, yes! It was so nice of them. Did you know about it?"

"Yes, I'm afraid I did. That's how I knew how long to give you for your goodbyes," he said as he grinned from ear to ear.

I gave him a mild shove and said, "Oh, you!" Then we laughed.

After we had been traveling for some time, Michael had me pull out the picnic basket. It was time for dinner. We ate it while riding to save time. Mrs. Taylor packed us a wonderful meal. There was chicken, ham, beans, biscuits, peaches, and pies. We had enough food to get us to where we were going.

It was almost dark by the time we stopped. We found a nice private place to sleep under the trees. As Michael got our bedding out and set up, I got our supper out and set it on the blankets. It was still warm out, so we didn't need to make a fire. We ate fried chicken, biscuits, beans and pie. It was a good supper. Then I cleaned up and got ready for bed, while Michael unhitched the horses and brushed them down.

As we lay under the stars, we snuggled some and talked about our future home. Then Michael leaned over and kissed me. It was a hungry kiss. One I hadn't experienced since our wedding night due to Michael's injury a week and a half ago. He then nibbled on my neck. He pulled me up and unfastened my dress, and it dropped onto the ground. Then he slowly took off my slip, then my corset and my undergarments until I was naked. He then pulled me into his arms and squeezed me tight as he kissed me. Then he laid me onto the blanket. I welcomed him with open arms. He was my husband and I loved him so. The scare I had at almost losing him was more than enough to last me a lifetime. It brought me closer to him. It was a beautiful way of spending the night with my only love, under the stars.

The next morning came before dawn. It was a cool morning. We gathered our bedding and loaded it into the carriage. We sat on the grass to eat and wait until it was bright enough to travel. We talked some while we ate, mostly about our new life together. It felt as if it would be a nice warm day, but not too hot. Michael then hitched up the horses, and we were ready to go.

By late afternoon, we were in Auburn. The house that Sheriff Mason arranged for us was on the outskirts of town here on the South end. It looked fairly new. It had a roof-covered porch that wrapped halfway around the house. There were flower bushes and trees all around the yard. It was big and beautiful.

Just as we were going to go inside, Michael suddenly picked me up and whisked me over the threshold. I giggled. He put me down and we looked around. The first room was the kitchen with a table and chairs, and a stove. On the right corner was a small room used to bathe. Going through the kitchen, I noticed a nice sitting room on the right, a dining room on the left, and four bedrooms down the hall on each side. The two back bedrooms were a little smaller than the ones in the front. *Nice and roomy*, I thought.

"Why don't you get us a little settled, and I will go check in with the sheriff's office. After I get back, we'll go eat then shop, all right?" Michael said.

"That sounds like a good idea to me," I told him.

After Michael left, I checked out the bedrooms first. The one on my left was a large room. It had a bed straight ahead between two windows with a stand on each side. In the far corner was an armchair with a fireplace next to it on the right wall. On the left wall were a wardrobe and a changing screen. A large chest sat at the foot of the bed. The blue curtains on the windows looked freshly washed. Our quilt was blue, so it would look very nice in here. The mattress looked like it was recently beaten to clean it. I opened the windows and pulled out our sheets, pillows, and quilt, and placed them on the bed. Then I left the room. The rest of the bedrooms had a bed, wardrobe, side tables, and a fireplace, which was on the same wall as the room next to it.

Looking at the kitchen, there was a fairly large pantry on the wall next to me at the far end. There was plenty of room to store food and whatever else I needed. On the right wall was the stove. Opposite of the pantry was the sink. There was a nice window over the sink with white curtains hanging there. I walked over and opened the window.

The table in the kitchen was big enough for ten people. It sat in the center of the room, with enough space to walk around when people were seated. There were shelves in the corner next to the sink to keep dishes on.

There was also a wash area just behind the left wall behind the kitchen door, and a fireplace on the wall of the kitchen in it. Shelves were up on the back wall of the room, and a tub was in the center. *This is a very nice room for bathing. I've never seen such luxury. Well, I better make a list, so I know what I need from the mercantile.*

Michael was back in no time, and we left for the mercantile. I noticed he was wearing a star-shaped badge. "I see you have your badge, my love," I said.

"Yes, I'm all situated as sheriff. Do you know what you need from the mercantile?"

"Yes, I made a list."

As we rode to the mercantile, we looked around the town. It was so nice, and it was even smaller than El Dorado. There was a mercantile, a blacksmith, two restaurants, two hotels, several saloons, the sheriff's office, a town hall, the stage station, even a trading post, and a few other businesses. There were many nice houses as well. People were walking around shopping or doing business and talking to one another. It seemed to be a nice quiet town, but a busy one at that.

Once in the mercantile, we noticed a very large variety of inventory, all kinds of canned food, beautiful material, linens, tools, and candy, just to name a few. This was a very nice place to shop. We went to the back and met the proprietors, Mr. and Mrs. George Jacobs. They seemed to be real nice too.

Mr. Jacobs was a short man, but a good-looking one nevertheless. He wore an apron over his tweed pants and brown shirt. His eyes were a deep blue, his hair had a sandy color, and he was just starting to loose his hair.

Mrs. Jacobs, or Madelyn, was about the same height as her husband, and a little more filled-out. She had brown hair and brown eyes with long beautiful eyelashes. She was a very nice-looking woman and had a very nice smile on her little round face. She didn't look much older than I was.

As we got our supplies, Michael ordered a rocking chair for me to put in the sitting room. I couldn't believe how many different things we were getting. Michael was getting things I didn't think of, and a few materials for me to make a few dresses out of. He said that when he saw what little I had packed when we left Aunt Janet's house, he had decided then to get material for me.

We got everything we needed to set up the house. We bought food, more bath sheets, linens, extra pots, a dutch oven, some tools, soaps, cups and beautiful crystal glasses with a matching pitcher. George and Michael loaded George's buckboard to take everything to our new home.

Michael and I got everything brought inside the house, and then he decided to take me out to eat. Once inside the restaurant, we took a table in the corner. The restaurant owner was Rainie Riverside. She introduced herself as Rainie when she took our order. She was a little older than me with blonde hair and green eyes. She was of average height and was also pregnant. She told us that her husband was Daniel, who was the town blacksmith.

The food was excellent, even better than the restaurant back home. We had pork chops, potatoes, biscuits, and cherry pie. We sat for a short time talking after eating. We needed to get back to our new home, but we just wanted to relax for a little while. The carriage ride took a lot out of me, and I thought Michael knew that.

When we got home, we started putting things away. "The rocker will be here in about a week," Michael said.

"Oh, I can't wait!" I exclaimed. We both worked together quickly so we could relax a bit before going to bed. "I think the kitchen is pretty well stocked for a little while. Where's the coffee?" Michael asked.

"It's in the pantry," I said.

When I reached for the coffee pot to make coffee, Michael took it away and told me he would make it since I was busy. "You can make it tomorrow," he said.

"I'm going to look at the sitting room. I got sidetracked earlier with my list that I forgot to see what it looks like and what's in it."

I entered the sitting room. There was a settee with a small table in front of it just opposite of the doorway, and two tables on either side of it. There were also two windows with white curtains on each side of the settee. On the wall to my right was a large fireplace.

On the wall opposite of the settee was a large armchair, and to my left was an oak desk. "Well, this room is nicely furnished," I said out loud and went back to the kitchen.

"Coffee's ready," Michael called out.

"Good," I said. We sat at the table and enjoyed our coffee together. "How did we come across this house with it furnished so nicely? I would have thought that whoever lived here first would have taken the furnishings with them, especially with furniture this nice.

"They had to go back east due to a family emergency and couldn't take this stuff with them. They decided to stay back in the east, according to the deputy. The money from the sale of the house was sent to the original owners."

"Oh, I'm sorry to hear it, but at least they received the money from the house," I said. "Well, the house is coming together quite nicely."

"Yes. We don't need any furniture in the sitting room?"

"No, it doesn't look like we need anything. Everything in there looks real nice. We'll need to get another wardrobe soon though. In the meantime, you could pull a wardrobe from one of the other bedrooms into our room."

"We can order that. Oh, I put the bath sheets and linens in the wash room for you," he said.

"Oh, thank you. I can't wait to take a bath."

"Well, we still have time before bed. What do you say, we heat up the water?" he asked. With a smile on my face, I got up and started boiling water. Michael started taking buckets of water and pouring them into the tub for me. In no time at all, I was in a nice hot bath. *Oh, how wonderful it is after such a long day.* I washed up and washed my hair, then leaned back to relax.

Suddenly, I wasn't alone. I opened my eyes to find Michael getting into the tub with me! I shrieked, then laughed and said, "You can't fit in here with me."

"Want to bet?" he asked, smiling from ear to ear. He had me move forward and he sat behind me. "See? I told you we'd fit," he said as he laughed.

After he washed up a bit, he pulled me close to him and began to wash me, working his way down. I rubbed his legs at the same time. "This is romantic, wouldn't you say, honey?"

"You're a rascal," I said and laughed. He began kissing the back of my neck.

"Your hair smells real good," he said.

"Thank you, my love."

When we finished, we rinsed off and dried off. He then picked me up and carried me to our room. "Good, I see you made up our bed," he said chuckling.

"You really are a rascal," I replied.

CHAPTER 12

I woke up this morning thinking of the splendid night we had together. It looked like we would have a splendid day as well. I went into the kitchen to make coffee. It was a chilly morning, so I went back to my room so I could put my robe on to keep warm. When I came back to the kitchen, Michael had come in with an arm full of wood. He lit the stove and the fireplaces to warm the house.

"Are you going to the sheriff's office today?" I asked.

"No, I'll start first thing tomorrow. We still need a few more things, and I want to help get this house in working order," he said.

"We don't have that much left to do."

"I have something in mind you probably haven't thought about," he said with a grin. *Uh-Oh*, I thought. "Make love to my wife," he said as a matter of fact. He came to me then, hugged me, and started kissing me.

"Now?" I questioned when I caught my breath.

"Why not? We did miss out on our honeymoon."

"I guess we did." We went to the bedroom then.

We spent the first part of the day in bed. Then we had our coffee and we talked. "Honey, you've come a long way in a short time. You're accepting our lovemaking without hesitation. That makes me very happy, especially knowing you enjoy it so well now," he said.

I blushed. I could feel the heat rising in my neck and face. "I'm pleased too, my love. Once I put my fear and shock aside, I realized how much I enjoy lovemaking."

"We missed breakfast, and I'm starved. It's time for dinner now," Michael said. So we went into the kitchen to prepare dinner.

After we ate, we finished organizing and making sure of what we had and still needed. We needed some supplies for the desk. I forgot to buy a broom yesterday, so we needed to get it today too. I also needed towels to clean with.

"Are we ready to go?" Michael asked. Before I could answer, a knock came at the door.

Michael opened the door to find a young lady holding a container of food. "Hello," she said. "I'm Gerri. I would like to welcome you to our town." Michael opened the door wider to allow her in. "You have a lovely home here. I hope you'll enjoy living in our town."

Michael introduced us. "Hello, I'm Michael Hallowell, and this is my wife Cheyenne."

"How do you do, Gerri," I said.

"Hello," she said. She walked to the table and set the food down on it. "It's fried chicken and biscuits. I thought it would help not to have to cook while you get settled." "Sounds wonderful. Thank you," I said.

Gerri was a beautiful woman. She had reddish blonde hair, bright blue eyes, and a lovely smile. She was just a little taller than me. "If you don't mind me asking," I said, "how old are you?"

"I'm twenty-one," she said with a smile. So she was three years older than me. She had a nice figure, not too big and not too skinny. "My husband, Mac, said we should invite you to dinner tomorrow night. Will you come?" she asked. I looked at Michael, and he nodded his head yes.

"All right, that's a date," I said. She smiled.

Gerri told us where she and Mac lived. "Well, I have a baby at home waiting for me, so I must go. We'll see you tomorrow. It was nice meeting you."

"It was nice meeting you too. We look forward to tomorrow." Michael said. We followed her out so we could go to the mercantile.

"Oh, you were on your way out, I'm sorry," she said.

"That's quite all right. We weren't in a hurry," I said.

We met several people in town today. All of them seemed very nice. It appeared we had a friendly town. I thought we would like it here. We could hear children playing and only one or two dogs barking. People were outside all around talking to each other. Yes, this was a quiet town.

When we arrived at home, Michael unloaded the carriage and took it around back. There was a big barn to keep horses and the carriage inside. A big backyard! There was plenty of room to grow here.

By the time Michael came in the house, I had supper on the table. As we ate, we talked about all the nice people we met. It would take me a while to remember all their names, I'm afraid.

Michael drank his coffee as I cleaned up. "It's getting late, we should go on to bed," he said.

"I'll be done in a minute," I replied.

As I cleaned up the breakfast mess, Michael was getting ready to go to the sheriff's office. He would be gone most of the day. I decided to make bread and pies this morning for tonight's supper. This afternoon I would start making a dress. It was going to be a lovely day.

Oh, it's all too amazing how quickly my life has changed, with everything being so different now. One minute I'm practically a slave to a man that beat me, and the next I'm married to a wonderful man and having my own life back. I have my own home. I can enjoy my own cooking and a husband who not only takes good care of me, but doesn't hit me too! It's just wonderfully amazing!

I started making the bread when someone knocked at the door. I opened it to find Gerri and a friend of hers standing there. "Hello, Gerri, won't you both come in?" I said.

"Hello, Cheyenne, this is a good friend of mine, Sandy," Gerri said.

"Hello, Sandy."

"How do you do?" she replied.

"Oh, just fine, thank you. Would you ladies like some coffee or tea?" I offered.

"Yes, tea would be wonderful," Gerri said. Sandy chose coffee. We talked and they offered to help me make three loaves of bread and two pies. I enjoyed having company. I wasn't used to being around people, but I liked it. I was free to do as I pleased. Before they left, I told them to take a loaf of bread home to their families. They thanked me and left.

It was early afternoon, and I was working on my dress when again someone knocked at the door. I opened the door and a strange man burst in pushing me backward while slamming and bolting the door.

"Who are you? Why are you here?" I screamed. He held me with his right hand then backhanded me with his left. I screamed as I tried to get away. I fought like a wild cat but without success. Then I quickly raised my leg and kicked him in his man parts. He doubled over. He almost lost his grip on me, but he refused to let me go.

"Leave me alone! Get out of my house!" I yelled. He dragged me to the sitting room where he proceeded to hit me. He punched me in the belly and in the face, and I fell to the floor.

"Shut up! This is for my brother!" he said.

"Who is your brother?" I cried.

"David. You sent him to prison!"

"I didn't, he tried kidnapping me, and he beat me. I did nothing to him. You're just like him!" He hit me once more.

My heart just sank. I thought I was done with that part of my life, done with being beaten. I didn't know how any man could treat a woman like this. My step-uncle never hit my aunt, but why hit me? I didn't know this man, never even seen him before. So then why was he hitting me? I did nothing to his brother David, except for what I was told to do. I didn't cause any trouble for him. All I could do was pray right now. I wished I could fight him off.

I was brought out of my thoughts when he suddenly shook me. "Aren't you listening to me, girl?" he bellowed.

I made the mistake of saying "No!" This time, it was just a slap, and not a backhand. I was grateful, but puzzled. He pushed me up against the wall and put his hand all over me. I screamed at the top of my lungs. "Get your hands off of me! I don't even know you, and you come into my house and start beating on me and touching me. Your brother caused himself to go to jail, and that still is no reason to hit someone!"

"Shut up, I didn't tell you to speak! I'd do anything for my brother, and he has no business being in jail, especially because of you! You're going to pay for it!" he shouted as he brought up his hand. I started screaming hoping someone would hear me. Being on the edge of the town, however, screaming may be a useless attempt. He shook me hard again and yelled, "Shut up, I said, or I'll kill you right now. Do you understand me?"

"Death would be better than this!" I yelled back. Tears began to well up in my eyes. *I must not cry, not in front of this animal.* I closed my eyes and waited for the next blow.

CHAPTER 13

Suddenly, someone was trying to get into the house. I screamed again, and he slapped me. "Shut up!" he said through gritted teeth. Then I heard a whishing sound go between us. He pulled me to the floor and reached for his gun, and I froze. He then shot his gun out the window. He pulled me into the hallway right by the doorway. He reached around the corner shooting through the window.

I didn't hear any shooting come from outside. I got worried that whoever that was either was shot or left. I guessed he thought the same thing because then he took me to my bedroom and threw me on the bed. He ripped my bodice and threw up my dress, ripping my clothes off underneath. I struggled, but to no avail. I was getting tired.

He then flipped me over onto my belly like I was a piece of meat. He took an undergarment and tied my hands behind me. He flipped me over again. He stared at me. I screamed, and he hit me again. Then he unzipped his pants, all the while telling me this was for his brother. I tried getting away but he had my legs between his, stopping me.

"Don't do this! Please don't do this!" He just grinned at me. I wiggled to prevent him from doing what he was about to do.

"Stop moving or else…" he said.

All of a sudden, he fell on top of me. He wasn't moving. I tried to push him off me, but he was too heavy. A second later, I felt him being lifted off of me. It was Michael! Michael threw the man on the floor; then he lifted me up and held me. He untied my hands. "Are you all right, honey?" he asked me.

"I am now," I cried. He called out to the deputy. When the deputy came in, he and Michael carried the man to the jail. He was just injured, so he would live.

On his way out the door, Michael said, "I'll be right back. You'll be okay until then?"

"Yes," I answered.

I went into the wardrobe to get undergarments and a dress to change into. After I was dressed, I went to the washroom to splash cool water on my face. By the time Michael got back, I was sitting at the kitchen table with a cup of coffee, and a cool rag on my face. He took my chin in his hand, turning my face toward him. The more he looked at me, the angrier he got.

"Oh, honey, do we have any salve for the cut on your face?" he asked.

"Yes, on the shelf in the washroom."

As he came back, he said, "I'm going to kill him!"

"Oh, Michael, you can't. That would be murder."

"Yes I know, but that's what I'd like to do."

"Why did those two hit me? What have I ever done? I don't even know that man!" I started to cry as I spoke. Michael was at my side in a split second. He picked me up and held me.

"It's going to be all right. I will take care of him," he said. After a few minutes, he put me down and put the salve on my face. "Did he hit you anywhere else? You hurt anywhere else? Do I need to go get the doctor?"

"No," I replied. "How did you—"

"Don and I were making rounds, and I wanted to include our house on our rounds. Luckily I did." he said, interrupting my question.

"How did you get in the house to save me?""I came in the back door, it wasn't bolted. I'm glad that this time we forgot to bolt it. Luckily he didn't notice that either. I want to go to the jail and make sure he is secure. I want you to go lie down, get some rest. Will you be all right until I get back?"

"All right, Michael, and yes, I'll be fine," I answered. He got me settled in bed before he left. He started kissing me and reassuring me that he wouldn't be gone too long. He bolted the back door before leaving.

"See you in just a little while. I love you," he said as he walked out the door.

Although I was shaking and still upset, I settled onto the bed to rest. *I can't believe this! I never even knew that man existed! I can't believe how some men think that women are to be treated with beatings and used like slaves! But a stranger? What gives him the right to just come into a stranger's home and treat a woman like this?* I was no longer upset, but I was getting angry at the thought of what he did. What he tried to do. He tried to take a beautiful thing and make it ugly! Well, I wouldn't let that happen. He would get what he deserved, and I would disappoint him by continuing to be happy with my life and enjoy lovemaking as I was meant to.

>>><<<

"Hello, Michael," said Deputy Don Murphy as I walked into the office.

"Hello, Don. Is he situated back there?" I asked.

"Yes."

I grabbed the keys and started back there. "What are you going to do, Mike?" Don asked. I didn't answer him. Once I unlocked both doors, I calmly walked into Finch's cell.

Finch jumped to his feet. "What's going on? What are you doing in here? The judge can't be here yet."

"You come to this town just to hurt my wife?" I asked as I slowly stepped closer.

"Yup," was all that he said.

"Why? She's done nothing to you or your brother!" I said through gritted teeth. "How did you find her anyway?"

"I heard it in El Dorado."

I came nose to nose with Finch now. Then I punched him, picked him up and punched again. I got about five or six punches

NANCY WOLFE WITH MANDI CARRIGAN

in before my deputy came in. "Shcriff! He's had enough. You're going to kill him!" he yelled.

"Maybe I should and save us all the bother," I said as I gave Finch one solid kick in the jaw. Then I walked out of the cell with Don, close behind locking the doors. "I don't want him alone, so deputize an unmarried man to take over when you go home. It's a little better for a night shift to have an unmarried man working. Wives tend to hate the night shifts." Don nodded his head in acknowledgement. "I'm going to be with Cheyenne if you need me, which I hope you don't. Get him a doctor," I said as I walked out the door.

"All right, Mike, give my regards to Cheyenne."

>>><<<

I was resting when someone again knocked at the door. I must have jumped a mile high. I was very nervous to answer the door this time therefore, I grabbed the rolling pin and headed to the door. I asked who it was, and the voice said, "Gerri."

"Come in, Gerri." As she entered, she saw me and gasped.

"What happened, Cheyenne?" she asked. I told her all that had happened. She was flabbergasted. "Oh, dear, I'm so relieved you're all right! What happened to him?"

"Michael took him to jail," I said.

"Oh, I hope he rots."

"Would you like some tea?"

"Yes please," she replied.

We sat and talked for probably an hour before Michael came home. He and Gerri said their hellos.

"Are you all right, honey?" Michael asked.

"Yes, my love, I'm fine now," I reassured him.

"Well, he gave no answers except that he was trying to get revenge for his brother for going to jail. I think he's regretting his actions now though."

"Uh-oh, what did you do?" I asked.

"Just gave him a taste of his own medicine," he said.

90

"Michael, you didn't!"

"Well, served him right for coming here beating up my wife! Lucky for him that's all he got. I'm pressing assault charges and attempted rape on him," he said angrily.

"I only hope there are no other brothers," I said.

"Don't worry so much, all right? What's for supper? I'm starved," he said calmly now.

"Stew," I said and laughed.

"Well," Gerri suddenly said, "I guess I'd better get home. You take care of yourself. I'll come by again real soon."

"Thank you for sitting with me," I said.

"You're welcome," she replied as she was leaving.

"Thank you for coming." She nodded and left. I then turned to Micahel. "Supper is on the stove if it's not ruined by now."

"Let's eat then," Michael answered, giving me a kiss.

During the night, my belly was hurting terribly. In fact, it was an excruciating pain. I got up so I wouldn't wake Michael. It didn't work. I doubled over in pain and cried out, which woke Michael. He rushed over to me, picked me up, and put me on the bed. "What's wrong, honey?" he asked.

"Perhaps it's my monthly, but it never hurt like this!" I said as I curled into a ball. I cried out again in pain.

"I'm going for the doctor!" He kissed me and said, "Be strong, honey, I'll be right back." Then he left.

The pain was horrifying. I rolled on the bed crying in pain. *What is wrong? If this is not my monthly, then what is it?* It was then that I noticed the blood. It must be my monthly. Why else would there be blood?

A short time later, Michael came with the doctor. The doctor came in the bedroom, but asked Michael to wait in the other room. He did as the doctor asked.

The doctor introduced himself as Doctor Kiley. Walking over to me, he noticed the blood. "How's the pain, dear?" he asked as he began the examination.

"It's excruciating, Doctor," I said.

Doctor Kiley proceeded to examine my condition. "I'm afraid you're having a miscarriage, my dear," he said after finishing the examination.

As I grabbed my belly, I said, "I'm pregnant? I didn't know! Now I'm losing the baby? Is that what you're telling me?" I cried.

"I'm afraid so, my dear. I'm sorry," he said. I really started crying then. Doctor Kiley gave me some medicine and left the room.

A moment later, Michael came in with a real sorrowful look. He held me tight and kept saying, "I'm sorry, honey." Then he said, "Doctor Kiley said he doesn't know how long this will take. You have to be strong, honey! We'll have more babies, you'll see."

"Oh, Michael, our baby!" I cried.

"Shhh, it will be all right, honey. You may have a long time to wait, but we can have more children."

About seven hours later, I finally stopped hurting so badly. I was extremely sore, but the cramping finally quit. Earlier, Michael had put extra sheets under me to make it easier to clean up.

"You can take the sheets now since there's so much blood. I can't believe how much blood there is," I said.

As he did, we noticed a large ball, and looking closer, we knew it was our baby. I cried again. Michael took our baby then to bury him in the backyard. I said a prayer and just leaned back against the pillows. I felt so strange, like, empty somehow. My heart just ached. All I could do was cry and hold my belly. When Michael came back in, he just held me.

After a while, I finally calmed down some. Michael asked if I would like to eat something. "Well, I guess I probably should. I'm a little hungry," I said. He came back with a plate of eggs and some bread. I ate what I could and gave the plate back to him.

"Doc says you have to rest, so I'm going to stay home and take care of you today," he said.

"You know," I started, "with all the times I have been beaten, I've never felt such pain as this. Why, my love, why did I lose our baby? Oh, our beautiful baby." I began to cry again.

"I can't imagine what you're going through, but I do feel a sense of loss. So my heart goes out to you, honey. I'm so sorry," he said while holding me. "It will be all right, honey. We'll be able to have more children, I promise." What he was saying was sweet, but not something I wanted to hear right now. But I said nothing. I knew that he meant well.

"By the way, Gerri stopped by, and I told her what happened. She wanted me to tell you she will be thinking of you," Michael said.

"Oh, she's the best. I couldn't ask for a better or more special friend than Gerri," I replied.

CHAPTER 14

I
t was a fairly warm, mild day for October. The birds were singing, the sun was shining brightly, the air smelled crisp and clean, children were playing, and dogs were barking. Yes, it was a normal beautiful morning. It had been a little over a month since the loss of my child. Although it still pained me something awful, I was healed physically. Doctor Kiley said that Michael and I could start trying to have another baby next week. I was happy about that, it had been too long.

Michael had told me that on that frightful day, as Doctor Kiley was leaving, he had explained to Michael that we had to refrain from intimacy for about six weeks to give my body time to heal. This was exactly what we had done. It had been hard lately, but we knew we had to wait. When Michael got home, he would be happy to hear the good news.

After the doctor left this morning, I made bread and two pies for supper tonight. I would need to go shopping again before making any more bread and pies. I needed flour, sugar, and some fruit preserves. Today would probably be a good day to do that. I decided that while the pies were baking, I would start making Michael shirts for Christmas. It would be easy to keep it a secret since he wasn't home most of the day. He came home for dinner most days, so I knew when to put the shirts away. I already bought the material in white and tan colors. They would look great on him.

Michael came home for dinner. "What do we have for dinner?" he asked.

"We have leftover stew, biscuits, and pie," I said.

"That sounds real good," he replied. Just as we sat down to eat, I told him about the Doctor Kiley's visit this morning. "Well, I'm pleased that you're healing so nicely."

"That's not all you're pleased about, is it?"

"What?" he said in a dumbfounded way.

"Ohhh, don't play that game with me, mister. You know exactly what I'm talking about," I said as I giggled. I then threw a towel at him.

He laughed. "It's all good news, honey." He then got serious and said, "Are you sure you're up to it? I wouldn't want to hurt you."

"Yes, I am fine. If the doctor said we can, then you shouldn't hurt me. He wouldn't tell us it's all right if it isn't. I'll be fine, my love."

"Next week?" he asked.

"Next week," I answered with a giggle.

When we finished our dinner, Michael decided to take me in the carriage to the mercantile. "I think it's still too soon for you to walk that far," he said. I told him that I would be fine. "I'll bring you home and unhitch the horse before I go back to the office," he said, leaving no room for discussion.

"All right, my love. I won't be too long."

While we were in the mercantile, George, the mercantile owner, told us, "There's to be a barn dance near the end of the month to celebrate the harvest. Talk to Sandy about what to bring, she's managing that. And oh," he said, "the two rockers you ordered are in, I have them in back. Do you need me to deliver them?"

"Yes, that would be good," Michael said.

On the short trip home, we talked about going to the barn dance. Since I was better, we agreed that we would go, as long as I wouldn't stand on my feet too long. I promised I would after a little protest. I told him that I was fine, and that he shouldn't be so overprotective. "That's part of being a husband," Michael said.

"All right, I'll go see Sandy tomorrow," I said.

I would have to buy more material if we were going to a barn dance. I would need to make Michael another shirt. I would give him the white one I was working on for the dance, and then make a new one for Christmas. I would ask Sandy or Gerri tomorrow if they would pick up the material for me so Michael didn't find out. I had some money in the coffee can to pay for it.

The next day, I went to Sandy's house to find something to bring to the dance. "Hello, Sandy," I said.

"Hello, Cheyenne please come in," she said as she opened the door wider. We sat, and while drinking lemonade, we discussed the barn dance, the food for it, and the material that I needed.

"What shall I bring?" I asked.

"Since you make such good pies, I thought you could make a couple of those," she said.

"All right, I will." She was more than willing to get the material for me. I gave her the money and told her I wanted it in white. "Well, I'd better get going. I still have to get the shirt done in time for the dance. I'm going to surprise him with it. Thank you so very much." With that I left for home.

>>><<<

"Sheriff!" Deputy Murphy said as I came in.

"Yes," I said, "what is it?"

"We need to be on the lookout, three men robbed a bank in Topeka and were seen heading south."

"When did this happen?" I asked.

"A few hours ago, according to what the stage driver said."

"Did you get what they looked like?" He said yes as he handed me a piece of paper with the information written down. "Well, Don, I guess I better go talk to Jacob over at the telegraph office and talk to Mark at the newspaper office to fill them in about the robbery and the descriptions of the robbers," I told Deputy Murphy.

After getting what information the telegraph office had, which was sent over just a few minutes ago, I went to the newspaper office. I needed to get some posters made and put up. Once there, I asked Mark what he had heard. "Nothing yet," he said.

"Here are the descriptions of the three men. Can you get them ready as soon as possible?" I asked.

"Sure, sheriff, I'll have them for you before supper."

"Thanks, Mark, we really need to catch them," I said and then I left.

Back at the office, I told Don, "We need to warn the town folks not to let strangers in their homes. If anyone sees any strangers riding in on horseback, they should report it right away. I'll start at my house and work my way up. You start on the other end and work your way down, all right?"

"Sure thing, Mike," he replied, and we headed out. My first stop was home. Since the episode with Finch, I made sure that Cheyenne kept the doors bolted. I would have to knock to get in.

CHAPTER 15

As I was working on Michael's shirt, someone knocked at the door. I put the shirt away and went to the door. "Yes? Who is it?" I asked.

"It's your husband." Right away, I felt alarmed. Something wasn't right, he didn't sound right. I opened the door. "Hello, honey," he said as he kissed me. "Have you seen any strangers around today?"

"No, why?"

"There was a bank robbery in Topeka by three men, and they're headed south at last report," he said.

"Oh, no."

"Close the windows and keep the doors bolted. If you don't know them, don't open the door. I'll be back as soon as we notify everyone," he said.

"I won't, and I'll keep the doors bolted. You seem so worried."

"Yes, well, they're dangerous men. Please keep the house locked up tight." He gave me a kiss and left.

Later, Michael and I were sitting down to supper when Deputy Murphy came knocking at the door. Michael let him in.

"What's going on, Don?" Michael asked.

"Hello, Mrs. Hallowell," he started, "I got Roy Edwards as another deputy. Plus, I got four others to stand by in case of trouble."

"Sounds good," Michael said.

"Roy's at the jail now. He'll be there until morning."

"Good, have you heard anything?" "Just that the newspaper office sent over the wanted posters you wanted."

"All right then, we can distribute them in the morning, except for two. Will you take a poster to the hotel and one to the saloon on your way home? I would appreciate it."

"Sure thing, Mike, I'll be home early as it is, so Jeannie will be happy."

"Thanks."

After supper, Michael sat sipping brandy as I cleaned up the kitchen. When I finished, we went into the sitting room near the fire and talked about the barn dance. "I hope we won't have to cancel the barn dance," I said.

"No, I don't see why we'd have to do that," he said.

"The bank robbers are running free. What if they aren't caught by then?"

"Well, there's no guarantee that they will come by here," Michael began, "but if they aren't caught by then, we will use extra deputies to cover the dance. I'll be on duty then too, but I'll still be with you until it's necessary for me not to be."

"All right, my love," I said. "Do you think we could go back to El Dorado for Christmas?"

"I don't think we should plan that until after winter. I wouldn't want to take a chance of snow moving in because we may not be able to leave and go home, or worse, we may get stuck halfway through."

"Oh, I hadn't thought of that. You're right, of course,"

Just then, someone beat on the door. Michael grabbed his rifle and told me to hide in the wash room until we would know who was at the door. So I did. Then I heard Michael yell, "Who is it?"

"It's Roy, sheriff!" Michael let him in.

"What can I do for you? Shouldn't you be at the jail?"

"Someone broke into the jail, knocked me out while I was pouring some coffee, and released Finch. There were two of them that I saw before I went out."

"Are you all right?" I asked Roy.

"Yes, ma'am, I'm fine," he said.

"Oh, terrific, that's all we need right now! Who broke him out?" Michael asked.

"I don't know. But I think they matched the description of the bank robbers. I didn't get a very good look, it happened so fast. Sorry, sheriff," Roy replied.

"Go get Don, then gather a posse. I will join you shortly." Roy left. Michael looked at me then and said, "I want you to go to Gerri's house. You'll be safe there until I get back."

"You won't be gone long, will you?"

"I'm not sure. Please stay with Gerri until I get back."

"Yes, I will."

"Get some things together," he said, and I did as he asked. I gathered my clothes and a few things, including the shirts I made for him, which I put in a bag so Michael would not see. "I'm ready to go," I said.

"Good, let's go." We arrived at Gerri's house a few minutes later. Her husband, Mac, opened the door. Michael explained about the escape and that he wanted me to be safe. "Would you mind letting her stay with you until I return?" Michael asked.

"Sure, she can stay as long as she needs too. We have room for her," Mac replied.

"Thank you!" Mac just nodded. Michael looked at me then. "Remember, stay here until I get back."

"I will."

"I love you and I'll be back as soon as possible," he said. He kissed me then and left.

>>><<<

As soon as I arrived at the office, everyone started talking at once. "Sheriff, a lot of men are willing to join the posse," Roy said.

"All right, everyone, quiet down please," I began. "We are going to need men to go on the posse and some to stay behind to guard the town."

"Who is this prisoner?" several of the men asked.

"He's the brother of my wife's step-uncle, who is in prison. He thought he would get revenge on my wife for sending his brother to prison. He attempted rape and he beat her. This is why he was in jail. Cheyenne's step-uncle went to jail because he tried kidnapping Cheyenne and beat her almost to death. I don't know who busted him out but we have to find out. As long as Dennis Finch is free, he will be a threat to my wife."

Roy and Don pulled me over to the side. "Why don't you stay behind with some of the men since you know what this guy looks like? If he strikes again, you would be able to catch him again quickly," Roy said.

"I'll think about it."

"Well, if she's in danger, you're the best one to help her."

"We have more than enough men for the posse and to watch the town," Don said.

"I hear what you're saying," I replied. "Let's get this posse together and out of here."

I stood on the porch of the sheriff's office and quieted everyone down. "We are losing valuable time, gentlemen," I began, and they all quieted down. "Who wants to be on the posse and who wants to stay here protecting the town? The two men who broke Finch out of jail could be the bank robbers, so we might have four men to find. Even though Topeka has a posse out looking for the robbers, we need to go out as well to find Finch." I then turned to Roy. "Roy, will you check with the telegraph office to see if there's been any word on any of robbers being caught?"

Roy left to check on that information, and Don and I deputized the men. Fifteen men would go on the posse, including Don and Roy, while I would stay behind with the other twenty men. A few minutes later, Roy came back from the telegraph office.

"No word yet on the capture of any of the men," Roy said.

"Thanks, you head out with the posse. Make sure there are enough rifles and bullets," I said.

After the posse left, I made sure everyone was armed and had plenty of ammunition. There were a total of twenty-one men to guard the town, and we divided ourselves into three groups. Seven men formed a circle around the town to help prevent anyone from getting in without someone knowing, everyone being on horseback of course. The other fourteen were told to get some rest until their shift started. Every two hours, we would trade off. Just before I started, I quickly checked in on Cheyenne and told her what we were doing. Then I mounted up.

CHAPTER 16

Since Michael left, I have been real nervous. The longer he was gone, the worse I felt. *Oh, I pray he catches them soon.* I worked on his shirt, but my mind wasn't on it.

Gerri came into the room bringing her sewing with her. "How are you?" she said.

"I'm fine, I suppose. I was just thinking that I hope they catch these men soon."

"Who would help that horrible man escape from jail?"

"I don't know. If his brother were not in jail, I would say it was David. Since he's in jail, it can't be him," I replied.

"It sounds to me like you know them."

"Yes, well, I know David. He's my step-uncle. He's a horrible man! He beat me every chance he got. I pray I never see him again. Michael got me out of there."

"Oh, my, that's unbelievable!"

"Then before Michael and I got married, David attempted to kidnap me. He beat me half to death before we decided to head out of town. Sheriff Mason was hot on his trail though. He managed to rescue me before we got too far away. He was sent to jail for kidnapping, assault, and attempted murder for twenty years. With David's brother out of jail, I'm still in danger. I never met the man before, and he just came to my house to beat me up. Can you believe it?" I explained.

"Oh, how horrible for you," Gerri said. "I'm so sorry. I feel better that you're here while all of this is going on."

"It's not your fault, but thank you. I guess I'm safe here, he wouldn't know where to find me," I replied.

"Wasn't your husband a sheriff there?"

"No, he was a US Marshal then. He gave that up so he could have a family. Marshals do not get much time at home. They are gone all the time," I said.

"Oh, how nice. It's a good thing he did too," she said. "How is the shirt coming along, by the way?"

"It's good. I think I'll have it done the day after tomorrow. And yours?"

"I'll have it done in a week. I have so little time to work on it."

"I know what you mean. But then again, I don't have a baby to take care of." We both laughed, and then I said, "I wonder how long this is going to take. It's been four days already. Not that I don't appreciate your hospitality. I just would like to go home. I saw Michael for an hour four days ago and that's it since I got here. He doesn't want to give it away that I'm here," I said.

"I understand, no offense is taken. I think I would probably feel the same way if I were in your shoes," she said.

"You would think that if they were anywhere near here they would have been caught by now."

"I agree with you." After a while, she said, "Well, it's getting late. I think I ought to call it a night now. What about you?"

"Yes, I'm getting tired now too," I agreed.

Several days later as we were eating dinner, Michael came by. I was so happy to see him that I threw myself into his arms. "It's been five days since I last saw you! Why haven't you come by? I miss you so much. I can't wait to go home. Will it be anytime soon, you think? Oh, I'm sorry, I'm rattling on. I'm not even giving you a chance to answer."

"Well, I got a wire saying that the posse from Topeka caught two of the robbers, one of which was killed. The third one got away, but they didn't say if they saw Finch. I had to go there yesterday to see if either one of them was Finch," he said.

"Were either of them Finch?" I asked quickly.

"No, I don't know who the third guy is either. The prisoner won't talk. Just said he is called Doc. Our posse is on their way back. Don said they lost the trail about ten miles past the southern boarder of Kansas. I don't think they will be around here for a while, if at all. Maybe Finch learned his lesson while in jail here," he said. "We should still be careful though just in case he didn't. We'll all still patrol the town at night so that we can keep an eye on things. If the judge hadn't been so ill, this wouldn't have happened."

"Well, nothing we can do about that now," I replied, and he nodded in response.

"I have hired a woman to live with us and help you around the house so you won't be alone when I have to work at night. She's twenty-eight years old and a widow. She has no children. She needs income and a place to live in. I told her we couldn't pay much, but at least she will have food and a roof over her head."

"That's all right, I think. When can I go home?"

"Now, if you wish. I'm done for the day," he said. "Let's go home."

I immediately prepared all my things so we could leave. Then I hugged Gerri and thanked her.

After we got home, I said, "I have to talk to you. Why didn't you talk to me first before hiring someone? We never talked about such a thing."

"Well, honey, it was a sudden idea when she came to my office asking if I knew of anyone that would hire her. I gave her my answer right there. Please don't be upset. I just would feel better if you have someone here with you when I can't be," Michael said.

"All right, if you think it's best. What's her name?"

"Sally Shore, she's real nice. I think you will like her."

"When is she coming?"

"Sally will be here today because as of Sunday she will have nowhere to go."

"All right, my love."

A short time later, Sally knocked at the door. Michael let her in. She was a little taller than I was, with sandy colored hair and bright greenish, gray eyes. She was a bit thin though. She was wearing a black dress with a vale.

"Hello, Sally, I'm so sorry about your husband," I said.

"Thank you, he died seven months ago, Mrs. Hallowell," she said.

"Oh, please call me Cheyenne."

"Very well, Cheyenne."

"Would you like some coffee or tea? Maybe a slice of pie?"

"Sure, just tea, thank you." She sat down, and I served her some tea. About that time, Michael came in with her belongings. I told him to put them in the second bedroom on the right. This would leave us some privacy at night.

Sally and I talked for some time. Then I told her to go ahead and get settled while I started supper. She could start tomorrow morning. Michael had gone to check on things and said he'd be back before supper. I decided to make fried chicken, potatoes, and biscuits—his favorite dish.

Sally came in the kitchen and said, "After supper I need to go to the house for a little while. Someone is coming to take a few things out of the house that he wants to buy. The rest of the furniture will stay for the new tenants."

During supper I put water on the stove to boil for a bath, and then sat down to eat. Michael was pleased with supper tonight. We talked about the dance, which was going to be this coming weekend. We were grateful we wouldn't have to cancel. We both could use the break.

After supper dishes were done, Sally left, and I got into a hot bath. After I washed, my husband joined me. "You know, my love, you're not going to be able to do this—" I began to say.

"Want to bet? We may have to wait longer to get a bath, but we will," he interrupted.

"You're a rascal," I said as I giggled, and he laughed.

After our bath, we moved to our bedroom to finish what we started. We took our time enjoying each other, even though we were both anxious, as it had been a little over a week since we made love.

No sooner did we finish that a knock came at the front door. Michael answered it, and it was Sally. She too was ready to go to bed, so she said "good night" and disappeared. Michael came back to bed, and we held each other until we fell into a deep sleep. It felt good to be in my own bed and in my husband's arms.

CHAPTER 17

The barn dance was finally here. We were using a huge barn built especially for special social occasions. It was decorated so beautifully. There were streamers, banners, and ribbons and bows. There was punch and cider, food of all kinds, and even candy for the children. We also had music with a piano, fiddles, and a guitar.

The night was not too cold, in fact it was rather warm, not a cloud in the sky with beautiful, bright stars, and a bright full moon. You couldn't ask for a better night for a barn dance.

Everyone was dressed in their Sunday best. They all looked wonderful! I wore a beautiful brilliant blue gown made of shinny material that seemed to sparkle. Michael bought it for me in Topeka when he was there. Luckily, I didn't have many alterations to do. My hair was pulled up on the sides with a small bun on top holding a little baby's breath. I also wore a beautiful shawl to match.

Michael wore his good suit that he married me in. He looked so handsome. His suit fitted him like a glove making him much more attractive. The look on his face when I handed him the new shirt was memorable. He was surprised and loved it.

All the men were on their guard. They were all prepared for anything. If those men showed up, our men would be ready for them. The women were all a little concerned, but I hoped they wouldn't let that interfere with the dance. The whole town was still on edge because of the two men that were still waiting to be caught, hoping they wouldn't come here. Everyone here was talking about it. Word got around quick in a small community.

"Now I want you to have a good time, let me worry about other things," Michael said.

"Yes, my love." I giggled. Just then Sandy came over. "My, you look lovely tonight," I told her.

She was wearing a lovely white gown trimmed with red. Her hair was curled and put up at the sides.

"As are you, Cheyenne," she said.

"Where is your husband?" Michael asked.

"He's over by Mac," Sandy said as she pointed.

Michael kissed me and said, "I'll be back shortly for a dance."

"How are you doing?" Sandy asked me.

"I'm good, thank you. What about you?" I said.

"I'm fine, thank you."

"Are you enjoying yourself?"

"Oh, yes, this is a wonderful dance, don't you think? A gorgeous night to boot."

"Yes, I agree with you."

"Oh, Gerri is coming," Sandy said.

Gerri was dressed in a gorgeous blue shiny gown made of satin. Her hair was also put up in a bun at the top of her head. We said the same pleasantries, talked about the dance, and of course, talked about the breakout.

A while passed before Michael came for our dance. It was a wonderful waltz. As we danced, we talked more. "Are you enjoying yourself?" he asked me.

"Yes, even more now though," I said.

"Oh. And why is that?"

I smacked his shoulder and said, "You know why, you rascal." He laughed and twirled me around. "Everyone keeps talking about the jailbreak. I wish they wouldn't," I said.

"I know, honey. Everyone is still on edge about it."

"I know they are, but it just upsets me to think about it."

"Try not to think too much about it, honey. I want you to have a good time tonight. You deserve it."

"I will try. Maybe if we dance a lot and eat, there won't be much time for conversation."

He laughed and said, "All right, we'll try. But I warn you, I'm not the greatest dancer." We laughed.

That's what we did. We danced and danced, then ate and danced some more. By the end of the evening, I was exhausted. It was getting real late now, so we thought it best to head home. We said our goodbyes to people and drove home. The night was perfect.

When we got home, we sat down to cool off and wind down in the kitchen. We had some lemonade. Sally had arrived home soon after. We offered her some lemonade too.

"Did you have a good time, Sally?" Michael asked.

"Yes. I danced some, but mostly just visited with the ladies. It was a wonderful night and without any mishaps," she replied.

"That it was," I said.

After about a half hour, we said our good nights and went to our rooms.

"You really enjoyed yourself, honey?" Michael asked.

"Yes, I did. Didn't you?"

"I did." We undressed and washed up. Then we got into bed. Both being totally exhausted, we cuddled and went to sleep.

The next morning when I woke up, I didn't feel so well. Too much dancing, I supposed. Michael was already up, so I got up and put my robe on. Then I went into the kitchen.

"Morning, honey," he said.

"Morning, my love. Oh good, you made tea for me."

"Not me, it was Sally."

"Oh, where is she?"

"Getting dressed. Are you feeling all right? You don't look so well."

"As a matter of fact, I'm not feeling well. I guess we danced too much last night."

"Well, take it easy today."

"Yes, my love, I will." Sally came out then and heard the tail end of our conversation, but didn't say a word.

"Morning, Sally," I said.

"Morning, Cheyenne." Sally replied.

Just then someone knocked at the door. Michael asked who it was. "It's Gerri," a lady's voice said. He opened the door. When she came in, she was holding last night's food.

"I thought you might enjoy a day off, Cheyenne."

"Better believe it," Michael said. I gave him a funny look. He chuckled.

"He just wants me to take it easy today," I said.

"Then I'm glad I brought some food here. It's not that Sally can't handle things, but she would get a break too. Nothing better than enjoying good food someone else has cooked," Gerri said.

"Very true," I said. We all laughed then.

"I guess we have dinner and supper covered," Michael said.

Michael then left to check on things with the deputies and the telegraph office. He would be gone for a while. Gerri visited about an hour then she had to leave. Her husband was home with the baby, and he still had things to do. That just left Sally and me.

We talked about the dance a little and about her share of the duties. The chores would be fairly equal so that she didn't have to worry I'd take advantage. "Thank you for giving me this job and a place to call home," Sally said.

"It's our pleasure, Sally. I'm glad you're here."

We talked about our personal lives a bit to get to know each other better. "My husband was a good, good man. He was so handsome and kind. He would help me every chance he got. A perfect gentleman," Sally said.

"He sounds terrific. I'm sorry he's gone," I said.

"He was just perfect for me. He was so loving, thoughtful, honest, and delightful. I only wish I could have had his baby then he could have been with me forever," she said sadly. "We were saving money to have our own ranch. We had such plans."

"I'm so sorry again, Sally. It must be very hard for you."

"Yes, it is, but maybe it will be easier being here and helping you."

"Well, I hope so too."

We talked on some more until Michael came home. We then had dinner. After dinner, we decided to go sit on the front porch for a little while. It was such a nice evening today. We watched all the people and the wagons going by, and we talked about whatever came to mind.

"I wonder if we're going to have a mild winter this year. If we were to base it on the past few days, I would say yes," I said, and Michael agreed.

"They had a mild one this past winter so it's highly unlikely we'd have two in a row, but it would be nice," Sally said.

A short time later, Michael took my hand, and we went to the backyard. We stopped in the house long enough to get his rifle. "It's time to teach you how to shoot," he said.

"But why do I have to learn how to shoot?" I said, incredulous.

"Look, I've been thinking, you've been attacked twice now. With that Finch still on the loose, you need to learn to protect yourself in case I'm not around. We will do this every day until you can handle these two guns, understand?"

"Yes, Michael." Afterward, we sat back on the porch. After a while, I said, "I would say we had a pretty lazy day."

"Yes, we have," Sally said.

"We've talked so much that it's almost time for supper," Michael said.

"Are you getting hungry already?" I asked.

"Pretty close, don't you think?" he replied.

"All right, let's go have some supper." I laughed as I went inside, with Michael and Sally on my heels.

After supper dishes were done, Michael showed me how to clean the gun. "If you're going to handle a gun, you need to know how to take care of it," he said.

Then we went out for a little more target practice. I didn't do too badly for a beginner, and Michael said I was a natural. I didn't know about that, but at least, I wasn't afraid of them. When we were finished, we went in for dessert before going to bed.

CHAPTER 18

I t was almost thanksgiving, and we were planning a big feast and to invite Gerri, Mac, Sandy, and Mitch. I hoped I was up for it. Even though I had Sally's help, I just didn't know with the way I had been feeling lately. Michael was due home any minute for dinner, and I needed to hurry and get it ready for him. So I put down the menu for thanksgiving and prepared dinner.

Michael walked in the door just as I was ready to put the food on the table. I asked how his day was going, and he told me a little about it. By the time he was finished telling me, he had also finished eating. Then he asked how my day was.

"I went to the doctor today—" I started to say.

"Are you all right?" he interrupted before I could finish.

"Yes, yes I'm fine, my love. I don't know how to say this, so I'm just going to blurt it out. It's just that you're going to be a father," I said. He spit out his coffee that he had sipped as I said it. I giggled.

"What? How? Never mind how, I know how. But, really?" he asked.

"Yes, my love. Are you happy?"

"Happy?" he replied as he got up from the table and came over to me. "Of course, I'm happy! You just shocked me with it. I wasn't expecting it. You could have given a guy a warning, you know."

I giggled. "Now how could I do that? It's either it is or it isn't. There is no warning," I said.

"Is that why you've been sick?" he asked as he gently moved me away so he could look at me.

"Yes, I think so, that's what made me go see the doctor."

"Why didn't you tell me you were going to the doctor? I would have gone with you."

"I only decided this morning."

"Oh, all right. I'm sorry I'm just shocked, but very delighted too, of course. I'm not thinking clearly," he said. I giggled again.

"Me too, my love, me too."

"You're to take it easy, do you understand?"

"Yes, but the doctor said I have nothing to worry about. Everything looks good. I can go about my day normally."

"When is he or she due to arrive?"

"Early August."

"What a nice birthday present, Momma."

"I guess so," I said as I giggled.

"I want you to rest as much as you can, starting today," he suddenly said.

"I will do my best, darling."

Sally had come in then. She had been to the mercantile to get us a few supplies. "Someone is very happy," she said.

"Well, Cheyenne just told me that we're going to have a baby in August," Michael said.

"Oh, that's wonderful for both of you! Congratulations!" Sally said.

"Thank you," we both replied simultaneously.

"We're going to have to get some baby clothes together, get a cradle, and make some blankets then," she said.

"Yes, we do and we will," I replied with a smile. It was so nice of her to say "we". It made me feel that she was getting comfortable being here.

Michael chuckled and said, "I'm going to ask Mitch to make the cradle, so that will be done."

"Thank you, that would be wonderful," I said. Just then our guests arrived.

"Wow, the table looks wonderful!" Sandy exclaimed.

"I very much agree," Gerri said.

"Thank you. I had hoped it would," I replied.

"You plan on feeding the army?" Mac asked, and I giggled.

"No, just you three men," I said, and everyone laughed. "Please, everyone, sit down and we're happy to have you for Thanksgiving dinner."

After everyone was seated, Michael also thanked them for coming then he made the announcement that we were going to have a baby in August. They all congratulated us and said that it was good that Sally was here to help out.

"I was a little worried after you lost your first one," Gerri said.

"I know what you mean," I told her. "I was thinking I would never have children after that. Silly of me to think that, but I did. God is blessing us with this baby, and I hope the baby is healthy."

"I agree with that," Sally said.

"I do too," Gerri chimed in.

The dinner was grand, and there was enough leftover to nibble on later tonight for supper. The ladies cleaned up after dinner and had it done quickly while the men sat down, talking and drinking coffee. The ladies and I moved to the sitting room to talk, leaving the men in the kitchen. We talked until supper. We ate, then I served the pies and cakes. It was a fantastic day. Gerri and Sandy helped clean up before leaving. I was tired, but was also invigorated, if that made any sense.

Michael and I said "good night" to Sally and went to our room. Michael was obviously frisky, since he kept kissing me on my neck. He then began to undress me. Then he kissed my belly and asked, "This will not hurt the baby, will it?"

"No," I simply said.

He kissed me again, this time with so much passion that I thought I'd explode right then. As we made love, Michael was gentle so as not to hurt the baby.

It was such a wonderful night on top of the wonderful day yesterday. I looked out the window and noticed it was snowing. The fire needed to be built up, so it would warm up in here. So

I got out of bed and placed two logs on the fire. It was a cold morning. I hurried to dress and went to the kitchen to warm up, knowing Michael would have the stove on. I was pleased to be getting warm. I poured myself some coffee and sat at the table.

Just then, Michael came in the kitchen. "Oh, there you are. What were you doing, my love?" I asked.

"Had to get more wood. It's all on the porch," he said. "The snow is picking up."

"It's beautiful though, isn't it?"

"Yes, I suppose it looks nice. It's just that it's so cold."

Between the lit stove and the fire burning in the fireplace that was in the bathing room on the kitchen wall, it was toasty warm in the kitchen.

Michael came to me and hugged me. "How are you doing this morning, honey?"

"I'm doing just fine, my love. The baby is fine too."

"I'm going to make you some breakfast this morning, so sit and relax," Michael said.

"Thank you." He made some bacon and eggs with leftover biscuits from last night. "It all smells wonderful, Michael."

Sally came out then. "Sorry I'm late, I overslept. All because of the excitement yesterday, I suppose," she said.

"No need to worry, I planned on making breakfast myself this morning, anyway," Michael replied.

"Thank you," she said.

"We need to do a little target practice today if you're up to it," Michael said.

"I'm ready," I said.

After breakfast, we went outside for target practice. We had been practicing for a while when Michael said, "You have improved greatly. All the practicing is paying off. I hope you'll never need it though, but I feel better knowing that if need be you would be able to protect yourself."

"Thank you, my love," I told him.

As I cooked dinner, I noticed how hard it was snowing. "Michael, look, do you see how hard it's snowing?"

"I see that."

"I can't even see across the road."

"What do you expect for January?"

"Are we getting a blizzard?"

"Maybe. I think I'd better get over to the mercantile to be sure we have enough supplies, just in case."

"Okay, I'll get you a list."

"I too have to leave to go see Gerri, but I'll be back soon," Sally said.

"With the way that it's snowing, don't you think you should wait?" I suggested.

"No, I'll be fine, really," she said as she left.

While I waited for Michael, I thought of the last Christmas celebration we had. I could not have asked for a better one. Christmas was wonderful! I made Michael a scarf to go with the three shirts I made him. I had asked Sally to pick me up an extra bolt of material in blue so I could make Michael a third shirt. Michael loved his gifts. He had said he needed new shirts. I also made Sally a nightgown, and we bought her some nice smelling soap, made with honeysuckle. She loved them too.

Michael gave me some honeysuckle soap as well and a new beautiful shawl with a muff so I could keep my hands warm. He also picked up the cradle to surprise me with it. It was a grand cradle. It was made of cedar, which smelled lovely. It was nice and sturdy, and sanded to perfection. It was a lovely Christmas indeed.

Michael came in about an hour later. He had bought what we needed in case we got snowed in, which wouldn't surprise me by the looks of things. "It's really coming down out there. It doesn't look like it's going to end anytime soon," Michael said.

"Are you sure we have plenty of wood to last us?" I asked.

"I think so. If not, then I'll just have to find a way out to get more."

"Maybe you should bring the wood in just in case we get snowed in."

"I think you're right. At least, it'll be dry."

So we spent part of the morning loading the wood up in the wash area and putting a good amount in the sitting room near the fireplace. We also stacked a bit of wood in our room and Sally's room near the fireplaces, so they would be dry and ready.

By supper time, it was still snowing, not quite as hard though. I made stew for supper with biscuits and a cake for dessert. After supper, Michael opened the door to check the progress of the snow, and as he did, snow slid onto the floor. "Well, looks like we're only not in a blizzard, but we'll also be snowed in," he said.

"It's still snowing?"

"Yes, honey, it is. It's already now up to my knees. It snowed heavier during supper."

"I wonder how long it will take for the snow to melt, so we aren't snowed in too long."

"Depends on the sunshine, honey," he said, chuckling.

I smacked his arm and said, "I know that!" Suddenly, I remembered Sally. "Oh, Michael! What about Sally? She's still out there."

"She's at Gerri's, so she'll be just fine. I don't think she'll leave there now," he said.

"I'm sure you're right," I just said.

CHAPTER 19

Michael checked the snow out of the kitchen door. The snow was up to his thigh and still falling, just not as hard. It must have snowed all night long. "How long are we going to be snowed in?" I asked.

"I don't know. It doesn't seem to be as cold today, maybe it will stop snowing and start warming up to melt the snow quickly," Michael said.

"That would be nice. Being snowed in for only a few days isn't bad, but anything longer than that will drive us crazy."

The snow kept coming and coming. Is it ever going to stop?

Three days later Sally came home looking pale. We rushed her in next to the fire to warm up. She let us know that she had tried to come home that day but had turned back just part way through. The snow was just too deep, and she would not have made it home. The next morning she woke up sneezing and coughing; her entire was body aching with a raging fever.

Michael checked her head and found her burning up. He hollered to me to bring in some snow and a bath sheet. I did as he asked. He took the bowl of snow from me and placed a bath sheet with snow in it on her head. The snow melted quickly, but the bath sheet was still somewhat cold. "How does that feel?" he asked her.

"It feels good, thank you," she said.

"Make her some tea, honey," Michael said. So I did. Then he looked at Sally and said, "Make sure you drink your tea, too. The more you drink, the better you'll feel,"

I found myself hoping that it was just a cold.

I took the tea to Sally. "How are you feeling, Sally?"

"I'm all right, except for this sneezing," she replied.

"Hope it's just a cold. Now, drink your tea. If you need anything, just yell." She nodded her head.

"Morning!" Sally said a few days later.

"Morning, Sally," Michael and I said simultaneously.

"How are you feeling?" I asked.

"Fine, except for this cold," Sally said as she sneezed.

"Your head still bother you?" Michael asked.

"Just a little."

Michael checked on the snow; it was melting but not very fast, and it was below his knee. "A few more days," he said.

"I hope, my love,"

I decided that I would bake some cookies and a pie today. It was a good way to pass the time. Sally decided that she was going to clean the house while I baked. Michael was with me drinking coffee.

"When will the first batch be done?" he asked me.

I giggled and said, "Soon, my love. You're worse than a child."

He grabbed the towel off the table and swatted me with it. I turned to him with a giggle and said, "I'll get you for that."

"You promise?" We both laughed then.

"You really are a rascal."

For the next five days, we kept ourselves quite busy. It snowed a couple of times, but except for that, there was nothing else to worry over. The sun shone most of the days, which helped to melt most of the snow from the blizzard. There was still some snow on the ground, but at least we could get out of the house now. We had been stuck inside too long.

Michael and I went to the mercantile, while Sally went to Gerri's. It was a cold day with some clouds moving in, so we didn't want to be out too long.

We restocked the food, and I picked out some material for the baby. "How did you like our blizzard, George?" Michael asked.

"Not too good, it kept business away. Yet, I didn't mind a small vacation." He laughed.

"I can only imagine," Michael said.

I visited with Madelyn for a few minutes. "I hear congratulations are in order," she said.

"Oh, yes, thank you."

"You have some nice material for the baby?"

"Yes, you have a good variety of material. Are you all right? You're not looking well, Madelyn."

"I'm good, Cheyenne, really. How are you? It's good to see you."

"Thank you, it's good to see you too, and I'm good. Did you make out all right during the storm?"

"Yes, it was lonely though. No customers, you know."

I giggled and said, "I understand what you mean. Well I'd better be going. I want to beat the snow home. It has been great to see you."

"You too, Cheyenne. Take care of yourself and that baby," Madelyn said.

"I will, you take care too." I met up with Michael then.

No sooner did we get home that Sally came home. We put all the food away together. "Looks like we made it home just in time," I said. "It's snowing."

Michael came to look out the door. "At least it's not snowing too awfully heavy. Hopefully it won't last long," he said.

It was time to make dinner now that everything was put away. Then I would start working on the baby clothes a little before I had to make supper. Sally knew how to knit, so she was going to make the baby a special blanket for cold weather. I already made curtains for the baby's room, which was the one across from us, although the cradle would be in our room at first.

"While you fix dinner, I'm going to go over to the telegraph office to see if there is anything for the sheriff's office," Michael said.

"All right, dinner will be ready when you get back, unless you run there and back." I giggled.

"Maybe that's what I should do," Michael said as he laughed and walked out the door.

I heated the leftover stew and warmed some biscuits from this morning's breakfast. I made coffee and some tea. Just as I put the food on the table, Michael walked in.

"Just in time, my love," I said with a smile. However, I lost my smile when I saw his face. "What's wrong, love?"

"Well, it looks like the man that shot me in El Dorado was a man named Damian Swartz. He was in the posse with us when we went after those rustlers," he said.

"Who is he?"

"Apparently, he's a good friend of David and Denny Finch." Then he looked at me. "I think that's who broke Finch out of jail here."

"Oh, no," I said quietly.

We sat to eat dinner, both lost in thought. This could be real bad. Denny Finch had help. *What if they come back? What if they find more help to kill us both? Oh, dear Lord, please don't let that happen.* Just then, Michael noticed me and said, "Listen, I don't want you getting yourself all worked up over this. You have enough to tend with being pregnant and all. I don't need both of you getting sick."

"I won't," I assured him.

Michael decided to stay home. He said he had nothing pressing to do. I think he was worried about me though. "Where's Sally?" he asked.

"She has gone to see Sandy for a little while. She said she wouldn't be long."

"I think I'd feel better if she didn't leave you alone while I'm gone."

"What does it matter? There would be nothing she could do to help if they show up here."

"I would just feel a little better. She could find a way to get to me if anything happened to you. I'll talk to her."

He went to the desk in the sitting room, and I stayed in the kitchen to make some fresh cornbread for supper. I hoped they never showed up here ever again. Maybe they just left the state. That certainly would be great. Denny was just as bad as, if not worse than, his brother David. If only the judge would have been available and not ill, Denny would be in jail still. *I think they are both insane! I can't think about this or I'll go crazy. I promised not to get worked up, so I'd better focus on what I'm doing.*

CHAPTER 20

Michael woke me very early this morning by rubbing my thighs. "You woke me because you're frisky?" I teased. His only response was a loving kiss and a devious laugh. Oh, how I love this man. I see how much he loves me. I never thought I could be loved like this, that I could love a man this deep in my soul. I not only enjoy the sensations, but I also look forward to what was to come. He is an amazing, desirable, and caring lover. We made love quickly, but it was intense! What a great way to start the day! I couldn't be happier to have such a loving and kind man.

Afterward, we lay there just holding each other and winding down. "What are you going to do today, honey?" he asked.

"Well, after this I'm not sure, nothing can compare." I giggled.

He rolled over to look into my eyes and said, "No, nothing can compare, but you're even better than that, honey. Life would be miserable without you."

"Aww, my love, I feel the same. I love you." Then he kissed me. "How about I make a cherry pie with supper tonight?" I asked.

"Oh, that's my favorite! You don't have to bribe me to make love to you," he teased.

"Oh, you," I said as I pushed on his arm, giggling.

We got up and washed, then dressed for the day. I went into the kitchen to find that Sally had already started breakfast.

"It smells wonderful in here, Sally," I said.

"Thank you. How are you this fine morning, Cheyenne?"

"I'm wonderful, thank you. I can't believe it's almost the start of summer."

"I know, it just came so fast. I'm glad though, I really hate winter," she replied.

With breakfast on the table, we planned our day. Sally suggested we go to Gerri's today. It had been a while, she said. Then our day was planned: cherry pie and biscuits this morning and Gerri's this afternoon. Michael would go to the office.

After dinner was finished and we cleaned the kitchen, we left for Gerri's. When we arrived, not only was Gerri expecting us, but so was the whole town it seemed. They all yelled "Surprise!" when I walked in.

Oh, what a wonderful surprise it was! There were gifts, cake, lemonade, games, and beautiful decorations. "Oh, it all looks fantastic!" I said. I looked at Sally and said, "So this is why you have been coming here so much lately. I can't believe you pulled this all off and so well. I don't know what to say, except thank you."

"Yes, I had to have somewhere to go to set up this party for you and the baby," she said. I gave her a big hug as well as Gerri and Sandy.

"You both are the best!" They smiled.

"Let's get this party started," Gerri said.

"First," Gerri said, "you must put this ribbon on, and anyone who says the word baby loses their ribbon. At the end of the afternoon, whoever has the most ribbons wins the door prize." They passed the ribbons around so everyone had one.

"Now we have a list of words, each word is scrambled up, and you have to unscramble the words in just three minutes." There didn't seem to be enough time to do this, but I would give it my best. The time was on. When Gerri called "time!" everyone stopped. The winner was Jeannie. She won a bottle of Lemon Verbena. We all applauded.

"Our next game is who can guess the size of Cheyenne's belly. We have some yarn. Each of you, in turn, will hold the yarn out to guess what size Cheyenne's belly is without going near her. The one who guesses the closest will win," Sally said. Each lady had a chance to hold the yarn to see if they could guess Cheyenne's belly size. After everyone had a chance to play, the winner was announced. "The winner is…Kathryn Ellsworth!" Sally said. She won a lovely small flower vase. We applauded again.

"Our last game is Diaper the baby. Form two rows. You must 'undiaper' and 'rediaper' the baby doll while blindfolded. Then pass the blindfold to the next player in the row. The first row who completes this quest will win. Ready? Set? Go!" Gerri said.

Everyone was laughing and having a wonderful time with this game. It was exciting. Then the winner was announced, "The second row wins!" Gerri said. They each got a beautiful set of white knitted doilies. We all applauded then.

"Now we shall have some cake. Does anyone want coffee instead of lemonade?" Gerri asked.

Gerri and I went into the kitchen to make coffee and get cups for those who want coffee. "Thank you for such a lovely party Gerri!" I said. "It's so fun."

"You're welcome. It has been fun, hasn't it?"

I took the cups out and set them down on the table. Gerri arrived with the coffee a few minutes later. All the girls were talking among themselves, enjoying the visit, and talking about how much fun they were having. Ribbons were being passed around like crazy. One would get a ribbon, say "baby" and lose all the ribbons she has. It was so much fun!

It was time to open all the gifts. I got baby clothes, blankets, burp cloths, and such. Sally made a winter nightshirt-type blanket, and it was adorable. Everything that I got was just beautiful! A lot of hard work went into everything. I couldn't have asked for a better day. I truly needed this distraction. Won't Michael be surprised?

The party went on for another hour because everyone was enjoying themselves and enjoying the break in their normal routines. I had never felt so popular in all my life. Not even when I went to school.

At the end of the party just before everyone started to leave, Gerri announced the winner of the grand prize, which was a beautiful brooch that was made in an oval shape, made with silver, and with a turquoise stone in the middle. "The winner is Rainie!" We all applauded again.

Everyone said thank you and said good-bye. Sally and I were among the last to leave. "I want to thank you both again. It was a lovely surprise party." I hugged them both. "Let's go home, Sally. I can't wait until Michael sees what we have."

By the time we got home, it was time to make supper. Sally decided that I had a very busy day and should rest. She would make supper tonight.

After taking a nap for about an hour and a half, I joined Sally in the kitchen. She made fried chicken tonight. "Oh, Michael is going to love you!" I teased.

"I just hope he likes it," she said as she blushed.

"I'm sure he will, Sally," I told her. "He loves fried chicken and cherry pie. Those are his most favorite things to eat."

> > > < < <

"Sheriff, I have an urgent telegram for you!" Jacob said while trying to catch his breath.

"Let me see it." I read the telegram, silently at first, and then out loud. "There's been a prison break. Stop. We're on work crew when they escaped. Stop. Eight men total Stop. Reward dead or alive. Stop."

"That's it? No other information?" Don asked.

"That's all it says."

Don and I just looked at each other. "Eight men." Don said.

"Yes, eight of them," I replied. "We will need to keep our eyes open and let the town folks know to keep their doors latched and watch for strangers."

"I doubt they'll come here. Let's hope they don't," Don said.

The look on my face had to have been obvious, but nothing was said. I couldn't tell Cheyenne about this just yet. I didn't want her to worry right now, not until I knew for sure what was going on. "I think it's best to just tell the men for now. I don't want to alarm Cheyenne. If the women know, they may say something to her. Her condition is too delicate right now."

They all agreed.

>>><<<

Michael came home, and we sat down to supper. I then told him of the surprising day I had. He was surprised too. "How nice of you, ladies, to do such a nice thing for Cheyenne," he said.

"It was our pleasure. She was so surprised that it made the party that much better," Sally said.

"The grand prize was a beautiful brooch, silver with a turquoise stone in the center, and doilies, a vase, lemon verbena. Rainie won the brooch. She was so excited," I told him.

"What did you win?" he asked.

"Oh, silly, I won all kinds of beautiful things for the baby. I'll show you after supper."

Once supper was over, I showed him all the things from the party. He was just as impressed and pleased as I was. "With all this stuff, I guess we're pretty much ready for the baby to come, with everything you and Sally already made as well," he said.

"I think so too, my love. At least I hope we aren't forgetting anything. With all this nice stuff, I'm getting anxious for the baby to come. August can't get here fast enough."

"Be patient, honey, the baby will be here before you know it," he said as he chuckled.

"It's going to be difficult with as much trouble as I'm having getting around right now. I hate to think how it's going to be during the last month."

Michael laughed and said, "You look so cute though." I threw a pillow at him. He laughed even more. *Typical man* was all I could say. After I put everything away in the baby's room, I was ready for bed. It appeared Michael was too, he was dozing while I put the things away.

We went to our room. I didn't think either one of us was up to making love tonight. I changed into my nightgown and crawled into bed. Then he too climbed into bed. We just snuggled and went to sleep.

CHAPTER 21

It was a very hot day today, too hot to do anything, even take a nap. I stayed in the sitting room where it seemed to be the coolest place in the house. It was way too hot to sit outside. I found myself wishing for a little rain to cool it off some. I was glad I made my cake and bread early this morning. I wouldn't bake in this heat.

As Sally walked into the room, she asked, "Cheyenne are you doing all right?"

"Yes, considering. How are you feeling?"

"About the same, I suppose. What shall we do today?"

"Well, I think it's just too hot to do much of anything today,"

"This is just the beginning," she said.

"I know, don't remind me," I responded as I giggled.

Michael came home early. "Hello, honey, how are you feeling?" he asked.

"I'm doing all right, considering this heat."

"Well, I have some news to cheer you up a bit."

"What's that, my love?"

"A group of us is going to go to Miller's pond to swim and have a picnic supper. What do you think of that?"

I slowly got up then and with a big smile, I said, "Really? Oh, that sounds wonderful! I have nothing prepared and no time to do it now. We need to get some food and drinks put together."

"I figured, so I ordered something from the café for the three of us," Michael replied. I went to him and gave him a big hug.

"Sally, let's get our things together for a picnic and a swim," I said.

I gathered up linen napkins, cups for drinks, lemonade, and a table cloth. Sally grabbed a blanket and bath sheets, and helped me pack them all away. We changed into dresses that were older and better for outside activities such as this. A few minutes later, we were ready to go.

Once we got to the pond, we set up our picnic area before joining the others. I walked over to the water and held my dress up and waded in the water while Michael jumped in. We enjoyed the water and our friends. Don and Jeannie were here, and so were Gerri and Mac, Melanie Campbell, Sandy and Mitch, Roy, and Susan Johnstone.

Rainie wanted to come, but she couldn't leave the restaurant, and Madelyn and George couldn't leave the store too. The men swam in their long underwear, and the women in their slips. This was so much fun. I was so glad Michael thought of it.

An hour and a half later, we were sitting down to enjoy our picnic. We all had our blankets set out next to each other so we could visit. For our supper, we had cold fried chicken, beans, peach slices, and lemonade. Everything was delicious. Leave it to Michael to get fried chicken, he loved his fried chicken. I giggled.

"What's so funny?" he asked.

"Nothing, just you and your chicken."

After we ate, we sat around just talking and laughing for a little while before going back into the water. Today would not have been better if there had been rain to cool us off.

It started to get late so everyone got out of the water, dried off, and got dressed for the ride home. Just as we were loading up, shots rang out. Everyone ducked for cover, except Sandy, she fell to the ground before she could reach the wagons. Oh, no, she must have been hit. Was she dead? Mitch was furious! Oh, dear, Sandy! Mitch picked her up and running he carried her to the wagons. "Mitch is she all right?" Michael asked.

"No, she's dead!" Mitch yelled. My heart just sank. Oh, Sandy I'm going to miss you. I began to cry.

The men grabbed their rifles out of their buckboards and returned fire. Shots rang out everywhere, but they were not too far away. "Up in the trees!" Roy yelled.

"Now who would be dumb enough to shoot us from so close?" Mac yelled.

"Don't know, but we'll find out. Roy, you and Don circle around and come up from behind. We'll draw their fire," Michael said. "With the women safely down, we could do what we have to do."

I stayed on the ground. When the shooting started, I felt a burning in my shoulder, so I looked and found that I was bleeding. I couldn't tell Michael yet because he had to take care of those shooters. He couldn't be worrying about me, it wasn't that bad.

More shots rang out, but everyone else seemed to be fine. Michael, Mac, and Mitch were all firing as much as they could to give Roy and Don time to get behind the shooters as Michael suggested. It wasn't too long of a wait. "All right, give yourselves up! We have you surrounded! If you want to come out of this alive, give yourselves up!" Michael yelled.

Their reply was more gunfire. Suddenly, I saw someone stand to take aim at Michael, and just before I could scream, in a split second, Michael sidestepped and fired. The shooter missed, Michael didn't.

Either Roy or Don fired shots straight up into the air to show they had the culprits. "All right, boys, we're in the clear! Roy and Don have the shooters! Cheyenne, you can get up now, honey." Just as he bent over to help me up, he noticed I was bleeding. "Cheyenne! You're hit!"

Just then, he picked me up and put me in the buckboard, which he got from the livery. He yelled just as he climbed up, "Sally, gather our things and go with one of the others. I have to get Cheyenne to the doctor!" At that, he raced off as fast as he could.

Once we got there, Michael picked me up and carried me. He kicked open the doctor's door with his boot and yelled for Doctor Kiley. "Doc! Cheyenne's been shot. Get down here, I need you!"

A few seconds later, Doctor Kiley was at my side. He checked me out, but there was no bullet. It went into my right shoulder and went out the back of my shoulder. The bullet did not hit anything major so there was no real harm done. He cleaned me up and closed the wounds. "You're going to hurt for a little while, but you'll be fine so long as no infection sets in," Doctor Kiley said.

"Is the baby going to be all right?" Michael asked the doctor once he knew I was going to be fine.

"Yes, the baby is just fine. Nothing to worry about."

"You're sure they're both fine?"

"Yes, they're both just fine." Next thing I knew, Michael was yelling at me right in front of the doctor. "Why didn't you tell me you were hit when it happened? Why did you wait? Do you know what could have happened? I could have helped you! Don't you ever do that again! Do you understand me?"

"Yes, Michael, now calm down."

"How can I calm down? I could have lost both of you today. You could have bled to death! There was no telling how long the shooting could have gone on!"

"All right, Michael, I understand, now please calm down." At that moment he grabbed me and hugged me tight.

"Don't you ever do that again," he said more softly. I didn't know if I should leave it alone or strangle him for yelling at me in front of the doctor. I took into consideration that he just got scared half to death, so I'd let it go.

"Now, Cheyenne, you're going to need this sling for a little while, and I want to see you again in a week," Doctor Kiley said.

"Yes, doctor."

"You may take her home now, Michael," Doctor Kiley added.

"Thanks a lot, Doc," Michael replied. He paid Doctor Kiley and we left.

Once we were home, Michael got me settled and said, "I have to go to the office for a few minutes. I need to see who was shooting at us and make sure they stay put. I want to check on Mitch too."

"All right," I replied. "Sandy… I can't believe she's dead. She was a sensational person, and I'm going to miss her so much!" I cried.

"I know, honey, neither can I," Michael said as he hugged me. Then he kissed me. "I'll be back soon."

Sally was home when we got there. "Are you all right, Cheyenne?" she asked.

"Yes, I'm fine, and so is the baby."

"Did the doctor get the bullet out?"

"No, the bullet went clean through. He said I have to wear this sling for a little while. I go back in a week."

"I'm so relieved it only went past your arm, it could have been much worse."

"Yes, it could have been. The bullet went through my shoulder, but it didn't hit anything vital."

"Oh, your shoulder, I'm sorry. You were lucky. Do you want something to snack on?" she asked.

"No, thank you, I'll just wait for Michael to come home then I'll have some cake. Yes, I'm very lucky," I said.

"I'm so upset with what happened to Sandy though," Sally said sadly.

"Me too, I'm going to miss her so very much," Tears formed in my eyes as I said this.

"I know I will too, very much. She was a close friend," Sally started to cry then, and I held her.

"You're a great friend too," I told her, and we cried together.

Sally brought all the stuff that we took to the pond inside. She started putting them away when Michael walked in the door. "Hello, Sally, thank you for taking care of all this," Michael said.

"You're welcome. It's no trouble," she replied.

Then Michael came to me in the sitting room. "We have Denny Finch in jail. Damian is dead. They were the ones shooting at us. I've sent a telegram sending for the circuit Judge. I don't want him in town any longer than necessary. You all right?" he said.

"Yes, I'm fine. I hope he stays in jail this time."

"He will. I have both deputies on it and I've asked two more for the night shift. He isn't going anywhere until we ship him out of here."

"Do you want some cake now, my love?" I asked.

"Yes, that sounds real good," he replied. We went into the kitchen.

Sally was finishing putting everything away when we went into the kitchen. "Sally, will you cut some cake for us please?" Michael asked.

"Certainly," she replied.

"I guess you'll need to take over most things now, Sally. That is, if you don't mind?" Michael said.

"Not to worry, that's what you hired me for."

"Thank you so much," I told her.

"You're welcome. How's your shoulder feeling?"

"It hurts, but I'll be okay soon. I'm probably going to have a rough night though."

When we finished our cake, Michael and I went to our room. Changing into my nightgown was a painful experience. After I got it on, I climbed into bed. Since I had to sleep on my left side, I would have to have my back against Michael. "I don't mind, at least, I can hold you," he said.

"I'll miss holding you."

"I know, so you hold the baby and we will be good."

"All right, my love. I love you."

"I love you too." Then he kissed me good night.

The next morning, I woke up very sore from sleeping on one side all night. My shoulder throbbed. I tried to assist Sally in the kitchen, but I was basically useless. "You shouldn't worry, Cheyenne, I have everything under control," she said.

"I know you do, but it's hard to do nothing when you've been so used to working everyday."

"I understand. It shouldn't take too long to heal, should it?"

"I don't know. The doctor didn't say. I don't know what I'm going to do with myself until I can take off this sling," I said.

As I sat out on the porch waiting for Michael to get home and for supper to be ready, I had been visited by just about every woman in town asking how I was doing and if I needed anything. All I said was that they help me find something to do with just my one hand and everyone laughed. It was so nice of everyone to come for a visit. It was a great feeling to be cared about by so many.

"How did you do today, honey?" Michael asked as he was walking toward the house.

"I was bored out of my mind. I'm not used to just sitting around," I said.

"Be patient, honey, it'll get better soon."

"But sooner would be better," I replied. Michael just chuckled.

"How's our little one doing?" he asked as he rubbed my belly.

"Oh, just fine, kicking me a lot."

A week later, I went to visit Dr. Kiley for a checkup. "So, Cheyenne, how have you been feeling?" Doctor Kiley asked.

"I'm pretty good. The baby seems to be just fine, kicking regularly. The shoulder seems much better now too," I told him.

"Well, let's have a look." The doctor felt my forehead to be sure that there was no fever. He then examined my shoulder and then the baby. "It seems that you were a very lucky young lady. There's no fever and no signs of infection. The baby appears to be doing well too. I think you need to rest more often, however," he said.

"Oh, I'm so happy to hear that, Doctor Kiley."

"I think you can take off the sling for short periods of time, as long as it truly doesn't hurt. If it hurts, leave it on, all right?"

"All right, thank you so much, Doctor Kiley."

On the way home, I ran into my husband. "So, how did your appointment go?" he asked.

"The appointment went good. I'm fine and the baby's fine too. I can even take the sling off for short periods of time as long as my shoulder doesn't hurt," I told him.

"That's wonderful, honey! Now maybe we can have some time together."

"That's how it looks to me too, my love," I replied with a smile. He did want me to rest more, however.

CHAPTER 22

Denny Finch's trial was today. The judge came in on the morning stage. He was dressed in a suit and ready to do business. He was an older man with gray hair and mustache. He stood shorter than Michael and was a bit stocky. When he got off the stage, I didn't realize that he was the judge until I saw him in court. He was polite, but a little standoffish. Maybe he was just in a hurry to get things started. Maybe after court he may be more sociable.

As he got off the stage, we saw the two attorneys discussing who was going to defend and who was going to prosecute. They couldn't agree, so they flipped a coin. Michael and I just looked at each other and laughed.

Michael, Don, Roy, Mac, and Mitch all had to testify to the events of the shooting that took place a week and a half ago. They all pretty much said the same thing, describing how it all happened. They told the Jury of my being hit as well as Sandy's death, and about how we all were just minding our own business, having a picnic and swimming with friends. There was absolutely no cause for them to shoot at us. It was simple revenge on the part of Finch and nothing more.

The court was also informed that Denny Finch was in jail on charges of assault and attempted rape, and that he had escaped. He had not gone in front of the judge for that yet, so the prosecutor included them to Finch's new charges.

As they were testifying, I felt like it was happening all over again, with the fear, the anger, and the pain. All I wanted to do was run, but knowing I couldn't made it all that much worse. Remembering Sandy dead on the ground just angered and hurt me that I so wanted to go pound Finch into stew meat! If only I could. To lose such a good friend was more painful than my own injury of being shot. That man deserved life in prison. He deserved to never see the outside of a cell again!

After all was said and done, the jury found Finch guilty on assault, escaping from jail, attempted rape, intent to commit murder, attempted murder, and murder. He was sentenced to hang by the neck until dead at sunrise tomorrow. That pleased Michael, and especially Mitch, who was taking his wife's death very hard.

I didn't have to go to the hanging to know how it all worked out. Everyone in town was talking about it. They said it was, and watching a man hang by the neck was just plain horrific. Just the thought of it made me nauseous. They would be better off shooting them instead.

Gerri told me that people were coming from all over town just to see the hanging. I was shocked by this news, especially with women being present. That was just something I didn't understand. I guessed I could understand men attending, but not women.

Sally came into the sitting room and asked, "Would you like something to drink? You seem awfully quiet, are you all right?"

"Yes, Sally, I'm all right. Just a little put off over the hanging today. Yes, lemonade sounds good to me. Bring yourself some too, and we can talk," I replied.

"I would love too, but I need to run to the mercantile for a few things for supper tonight."

"All right, just hurry back."

"Dinner is ready, and Michael will be home soon. Will you be all right until he gets here?"

"Oh, yes, I'll be just fine. You go ahead," I told her. Before she left, she brought me some lemonade.

Not long after Sally left, Michael came home. "Hello, honey, how are you feeling? Where's Sally?" he asked.

"Sally went to the mercantile. She just left a few minutes ago. I'm all right, I'm just a little disturbed by today's event. Otherwise, I'm fine," I replied.

"I had to be there, but I'm glad you decided not to go. It was a bit hideous, especially for a pregnant woman. It's over now, so why don't you try to forget about it, and let's go eat dinner?" Michael said.

"I don't know if I can."

"You need to eat, honey."

"All right, I will try."

I ate very little, but at least I ate enough to satisfy Michael. With a worried look on his face, Michael said, "Honey, you can't go on getting yourself all worked up like this. It's not good for you or the baby."

"Oh, I know, my love. It's just that I'm experiencing something new, so I just need a little time."

"All right, maybe you could take a nap today. You're getting close to your delivery. You could probably use the rest, anyway," Michael said.

"Yes, I will try, my love."

I woke up suddenly realizing that it must be close to suppertime. When I went into the kitchen, Sally was already getting supper ready. "Hello, I didn't realize I had slept so long. Why didn't you wake me?" I told her.

"You were sleeping so soundly, and I thought I can manage supper, anyway."

"I know you can. I just don't want to seem like I'm taking advantage," I explained.

"You wouldn't be, I was hired to do these things, remember? I don't mind at all."

"All right, thank you, Sally."

I began to clean the kitchen and suddenly my belly started to cramp. It wasn't cramping real hard though, so I didn't think it was labor. I decided to continue what I was doing.

"Are you all right?" I heard Michael say.

"Yes, my love, I'm fine. Just a little cramping is all," I replied.

"Why don't you let Sally do that and you go rest?" he suggested.

"I rested all afternoon, I'm not tired. I can't live in bed, you know," I said.

"Well, take it easy then. Go read your book or sew something. Anything just so you get off your feet," he insisted.

"All right, Michael." So I got my book and went into the sitting room to read a little. It was still light enough to see the pages if I sit by the window, and it wouldn't be long until bedtime, anyway.

Later at night while I was asleep, I suddenly felt pain in my belly. It felt very sharp and strong that it woke me up. But I didn't want to wake Michael, so I went into the kitchen, and made some tea with honey. *Maybe this will help so I can sleep.* But an hour later, I felt the pain increase more. I groaned and thought this wasn't normal pain. My lower back was beginning to hurt now too. I began to pace the kitchen. Michael came in then.

"What's wrong? Why are you up?" he asked.

"Because this pain i-i-is getting worse," I groaned out. Michael grabbed me around the waist, picked me up, and carried me to bed.

"Honey, are you all right?" he asked.

"No, my love, it comes and goes, but when it hits, it really hurts." I said as I gritted my teeth.

"Shall I go get the doctor?"

"No, not yet. If I'm in l-l-lab-b-bor—*oh!*—it will be a while from what Gerri and Rainie told me," I managed to tell him.

As the sun rose, so did the pain. "Michael, I think it's time to get Doctor Kiley." Michael kissed me, went to get Sally, and then left. I got up to walk around a little hoping to keep my mind off of the pain. That didn't last long, however, so I climbed back into bed.

Doctor Kiley arrived in no time. He asked Michael to stay in the other room, and began examining me then. "Yes, my dear, you're in labor. I don't think it will be too much longer though. At least, I hope it won't be," he said. "I can see the baby's head now. It's getting ready to enter the world."

"I'm having back pain too. Is that normal?"

"Yes, it is."

"Oh, how much longer before all this is over?" I said through gritted teeth.

"Not much longer, dear."

"Good, I hope you're right."

Around breakfast time, the pain became more excruciating. Now I felt my body pushing, so I couldn't help but push. Doctor Kiley checked again. "The head's coming out, so push, honey." So I did, and I also screamed in pain. It felt like my insides were coming out and not just the baby. I began shaking and sweating from the pain and pushing.

"*Aaahhh*! Is it ever going to quit? I'm so tired. I don't know how much longer I can do this!" I shrieked.

"You can do it, Cheyenne, now push, honey!"

"I can't do this anymore, I'm so weak. Is this pain ever going to quit?" I moaned. "What's taking so long?"

CHAPTER 23

Doctor Kiley chuckled and said, "Yes it will end soon, my dear. Push once more." I pushed with everything I had, and the next sound I heard was my baby crying. "You have a daughter, Cheyenne!" he exclaimed.

It seemed to be taking him a long time to let me see her, so I asked, "Is she all right? What's wrong?" Doctor Kiley didn't answer. I was beginning to panic. I was exhausted. I felt so weak, but I guessed that was normal after giving birth. "Doctor Kiley? What's wrong? Is the baby all right? Please answer me." I was practically hysterical now.

"She's fine. It's just that you and I were not done yet. You had a lot of bleeding I had to tend to. You're going to feel weak and tired for a while, so I want you to stay in bed for the next couple of days."

"All right, I will," I said. *A girl. I have a daughter.* He wrapped the baby up and brought her to me. Then he left the room.

My baby daughter, I couldn't believe it! Just then Michael came in. "Look at our daughter, Michael. See what we did." I couldn't help but cry and laugh at the same time.

"Oh, she's beautiful! Just like her mother. Except for her hair, she looks like you," Then he kissed me. We talked a little about names until we decided on Lucy Kathryn. "It suits her," Michael said.

"Hello, Lucy my darling," I said. She had little hair but black like her daddy and beautiful, bright blue eyes.

"She is so tiny." Michael realized as he held his daughter. "She's beautiful, honey."

"You said that already." I giggled.

Sally knocked at the door then. "Come in," I said.

"I brought you something to drink and eat. I thought you'd be hungry by now," she said.

"Yes, I am starved, thank you." While Sally and Michael admired the baby, I ate my breakfast. I had peaches, homemade bread with butter, and eggs. They all tasted so good today for some reason. Maybe because I worked so hard that I built up such an appetite.

"Doctor Kiley wants you to rest for the next few days. He said you lost a lot of blood. So no working around the house or going to the mercantile or anything like that for you. All right?" Michael insisted.

"All right, I'll stay in bed as the doctor ordered or sit in the sitting room or the porch. That wouldn't hurt, right?" I replied.

"That would be fine. Thank you, honey."

"You're welcome, love." With that, he kissed me.

We had many visitors today. I was glad that even though I was suppose to rest, I, at least, was able to get dressed. Everyone had been so wonderful. They fussed over Lucy and agreed with Michael that she looked like me, except for the black hair. They even gave me a couple of gifts. There were flowers, sweets, and some food. Even the children were great with Lucy. They were all so sweet! I couldn't even think how to thank them for their kindness. I would remember this day always.

Mark Esterbrook at the newspaper office printed up an article about Lucy's birth in the paper: "Lucy Kathryn Hallowell born July 28th, 1854". And I realized it also happened to be my parents' wedding anniversary! What a special day for my Lucy. Having the newspaper article to keep, I thought that was amazing.

Lucy was a good baby. She didn't cry that much except when she was hungry. She slept a lot too, very tiny considering how big I was.

I hoped I was going to be a good mother. I didn't want to disappoint my child. This was all so new to me. I was around for my nephews when they were little, but my Aunt took care of them. I guessed every mother really worried if they would turn out to be good mothers.

"Happy Birthday, honey," Michael said as he kissed me.

"Thank you, love," I said.

"Come outside, I have a special gift for you."

"What on earth could you possibly get for me that would be outside?"

"Just come and look." He took the baby from my arms.

Once we got outside, there was a gorgeous palomino mustang. "Oh, my Michael, she is just gorgeous! Is she for me? I don't believe it!" I couldn't believe it.

"Yes, she's all yours. What do you want to name her?" he asked.

"'Whisper'! 'Whisper' is a good name," I told him. "Oh, Michael, thank you so much!" I hugged him, and then kissed him. He returned the kiss with great enthusiasm himself, and I laughed. "I haven't ridden a horse since I was little," I told him.

"Don't worry, a refresher course is all you would need for it all to come back," Michael said. "You know how to take care of a horse?"

"Yes, I had to do it at Aunt Janet's."

We went back into the house to eat breakfast. Michael put Lucy into her cradle. She shouldn't need to eat again for the next couple of hours. I couldn't believe Lucy was almost two weeks old. I still had winter clothes to make for her. Hopefully I would have them done on time.

"You know, Sally, Saturday is Box Dinner Day. You should make your fried chicken dinner. It tastes so good," I suggested as we ate breakfast.

"I don't know if I'm ready for that, Cheyenne," she said.

"It's just for fun and for a good cause. There's nothing to worry about. It's all right if you participate."

"You really think I could?"

"Of course I do."

"All right, I'll think about it."

"Good. I think it would do you some good to go out and enjoy yourself."

Suddenly, Michael pulled me into our room and said, "You should not get involved in Sally's personal life like that."

"I just want to see her have some fun, to be happy."

"That's none of your business. Leave it alone."

"Oh, Michael—"

"Please, just do as I ask," he interrupted me.

"Oh, all right." I just gave out a huge sigh.

CHAPTER 24

S aturday had finally arrived. It was going to be a fun day. "Sally, do you have everything ready?" I asked.

"Yes, I got everything now. I even threw in some peppermint sticks."

"Good idea," I said. We got into the carriage then and off we went to the social barn.

"Are you nervous, Sally?"

"Oh, yes. This is new for me, and I'm not even sure if I'm ready." As she said this, I noticed she was nervously playing with the box on her lap.

"It will be fine. Just remember it's for a good cause. Giving to the church for the needy is an important reason to do this, Sally. Try to relax. You'll have fun, you'll see," I said, and Michael gave me a hard look.

A lot of people had shown up for this event, and I thought that was a good sign. This event would be a success. At least I hoped so. After gathering our things out of the carriage, we went inside. We saw almost all of our friends and some new people as well. Tables holding all the box dinners arranged nicely and neatly on white table cloths were all lined up. Streamers and ribbons and bows were hanging nicely. There was also a banner hung over head that read, "Box Dinner Social," and benches were all lined up in two rows starting up front. Everyone was mingling before the bidding started. Michael went over to talk with Roy while Sally and I got her box dinner set up and took our seats up front.

Melanie Campbell came to sit next to me. "Hello, Melanie," I said.

"Hello, Cheyenne and Sally," Melanie said.

"Do you have a box dinner going up for auction?" I asked.

"Yes, I figured it was time to get out and mingle," she replied.

"It's good to see you out and participating in such an event," Sally said.

"It's good to see you, two, too."

Daniel, Rainie's husband, was the auctioneer. He stood up and went to the front of the room. He raised his hands and called for everyone to take their seats, so we could start. Michael found me, and Sally moved over for him to sit next to me.

Once everyone was seated, Daniel announced, "This is how it works. You men will bid on a woman's Box Dinner. The winner of that bid will not only get the dinner, but the lady's company for the afternoon as well. Remember, boys, they *are* ladies. It's that simple. Shall we start the bidding?"

"The first box dinner belongs to Elizabeth Cantrell. Bidding starts at twenty cents," Daniel said.

All the single men and widowers started bidding. Twenty cents, thirty cents, fifty cents, seventy five cents, all the way up to the final bid of one dollar and ten cents, which apparently went to our deputy Roy Edwards.

"The second box dinner is from Melanie Campbell. Who wants to start the bidding at twenty cents?" Daniel asked. The men started bidding again, twenty cents, thirty cents, all the way up to a dollar and twenty cents. "The bidding stopped at one dollar and twenty cents this one goes to Jacob James from the telegraph office."

"The next box is from Sally Shore, who will start the bidding at twenty cents," Daniel announced. Again, the men bid. "The final bid of two dollars goes to rancher Dean Ranson!" The bidding kept up until the last box was won by newspaper man Mark Esterbrook. Susan Johnstone will be joining him.

"Oh, Sally, Dean is a handsome man. I hope you have a wonderful, fun afternoon!" I told her.

"I hope so too. Yes, Dean is handsome indeed," Sally replied.

"You better go meet Dean for dinner, Sally," Michael said giving me a stern look. At that moment, Dean came over to escort Sally to their dinner. We said our pleasantries, and they were off.

"Oh, Michael, I hope she has a good time," I said as I watched them walk away.

"I'm sure she will. But you need to stop pushing her," he said sternly, and I couldn't help but wonder.

A few hours passed by until it was suppertime, but Sally wasn't home yet. Michael and I went ahead with supper. "She must be having fun to be gone this long," I told Michael.

"I'd have to agree, honey. She has been gone quite a while."

Just as I finished cleaning the kitchen after supper, Sally walked in the door. "Oh, hello, Sally," I said.

"Hello, Cheyenne," she answered.

"You must have had a nice time for you to have been gone so long."

"Oh, yes, I had a wonderful time! Dean is so nice. He is Melanie's cousin. He's a rancher and new here. He bought some property about a mile south of town, and he's never been married. He loved his box dinner too, he had said," Sally replied.

"It sounds like you like him."

"I think I do. But don't you think it's too soon for that?" she then asked.

"No, I think it's a good time to put your mourning aside. You'll always love and miss your husband, but it's time for you to go forward with your life."

Just then, Michael walked into the room. "Hello, Sally, did you have a good time?"

"Oh, yes, it was wonderful. Better than I expected."

"Well, I'm happy to hear it, Sally. You deserve it. You need to get out and have fun."

"Thank you. Yes, I suppose I do need to have some fun," she said as she blushed.

Since then, Sally started going out a little more with Dean. When he was over for supper last night, he was very polite, considerate, and helpful. He had insisted that he and Sally make supper for me and Michael tonight. They made steak and potatoes with biscuits. It was delicious. All I could hope for was that he would stay that way, even after he would marry someone. I was very happy to see them get along so well. It seemed that he was treating her very well, at least, he did in front of us. He did seem to be a good man, so I should trust that. I guessed I was just on edge these days. I was sure though that everything was going well with them, and I could never be any happier for Sally.

CHAPTER 25

"Do you have everything ready to go?" Michael asked.
"Yes, love, it's all over there. You can load it anytime," I replied.

"Are you sure we have enough stuff for the baby?"

"Yes, love, and Lucy is ready to go now too. I just finished feeding her, so she should be good for a little while. I swear that child's appetite is growing faster than her nails do." I laughed.

"I'm going to load all of this now. I'm glad we have a double-seated carriage," he said as he laughed and walked out the door.

After Michael helped me and Lucy into the carriage, we were about ready to leave. Michael climbed in and grabbed the reins.

"Oh, Michael, I can't believe we're going back home to see everyone! It's been too long," I said excitedly.

"It'll be a long ride, as you well know. Are you sure you're up to it, honey?" He looked at me to see my reaction.

"Yes, love, I'm going to be just fine. Don't worry so much," I replied with a giggle.

It was a long ride indeed. But having Lucy with us seemed to have made it quicker though. I guessed it was because I was so busy with her that she kept my mind busy as well. When it came to her bedtime, she gave us no trouble. She slept under the stars just as if she were born to it. She was so good.

We were almost to the boarding house when we saw a few people we knew and we waved to each other. We'd get to visit everyone while we were here. A week long visit would be a good amount of time to spend with friends.

Just as we pulled up to the boarding house, Tami came running over. "Cheyenne and Michael, what a pleasant surprise! Is Mrs. Taylor expecting you?" she asked.

"No, we told no one we were coming. Michael just decided it was time for a visit," I told her.

Michael came around the carriage to get Lucy from me. Then he helped me out. We went into the boarding house and saw Mrs. Taylor in the dining room. "Cheyenne! Michael! I can't believe you're finally here," she cried. She came to me and hugged me. Then she turned her attention to Michael, who was holding Lucy. "Oh, my, she is beautiful, Cheyenne! Congratulations to you both," she said. We thanked her and watched her take the baby from Michael.

Carol came downstairs and came over to give me a hug. "Oh, Cheyenne, it's so good to see you! How are you?" she said.

"Hello Carol, it's good to see you too. I'm fine. How are you?"

"I'm good. Where's the baby?"

"Mrs. Taylor has her, she moved into the sitting room as you came down the stairs." We both turned then and went into the sitting room.

Mrs. Taylor was fussing over Lucy. She told Michael to get our things and take them upstairs. My old room was available. Carol walked over to Mrs. Taylor to see Lucy and said, "Oh, she is so lovely, Cheyenne!"

"Thank you, Michael says she looks like me, except for her black hair," I replied.

Mrs. Taylor handed the baby to Carol and said, "Cheyenne come help me in the kitchen, so we can visit while I prepare supper." So I followed her. We cooked and cleaned while we talked about what had been happening since last we saw each other.

Michael came into the kitchen then. "I put everything in our room, honey. I'm going to run over to the sheriff's office. I'll see you at supper," he said.

"All right, see you later." I gave him a hug and a kiss and whispered in his ear, "I love you." I then turned to Mrs. Taylor and said, "If you don't need me anymore, I'll go upstairs and take care of everything before supper."

"All right, dear, see you at supper," she said.

"See you at supper."

Not too long after I got everything organized and went back downstairs, Lucy wanted to be fed. I took her from Carol and then went back upstairs to feed her. I relaxed on the bed while Lucy ate, holding her close to me. I must have dozed off because next thing I knew, Michael was standing over me. "Ready for supper?" he asked.

"Yes, yes, give me a few moments," I replied. I looked down at Lucy and she too fell asleep. "I guess I didn't realize I was so tired,"

"It's all right, honey. A nap was probably a good idea. I'd like one myself," he said. A few minutes later, I was ready to go to supper.

I woke with the sounds of thunder crackling outside. *Oh, dear, I have plans to go see Mrs. Carey today too. I'll probably just go later when the storm's over.* Michael was already up washing. "Morning, honey."

"Morning, love," I replied sleepily. "What are we going to do today with this storm?"

"We'll just have to wait and see when the storm passes," he said.

I was getting up to wash and dress when Lucy started crying. I picked her up. "I suppose she doesn't like the storm, my love."

"Probably not, honey," he agreed. "I'll take Lucy so you can dress. I'm starved and want to go to breakfast." I laughed and gave him the baby.

After breakfast, Mrs. Taylor and I were in the sitting room sewing when a very loud crack of thunder sounded. We jumped. "This is becoming a bad storm," she said.

"I hope it doesn't get much worse," I replied.

The rain was pounding the windows, and the thunder was horribly loud. And it seemed lightning was flashing everywhere too. So far though, we hadn't had any hail. Lucy began to cry again. This time she needed to eat. "Excuse me, Mrs. Taylor, I must go feed Lucy. I'll be back down soon," I said.

"Go on then, dear, she needs to eat. See you later."

By dinnertime, the storm had passed. I hoped I could salvage the day and go see Mrs. Carey. I hadn't seen her since I left. She has a baby boy now that I couldn't wait to see. He was six months older than Lucy. I went outside to check the sky to see if the clouds had passed. They did. Now I could go see Mrs. Carey.

Lucy and I went into the dress shop. Mrs. Carey looked up and dropped what she was sewing to come give me a hug. "Cheyenne! How good it is to see you! It has been too long," she said.

"Yes, it has. It's great to see you as well, Mrs. Carey," I replied.

"Please call me Annette. You too had a baby!"

"Yes, her name is Lucy. She was born July twenty-eighth," I said as I handed Lucy to her. "Where is your son?" I asked, and she pointed over to a blocked-in area made of crates in the corner where the baby was playing. I laughed and said, "You have a good way of keeping him safe and a room to play."

"It was the only way I could bring him with me."

I walked over to him as I asked, "What's his name?"

"Benny," she replied.

"He's as handsome as can be! Hello, Benny," I said as I picked him up. "How has business been for you?"

"Oh, a little slow, but at least it's going."

"Thank you again for the beautiful shawl and wedding dress you made for me," I said.

"Oh, Cheyenne, it was my pleasure. I never made anything more beautiful. It was a joy to do," she replied.

We talked a while as she worked. I filled her in on everything that had happened since we last saw each other.

"My, I can't believe anyone would want to harm you, especially a stranger! I'm so sorry," Annette said.

"Don't be. It isn't your fault. I thank you for the support though. With Denny being dead and his brother, David, in jail, I should be safe now. That's the important thing."

"Yes, that's the most important thing. Those things should never happen to a woman. It's more than cruel. It's downright evil. I'm so happy you were able to have a baby," she said.

"Oh, I agree, and I'm truly grateful. I've been blessed. "Well, I must go so I'm not late for supper. I'll see you again before I leave. Thanks for everything, Annette," I said as I hugged her.

"Thank you for the help, but I miss you. I'm so happy for you, for the baby, and that you are safe. Take good care of yourself and I will see you soon," Annette replied.

On the way back to the boarding house, I realized that it turned out to be a very nice day. A few white fluffy clouds were passing by, but the air was fresh and clean-smelling, and the sun was bright and warm. Nightfall would be upon us very soon though.

After supper, I helped everyone clean up. It was not normal for everyone to be cleaning up, but I bet Mrs. Taylor was happy getting so much help. "It was a lovely supper, Mrs. Taylor, thank you," I said.

"I'm glad you enjoyed it, Cheyenne. I thank everyone for the help. It gets things done much more quickly."

"It's not any trouble though," Carol said, and the others chimed in with her.

Michael spent the afternoon visiting as well. I guessed he had some business to tend to first, however. He got back just in time for supper. We all talked about our day at supper. How nice it was to see everyone again. It was like having a big family at home. I hadn't felt this good since I was a little girl with my parents.

Deputy Jackson burst in unexpectedly. "Mike!" he yelled, breaking my reveries. "We have trouble. Sheriff Mason asked me to come get you."

Michael looked at me and said, "You stay put. I'll be back soon." He kissed me before he grabbed his rifle and ran out of the house.

"I wonder what in the world is going on," Mrs. Taylor said.

"I don't know, but I hope it isn't serious or too dangerous," I replied.

"I agree, it's been pretty calm around here these days, and I like it that way," she said.

CHAPTER 26

"So, what do we have?" I asked.

"Well, Mike, we have several strangers in town. They are causing trouble at the saloon right now," the deputy said.

"Let's see if we can take care of it, huh?" I said.

When we got to the saloon, the sheriff was having a little trouble containing the strangers. There must be seven of them. I cocked my rifle and walked into the saloon. I wondered if any of these men were some of the escape prisoners.

"Okay, gentlemen, let's simmer down now!" I yelled.

"Who do you think you are, mister, coming in here telling us what to do?" one of the men said as he grabbed a girl.

"We're having a bit of fun is all," another man said. He was tall and lean, and his clothes were all black, including his hat. He was a little broad in the shoulders with muscular arms, but otherwise he was lean. He must be the leader.

"Your men are causing trouble in here. This is a peace-loving town and I expect everyone to abide by our laws. One of those laws is to not cause harm to anyone. You're hurting the lady and I won't tolerate that, even if she's just a saloon girl. Follow the law or leave town!" Sheriff Mason said.

"All right, sheriff, we won't hurt no one," the man in black said.

"Mind your own business and leave people alone," Mason countered.

All of a sudden, there was a scream coming from one of the upstairs rooms. I ran up the stairs, two steps at a time. I listened for the scream, which came as soon as I reached the top step. I ran down the hall to the third door on the right. With my rifle ready,

I kicked in the door. What I found was unbelievable. One of the saloon girls, a tiny brunette, was on the floor all cut up in a pool of blood, and bright, deep crimson covered the walls. She must have been stabbed at least a half a dozen times, her face almost unrecognizable. No one else was in the room.

I looked around for clues of who may have been responsible. The window was open all the way, and a cool breeze blew the curtains as it entered the room. I looked out the window to find no one there. There wasn't any sign of clues, except some deep, dark brown hair in the girl's hand. She must have pulled them out as she tried to fight for her life. I had a funny feeling that it may be one of those men that rode into town.

I went downstairs and reported everything to the sheriff. We looked around the room but saw nothing to hint us of the girl's killer.

"Her name was Sadie," Sheriff Mason said. "She had been abandoned at a very young age, so she had to fend for herself. She was barely eighteen."

"Who and why would someone kill her, especially in such a brutal way?" I asked as we walked out the door.

"I don't know, but I hope we find out before it happens again," Mason said.

We looked around outside but there were no fresh hoof prints, except where the horses stood. Out back where the stairs from the saloon were, there were no signs either. We couldn't see footprints on the dirt to tell if anyone stepped there recently, especially with the wind blowing the dirt around.

Up on the balcony however, we found a bloody bootprint and one smudged bloody print from the same boot. The long smudge lightened dramatically before it stopped. The killer must have stepped in the blood by the window just as he climbed out. Then tried to wipe it clean by sliding his foot on the floor of the balcony. Aside from these, they're all we had to go on.

"Before I came back downstairs from the room, did anyone new come into the saloon?" I asked.

"No, not a soul," Sheriff Mason said.

"We need to go into the saloon and ask the leader if they plan on staying or just passing through," I suggested.

That was what we did. The leader, who was the one dressed in black, was called Hendrix. Hendrix said they were just passing through and that they weren't planning on spending the night in town. So then where did the killer go? "Did you get a good look at the strangers in the saloon?" I asked.

"Yes, I did. There were seven of them. I'd recognize them if I see them again. Did you see them too?" Sheriff Mason asked.

"Yes, I noticed seven of them from what I could tell. I too would recognize them again. Has anyone moved here since we left?"

"Nope."

"So there were seven in the saloon before I heard the scream. Which means that either there is one more drifter or someone in town did this murder," I stated.

"So we will sit on the walk of the sheriff's office and see if there is an eighth man or not. If so, we will go after them. If not, then we have to figure out who did this," Mason said.

"Max, the saloon keeper is real angry over losing one of his girls. He was about ready to throw them all out just because of how they were treating the girls," Jackson said.

We made ourselves comfortable until the strangers came out of the saloon. Seven men mounted up and started out of town. "I think we should follow them, even though there are only seven of them. The murderer could have left town as soon as he was done killing. He may be waiting for Hendrix and the rest of the men to come," Mason said.

So Mason, the deputies, and I mounted up and followed slowly behind them so as as not to bring attention to ourselves.

About a mile outside of town, the men stopped where there was already smoke from a fire. *So there is an eighth man, Mason was right.* We watched them as we slowly crept up close to them in the tall weeds. When the men were settled down, we started to move in.

"All right, all of you put your hands in the air and no one will get hurt!" Mason yelled at the men.

>>><<<

"What could possibly be keeping Michael? Oh, I hope nothing is too terribly wrong. It's getting real late."

"I'm sure he's all right, Cheyenne," Carol said.

We were in the sitting room sewing and talking as the evening grew late. "Maybe you should go upstairs and try to get some rest, Cheyenne," Mrs. Taylor suggested.

"No, I think I'll wait just a bit longer. The baby is due for feeding in an hour, so I'll just wait until then," I replied.

Tami had already gone upstairs to her room. I was getting sleepy and at the same time, too nervous to really relax. Mrs. Taylor didn't seem to be relaxed either. She seemed just as concerned as I was. I didn't know what Carol was thinking or why she was staying up so late. Maybe she was a little nervous too. She kept looking at the doorway.

"Are you not sleepy yet, Carol?" I asked.

"Not really, I'm just waiting to see what's happening. If I may say though, I think I'm worried about them too. It's not usual for the sheriff to be called out this late for trouble," Carol replied.

"Carol, if you don't mind my saying, is interested in our deputy sheriff Bob Jackson. They have seen each other a few times in the last two weeks. He has been busy lately with fixing up his place as well as being deputy." Mrs. Taylor said, and Carol blushed.

"He's such a sweet man. When he sees me, he always comes to say hello or help me if I'm carrying packages. Stuff like that can entice a woman, you know," Carol began. "He asked me to dinner one afternoon two weeks ago. I have seen him about four times for either dinner or supper. We enjoy each other's company very much, I think. As a matter of fact, we're supposed to go to supper tomorrow night."

"Oh, Carol, I think that's wonderful!" I said.

"Yes, I think she's smitten," Mrs. Taylor said as she giggled.

"Oh, Mrs. Taylor!" Carol exclaimed in surprise.

"He's a good man. He helped the sheriff take good care of me when Michael was out of town. I must say he isn't bad to look at either," I told Carol as I giggled. I thought I blushed a little at that one.

We talked for another hour until Lucy began to fuss. "Well, I'd better get her taken care of. I'll see you ladies tomorrow," I said.

"Would you like a snack before you go to bed?" Mrs. Taylor offered.

"Oh, yes, that would be lovely. Thank you," I replied as I picked up Lucy.

"I'll bring it up in a few minutes, Cheyenne," Mrs. Taylor said.

Just as I finished cleaning Lucy up and putting her in her nightgown, someone came to the door. Mrs. Taylor came in with a piece of apple pie and lemonade.

"She is such a doll," Mrs. Taylor said as she fussed over Lucy.

"Yes, she is. She's a good girl too," I agreed. Mrs. Taylor held Lucy for a short time until Lucy began to fuss, wanting to eat.

"You know, Cheyenne, I'm going to miss you and this little angel when you leave."

"I will miss you very much too, Mrs. Taylor. You've been wonderful!" She hugged both me and Lucy before she left.

I sat down on the bed and began to feed Lucy. I was a little choked up over what Mrs. Taylor had said. I loved her so. She had been a combination of a sister and a mother to me. I would surely miss her once I would have to go back home.

I ate my pie as I fed Lucy. It was so good. It had been a while since supper, so I was glad Mrs. Taylor thought of bringing me a snack. I began to think of Michael again. I was getting worried.

He was taking so long. I figured he would be back by now. What could possibly be keeping him this long? Even though it was late, I would think that if anything had happened to Michael, someone would have already come to tell me. So I must think positive that all was well.

CHAPTER 27

Just as one of the men was reaching for his gun, the deputy shot him. "Don't move or someone else could get hurt. You, mister, stand up," Mason said. He was looking at a man who was wearing brown pants and shirt with a long, black coat and wide-brimmed, black Stetson. We couldn't see his face in the darkness and under his hat. Slowly the man stood. "What do you want?"

"Let me see your boots," Mason said.

"What for?" the man asked rudely.

"Just do it or I will shoot you and take them from you!" Mason ordered heatedly.

The men all looked at each other and the leader stood up and began to speak, "We've done nothing wrong, so why are you bothering us?"

I pointed my rifle at him and said, "You say one more word, and it will be your last. Stay out of this."

Hendrix looked at the man in brown clothes and said, "Do what they want Jenkins." One at a time, Jenkins took off his boots and threw them at the sheriff. Mason picked up the boots and looked at them. Then he looked at me and nodded.

"Watch them closely Mike as I arrest this man," Mason said. He then looked at Jenkins and said, "Walk over here slowly with your hands up high."

The man did what he was told, but he complained. "I didn't do anything. What do you want me for? You have no—"

"Quiet!" Mason interrupted. Once Jenkins was in front of the sheriff, Mason took Jenkins's gun and tucked it into his belt. "Now turn around. You are under arrest for murder." Sheriff Mason tied

Jenkins's hands behind his back. "Let's go." As they backed out, they warned the others not to cause trouble.

"Jenkins is a suspect for the murder of that saloon girl today. His boots will prove it, so stay put."

"I didn't kill no woman!" Jenkins yelled.

Mason just tugged Jenkins's arm, pulling him away. Once they got to the horses, they mounted up and began heading to town.

"I wonder why they ain't shooting at us by now," Deputy Jackson said.

"I don't know, but hopefully there will be no more trouble. I'm supposed to be on vacation," I said as I chuckled.

"Well, Mike, let's just hope the others stay away so you can finish your vacation," Mason said.

Once they got back into town, I helped lock up the prisoner. "Well, if that's all, I'm headed back to the boarding house. Just yell if you need more help."

"Sure thing. Thanks Mike. See you later," Mason said. At that, I nodded at the deputies and headed back to the boarding house for some much-needed rest.

>>><<<

Michael came into our room just as I dozed off. I woke and was so happy to see him. Lucy was sleeping in my arms. "What happened? Where have you been, my love?"

"We had to go after a murderer who tried to escape town," Michael said.

"Oh, my, a murder! Who?" I asked.

"A saloon girl. When we went to the saloon to check on the trouble going on there, we heard the poor woman screaming. By the time I got up there, she was dead."

"It isn't someone we know, is it?"

"No, no one we know. We had strangers in town. One man had blood on his right boot, which will probably match the bloody print we found. If it is the same size, it's a pretty good bet he is the killer. When we searched him, we found a knife on him. He wiped the blood away, but it just seems to fit together," Michael explained.

"Oh, I see. Will the others come after him?"

"I don't know, honey. Let's hope not." After a while, he said, "Let's get some sleep, huh?"

We were rudely awakened by the sound of gunfire. We jumped out of bed. "Get down, get the baby and stay on the floor," Michael whispered.

I did as he said. I put Lucy underneath me to protect her better. After pulling on some pants, Michael went running out of the room. The gunfire was rapid and sounded like an army! *Oh, Michael, please be careful.* I knew he would go outside to see what was going on and who was responsible for the shooting.

After several minutes, the gunfire finally stopped. Shortly after that, Michael came back. "Are you all right? You're not hurt? How's Lucy?" he asked as he helped me and Lucy get off the floor.

"Yes, I'm fine. Lucy is fine too," I said. "What was that all about? Who was it?"

"I didn't get a good look, by the time I got out there, they were already across town. If I had to guess, I'd say it was Hendrix and his boys."

A knock came at the door, and Michael went downstairs to see who it was. I followed behind, still holding the baby. "Sheriff Hallowell, its Deputy Jackson," a voice said. Michael opened the door to let him in.

"What on earth was that all about?" Michael asked.

"It was Hendrix and his men shooting up the town. Some people were injured. No one was killed except for one of Hendrix's men. Are you all right?" Deputy Jackson said.

"Yes, we're fine, thank you. Did the rest of them get away?" Michael asked.

"Yes, but we know who they are now, so we can either go after them or wait until they come again," Jackson replied.

"The prisoner is still in jail, right?" Michael asked.

"Yes, he is."

Everyone was up now and looking at each other still very sleepy. Mrs. Taylor was obviously shaken up. No one said a word we just listened to what was being said.

Michael looked at me and said, "Stay here and keep both doors bolted, all right? I need to go to the sheriff's office. I'll be back as soon as I can."

"All right, my love, I hope you hurry back," I said. He kissed me, grabbed his rifle and went out the door with the deputy.

Although I was tired, I was too shaken up to sleep, so I decided to make some coffee. I guessed those men were a bit angry that their friend was in jail. But I wondered why they were shooting up the town though instead of trying to bust out their friend. Oh, I hoped Michael wouldn't be too long. After all, there isn't much they could do in the dark. I asked everyone if they wanted to stay up with me. The only one who said yes was Mrs. Taylor.

I decided to keep Lucy with me in the kitchen until Michael returned. I wanted to be sure it was over and that we were safe. Lucy was fast asleep, not having a care in the world. Bless her little heart. She's such a good baby.

"I hope no one is seriously hurt. It's bad enough people were shot at in the first place," Mrs. Taylor said.

"I know what you're saying. I hope you're right."

"I can't believe this is happening. This kind of thing just doesn't happen here. We have a good, quiet town."

"I've never experienced anything like this, people just shooting at anyone and anything for no reason at all."

Just then Michael knocked on the door. Mrs. Taylor let him in. He got himself a cup of coffee and sat down next to me. "Well, we can't go after them in the dark, especially since we don't know where they are. Three men volunteered to stay at the jail with Don to help guard the prisoner. Hopefully they won't be back tonight," he explained.

"What about those who were shot? Any serious injuries?"

"Only one is in serious condition. Mr. Cooper. The doctor is with him now."

Mrs. Taylor and I just looked at each other. "Let's drink our coffee and go back to bed," Michael said. Mrs. Taylor and I nodded in agreement.

Now that we knew who it was and that the prisoner was still in jail, maybe we could get some sleep. I hoped they didn't come back. I'd hate to think what those men are capable of. I yawned. I felt better just knowing Michael was back. "Why do you think they didn't try to break their man out of jail?" I asked.

"I don't know, honey, but that could be their next move. That's why there are four men guarding Jenkins. Come on, honey, let's go back to bed," Michael said.

CHAPTER 28

We woke to a gorgeous morning. The sun was just rising, making a beautiful colored sky. I stretched and looked over to my handsome husband, who was holding our darling daughter. I got up to open a window to get some fresh air. It smelled so sweet with hardly a breeze at all. It looked like it would be a good day.

"Morning, honey," Michael said.

"Morning, my love. What are you going to do today?"

"After breakfast I think I will go over to the sheriff's office and just relax. It's almost time to go home, day after tomorrow."

"Yes, I know. I have enjoyed so much our visit with everyone, but I'm looking forward to going home," I told Michael as he relaxed on the bed and I fed Lucy.

"I am too." We talked for a little while until Lucy was finished eating. I handed Lucy back to her father. "Maybe we can come back next spring if all goes well."

"That would be wonderful." I got cleaned up and dressed then, and then we headed downstairs to have breakfast.

"Morning, everyone," I said as I sat down to eat. Everyone responded in kind. I looked at Mrs. Taylor as she brought the last of the food in. "We go home the day after tomorrow. I've enjoyed so much my visit with all of you," I said.

"Yes, I too have enjoyed spending time with you and especially the baby," Mrs. Taylor said. We all laughed then.

"Oh, I see how you are," Michael told Mrs. Taylor as he laughed. We all talked of enjoying our time together and of coming back again in the spring.

When Michael finished his breakfast, he got up from the table. "Well, I'm off to the sheriff's office. I'll see you later." He leaned down to kiss me and Lucy.

As he left, I handed Lucy to Mrs. Taylor so I could finish my breakfast. Carol excused herself to run upstairs, but just before she could go up, I heard her talking. It seemed like someone came into the house. "Can I help you, sir?" Carol asked.

"Yes, I would like to see the proprietor," he said.

"Just a moment," Carol told him.

Then she came to the dining room doorway and told Mrs. Taylor about the gentleman who came in. Mrs. Taylor handed Lucy to me then went out to talk to the stranger. We were all quiet since it was odd to have a strange man come to the boarding house.

"I'm sorry; sir, but I have no more rooms available. Perhaps you can check—"

Mrs. Taylor didn't finish what she was about to say. The man suddenly grabbed and pulled her back to his chest, with his revolver drawn. They took a step into the doorway of the dining room, and he said, "How many people are here?"

"There are five of us right now," Mrs. Taylor said.

He pushed her to the chair, and then looked at Carol. "Where's the fifth person?"

"In the kitchen," Carol said with some fear in her voice.

"Well, go get her!" Carol did as she was told and brought Miss Sheridan into the dining room.

"Sit down all of you," the man said.

"What's this all about?" Mrs. Taylor asked.

"Never mind. You!" he said pointing to Carol, "go open the back door." She went to the backdoor and opened it.

There came another man's voice saying, "Get moving, lady" as he shoved her back into the dining room. Both men had their revolvers drawn. "Go sit down," he told Carol as he gave her a shove.

"What do you want? There are only women here," I said.

"Be quiet," the second man said.

Mrs. Taylor was getting agitated. "What is the meaning of this?"

"Well, lady," the first man said, "our friend is in the jailhouse and you, ladies, are going to help me get him out. Now shut up!" He then looked around the room and pointing to Miss Sheridan, he said, "You go to the jail and tell the sheriff that I want Jenkins released, or I will shoot one of these women in one hour." He then raised his voice. "I'm not playing around! You tell 'em that!"

Slowly Miss Sheridan got up, shaking; she started out of the room. As she did, the first man grabbed her arm and then told her, "You tell 'em that Hendrix sent you. Do you understand?"

Nodding her head, she shakily said, "Yes sir." Then out the door she went.

From where I sat, I could see the street out of the window. A short time later, I saw several men take cover across the street. And then I heard Sheriff Mason yell, "All right, Hendrix, we are here. Let those ladies go!"

Hendrix broke out the window. Showing his gun, he yelled, "Let's see Jenkins!"

Mason made Jenkins stand up, but that was all. He then pulled Jenkins back down. "Now, how do you propose we do this? I want those women unharmed and free."

"I have four women in here, I will release one at a time as you let Jenkins walk over here," Hendrix said.

As Jenkins walked across the street, Hendrix allowed Tami out first, and then slowly let Carol go. I was getting real nervous. I was hoping he would let us all go. I didn't want any harm coming to my baby.

Just as Jenkins hit the porch, I was released with Lucy. Once Jenkins was in the house, Hendrix said, "Now, I'm going to keep this last woman until we are safely away from here then I will send her back. I will kill her if you follow us. Do you understand?"

I was safely across the street, and Michael reached for me and just held me. "Oh, Michael, what about Mrs. Taylor?" I asked.

"Don't worry we will get her back, all right? Now you go to the restaurant and I'll be there shortly," he replied.

I kept looking back, wondering what they were going to do and how they would get Mrs. Taylor back safely. If they followed those men, then Mrs. Taylor would be killed. But if they didn't follow Hendrix, they wouldn't know where to find them to help Mrs. Taylor. As I was walking, I saw those men leave, taking Mrs. Taylor with them on the horse in front of Hendrix. *Oh my, I hope she will be all right.*

Once in the restaurant, I took a table by the window so I could watch for Michael. He came in a few minutes later. He came to the table and sat down. "In a few minutes, we are leaving to go get Mrs. Taylor. I want you to stay here and get something to eat. Don't go to the boarding house alone. I've asked Carol to come sit with you. Then I've asked Artie Phillips to escort you to the boarding house and stay there until we return."

"I'm not hungry. It's not even dinnertime yet. If you follow those men, they will kill Mrs. Taylor!" I said.

"It will be dinnertime shortly, so eat something. You're still eating for two," he chuckled. "As for Mrs. Taylor, we'll bring her back safely, just leave that to me. Don't worry so much."

"That's easier said than done, my love." I replied.

"I know, but you need to try, all right?" he said. I nodded but didn't say anything else. Michael got up, kissed me, and left.

Carol and Tami came in the restaurant then. I invited them to sit down. "I've never been so scared," Tami said.

"I know what you mean, Tami," Carol said. "Are you and Lucy all right, Cheyenne?"

"Yes, we're both just fine. I'm worried sick over Mrs. Taylor though. I hope she'll be all right," I said.

"I know. We are, too. I hope the posse can get her back," Tami said.

"Me too, I don't know what I would do if anything happens to her," I replied. We ordered dinner. "After we eat, I must get back to the boarding house to feed Lucy. Michael will not let me go alone. I must see Artie Phillips to accompany me. Would you like to go back as well?" Both Carol and Tami said they'd go back too.

We talked, mostly about Mrs. Taylor, while we ate. We were all so worried about her. I wondered how they were going to get her back safely. "I'm sure she'll be fine, and the posse will have her back in no time," Carol said.

"I'm sure you're right, Carol," I said. "Well, are we ready to head back?"

"Yes," Tami said.

Once we were in the boarding house, we locked both doors, even though Mr. Phillips was here. I was just a bit nervous now, I guessed. I went upstairs to feed Lucy, and the girls went into the kitchen to prepare supper. I figured I would just help with that as soon as I was done with Lucy. We wanted to be sure it was ready when Mrs. Taylor got home.

I baked two apple pies as Tami and Carol made supper and bread. We had a lot to do to keep us busy, and we talked at the same time.

"So you are leaving day after tomorrow?" Carol asked.

"Yes, I'll miss you all very much, but I think I'm ready to go home," I said.

"I can understand that," Tami said.

"I would like to come visit you. Maybe I should plan that for next month if that would be all right with you, Cheyenne," Carol replied.

"Oh, that would be wonderful, Carol. We have an extra room so you won't need to stay at the hotel."

"Oh, Cheyenne, that would be great! Thank you. It's settled then.

We finished making everything for supper just before five o'clock. There was still no sign of the posse and Mrs. Taylor. I hoped it wouldn't be too much longer. Miss Sheridan came back just before we had supper finished. She set the table.

"Are you all right, Miss Sheridan?" I asked.

"Yes, I am fine now. I was so scared. I'm so sorry about Mrs. Taylor though."

"We understand, we feel the same," Tami replied. "Mrs. Taylor is a strong woman she'll be just fine and home soon."

"I agree," I said. "Shall we eat?" The ladies all said yes. We made a plate for Mrs. Taylor and Michael, so they could eat as soon as they get back.

I was upstairs in our room feeding Lucy when I heard a ruckus downstairs. At first I got very nervous. Then I realized that it was a sound of celebration. I finished feeding Lucy and put her in her bed. I then ran down the stairs. "Michael!" I yelled. I went into his waiting arms. "Mrs. Taylor?"

"She's fine and in the dining room. Go see her," Michael said.

I went into the dining room where Mrs. Taylor was sitting at the table. "Mrs. Taylor! Are you all right?"

"Yes, dear, I'm fine now," she said while we hugged.

"What happened?" I asked.

"Well, honey, have a seat and I will fill all of you in on what happened," Michael said. We all sat down and waited.

"We followed the tracks, what we could anyway," Michael began. "The wind was blowing fairly strong. We heard them talking from a distance, they were being very loud. So we dismounted leaving the horses there, we walked over to where the voices were coming from. We stood in the trees and spread out—"

"Your husband was behind me appearing out of nowhere. I never heard him coming. Neither did those awful men," Mrs. Taylor interrupted before Michael could finish. "He untied me and told me to stay down but very slowly back up. I did as he said. Those men weren't paying any attention to me. Once I was behind the tree line, he told me to lie flat on the ground, so I did.

Then Sheriff Mason yelled to the eight men to put their hands up high and not move. The next thing I heard was gunfire."

"Some of the men put their hands up and some didn't," Michael said. "Instead, they reached for their guns, dropped to the ground, and started shooting. We had two of our men injured, but Hendrix and Jenkins are dead, one of the men was injured, and the other four are in jail. They didn't even have a chance to notice Mrs. Taylor was gone."

"How badly hurt were our two men?" I asked.

"I really don't know yet, they're with Doctor Comings now," Michael replied.

"Oh, I hope they will be okay and not seriously hurt," I said.

"Is everyone here all right?" he asked.

"Yes, we're all fine. Lucy is upstairs sleeping peacefully. Are you hungry? We put some food up for both of you."

"I'm starving," he said.

"I could eat something too," Mrs. Taylor said.

I was so happy that Michael and Mrs. Taylor were home. "I'm relieved you're both safe."

As we ate, we all talked for a little while then we went to our rooms. Michael made love to me as if he were desperate, like it would be the last time. It was strong and possessive yet very passionate. I guessed what happened today scared him more than he was letting on, even though it wasn't me who those evil men took. The relief on his face when I crossed the street was obvious and intense. Oh, how I loved this man!

CHAPTER 29

I walked into the house with Lucy, and Michael followed behind with an armful of our bags. It sure felt good to be home. It was a nice quiet ride home too. The air was crisp and clean, the sky was clear with few clouds, and the sun was shining brightly and warmly on the cool day, making the ride very comfortable. Today wasn't much different. It was a cool day so far, and I didn't think it would get very hot again today. That was all right though. It had been a very hot summer lately, so the cool days had been very pleasurable.

We had a wonderful week visiting in spite of the troubles we had. I would miss them very much, but I hoped all would go well, and Carol would come visit in a month as we planned. "Did you get everything, my love?" I asked Michael.

"Yes, now comes the joy of putting it all away," he teased.

"Well, I'd best get started. With Lucy sleeping, I should be able to have it all put away in no time at all."

"I need to check in at the sheriff's office first, so I will see you in a little while, honey."

"Okay, see you later."

With everything put away now, it was time for me to get supper started. It would be nice to sleep in our own bed tonight. That was the only bad part about going away to visit; you missed your own bed.

Just as I began supper, Sally walked in. "Hello, Cheyenne, it's good to have you back," she said.

"Hello, Sally, it's good to be back home," I replied.

"How's Lucy?"

"Oh, she's fine. She's napping now. She had a busy week."

"I'll bet, so tell me about your visit. Did you enjoy yourselves?" she asked, so I told her everything about our visit, including the trouble with those men. "You had quite an adventure, it sounds like. I'm very glad everyone is all right," she said.

"Me too, it scared me to death when they took Mrs. Taylor. She's been like a mother to me. I don't think I could have handled the loss very well if something had happened to her. I'm so grateful that didn't happen."

"Yes, I am too, for your sake."

As I made the bread for supper, Sally told me about her week. She and Dean spent quite a bit of time together. It was nice to see her happy. But I would miss her very much if she and Dean got married, which I thought they would. Sally started making a cake as the bread baked. The house smelled real good now. I love the way it smells when we cook.

"I so enjoy his company. He's so good to me, Cheyenne," she said as she brought me out of my thoughts.

"I'm so happy to hear that. Do you have plans for this evening?" I asked.

"Yes, Dean will be here after supper."

Lucy woke up then, so Sally went to get her. She missed her as much as she missed us. She came into the kitchen and said, "She has grown. I've missed her so."

"I'm sure she's missed you too, Sally. She's such a good baby. I hope if I have any more babies, they all will be as good as Lucy."

"I hope someday I'll be able to have children."

"I'm sure you will, Sally."

Just as we put supper on the table, Michael came home. "You must have smelled dinner just when we were putting it on the table." I giggled.

He gently swatted my backside and said, "You making fun of my nose, lady?" I giggled again.

"No, just your timing, my love." Then I asked, "So how are things at the sheriff's office?"

"Just fine, it's been very quiet while we were gone. No problems to speak of. A couple of bar fights and that's about it. Let's hope it stays that way, for a while at least."

"Let's hope so."

When supper was over, Dean came by to get Sally. They were going out for the evening. While I washed up the dishes, Michael came up behind me and started to rub my sides and my hips. "My love let me finish the dishes." I giggled. He didn't listen, however. He began nibbling my neck as his hands roamed. Finally when I knew he wasn't going to let me finish, I turned in his arms. Next thing I knew, he was picking me up and carrying me to our bed. We made hot, passionate love. It seemed powerful, like it was a celebration of being alone. He always knew how to make me feel loved. He was a man of great passion and desire. A hungry man.

Afterward, Lucy woke up to be fed. When I finished feeding her, I got into a nice hot tub. It felt good to get the dust off like this than just washing up. Michael came in as I finished washing my hair. He came over and took the sponge from me and began washing me. I giggled. "You think you can just come help yourself anytime you want, sir?" I said.

"You better believe it," he said in a very passionate tone.

I giggled again. "Anytime..." he interrupted me with a hot kiss.

He stopped the kiss and nibbled on my neck and said, "You're mine." And he continued to nibble some more. "I can't get enough of you," he said as his hands roamed everywhere until they reached my most sensitive areas.

After I exploded in sheer ecstasy, he pulled me out of the tub, covered me in a bath sheet and carried me to our bed. This was where we made long passionate love. Then we held each other and fell into a much-needed sleep.

It had been hot the last several days. After supper, we would sit on the porch enjoying a light cool breeze. I enjoyed our time very much just relaxing in our rockers after a hot busy day. It was so peaceful this time of day. I thought Lucy liked being out here too. She was so content in my arms.

Sally had been out with Dean every evening. I think it was getting serious between those two. They hadn't spoken of it, but it just seemed obvious with the time they spent together. I was happy for them if they were. If they married, I didn't know what I would do without Sally.

"What will we do without Sally if she marries?" I asked Michael.

"Look for someone else, I guess," Michael replied.

"It won't be the same."

Our wedding anniversary was in a few days. I would give Michael a new hat that I ordered from the mercantile. His hat was pretty worn so, I thought he would love the new one. Sally was going to take care of Lucy for me, except for feeding time, so we could spend time together then go out to supper. Sally said she would take Lucy to Gerri's between feedings during the afternoon. Michael was taking off that day too. It should be a wonderful anniversary. I can't wait!

Sally came into the kitchen and said, "Looks like we'll be getting some rain today. There are dark clouds coming."

"Well, I hope it will cool us off a bit. We can use the rain though. I guess I'd better get to the mercantile now before the rain comes. Will you mind Lucy please? I won't be gone long," I said.

"Yes, of course, but try to hurry back before it rains." So I rushed out the door as soon as I could.

I saw George as soon as I entered the mercantile. "Hello, George, how are you today?"

"Hello, Cheyenne, I'm good. And you?" he replied.

"Oh, just fine. It's been very hot the last few days. Where's Madelyn? I hope she isn't under the weather today."

"She's resting upstairs, she's sick."

"Oh, I hope she'll feel better real soon."

"Thank you, Cheyenne. So what can I do for you today?"

"Did Michael's hat come in yet?" I asked.

"Yes, it's here. Would you like me to wrap it for you?"

"Yes, please." I picked up a few things and then went home as fast as I could.

The thunder boomed and shook the house. The lightning must have been close being so loud. The lightning lit up the entire room. I looked out the window to check on things. It was very dark out there, but there was nothing out of the ordinary. I turned back around and hid Michael's gift under the bed. Lucy still slept peacefully.

Michael came in the house just before the hail came. The hail hit the roof so loudly it sounded like it was going to come right through it. The hail hitting the windows sounded like it would break the glass. I just entered the kitchen in time to see him pull off his shirt and boots. "I'll get you a dry shirt, Michael," I said. I went to our room and grabbed Michael a shirt. Now he was wearing the blue shirt I made for him for Christmas, and he looks so handsome in it.

"It's pretty bad out there," Michael said.

"It sounds like it," I replied.

We all listened to the sounds of the rain and hail. *Ah, this sounds like a twister.* I decided to bring the baby into the kitchen doorway. It was the only area that had no windows. If the windows broke, I didn't want to risk Lucy being hit with the glass. She still slept soundly even though her papa carried her to bed. She should be waking soon to eat, however.

"The wind has picked up real good, but I don't think we have anything to worry about," Michael said.

"I hope you're right. Twisters scare me half to death," Sally said.

"I hope the hail stops soon," I said as I looked out the window. "There's so much hail now that it looks like snow out there."

"It does, doesn't it?" Michael replied.

"Well, we better get supper on the table," I said.

The storm finally passed. We had just finished supper when Don knocked at the door. "Mike, we have to get out to the Chesterfield place. The high winds knocked down their roof, and it fell in on top of them. We have to dig them out. Doc Kiley will be going with us to help the injured," he said.

"All right, I'm coming. Did you gather up some help?" Michael asked.

"Yes, we have a lot of help coming."

"Let's go then."

"I'll be there just as soon as I'm done feeding Lucy," I said. "I can help take care of the wounded."

"All right, see you there, honey," Michael said as he kissed me.

The house looked terrible! More than just the roof caved into the house, one of the walls did too. There were so many people here that you would think there was a town meeting or something. Men, women, and even some children were all helping. It was a sight to see. The more there were, the sooner they could dig the Chesterfields out.

I was a bundle of nerves seeing this site. Just knowing there were people under all that mess broke my heart. How could anyone survive this? Oh, I mustn't think that way. I didn't know them very well, but I certainly didn't want them to die or be hurt. If they survived this, I was sure they would be injured. I hoped they weren't seriously hurt and that none died.

First, they pulled out Mrs. Chesterfield and the baby. They still had a ways to go though. I went over to Doctor Kiley to see if he needed any help. "Hello, Doc, how is she? I came to help, so just tell me what you need me to do."

"She's not too bad, considering. She has a badly broken arm I need to set. If you can get someone to tend to the baby, you can help me with Mrs. Chesterfield. The baby only has bruised ribs. Mrs. Chesterfield was partially on top of him in the rubble, so he didn't get hit with anything but his Momma," he said.

I found Melanie Campbell and asked her to tend to the baby. She said she would be delighted. Melanie found a blanket and went over to a tree to put the baby down on the blanket. She sat down next to him and started to play and laugh with him. I thanked her and went back to Doctor Kiley.

"All right then, let's get this arm set, shall we?" he said. We went to work fixing Mrs. Chesterfield's arm.

Shortly after we were done, another little boy was brought over. He was badly bruised and had some cuts but appeared to be okay otherwise. We cleaned him up and checked him carefully. Nothing appeared to be broken.

Soon after treating Mrs. Chesterfield, Gerri brought their four-year-old boy over. He had some injuries, a broken wrist and a bad cut on his leg as well as bruises and cuts all over his body. He was very lucky that he wasn't injured worse than he already was.

We waited a little while until they brought over Mr. Chesterfield. He too was all battered up with cuts, scrapes, and bruises everywhere but didn't have anything broken. He also had bruised ribs. He complained of his head hurting however. Doctor Kiley checked him out and said, "You have a concussion, but otherwise I think you're okay. There are things to watch out for, so I'll tell your wife so she can keep an eye on you."

"How is my wife?" Mr. Chesterfield asked.

"She's okay, except for a badly broken arm. She'll need help around the house for a while and tending to the children," Doctor Kiley replied.

"What about my girls?" he asked.

CHAPTER 30

S till missing were the Chesterfield's two daughters. Oh, I hoped they got to them and that they would be okay. Everyone was frantically searching for the girls. There was still more rubble to go through. Looking at the house made me wonder how the others made it out without serious injury or anything worse. The wood was heavier due to all the rain we had today. There was still hail on the ground, which made it look like it snowed instead of rained.

About twenty minutes later, they brought over their older daughter. The younger one, however, who was only six years old, didn't make it. Oh, that was going to be so hard for the Chesterfields to hear.

Michael came over then and said, "I need to go tell the Chesterfields about their youngest daughter. I can only imagine how I'd feel if I were in their shoes."

"All right, my love," I said with tears in my eyes.

They appeared to take the news very hard. Oh, how my heart was breaking for them. I went to Mrs. Chesterfield and held her as she held her younger son. Her husband just walked away. I guess he needed some time to himself to absorb the news of his daughter's death.

Their oldest daughter, who was eight years old, had some serious injuries. She had a piece of wood stuck in her back, a sprained wrist, a broken ankle, and a few cuts and bruises. Doctor Kiley carefully took the wood out and checked to see if he could see any damage. He would have to take her back to his office to take care of that. He wrapped the wrist and set the ankle. He asked Mac to take her to his office in their buckboard.

I took the little boy, Henry, over to Melanie. She was very willing to help, and that made me feel good. "Would you mind watching Henry too, Melanie?" I asked.

"Not at all, I'm here to help. The baby is doing real well. You would never know he has bruised ribs with the way he is playing." She giggled as the baby giggled at her.

"That's good. His ribs probably don't hurt too badly. By the way, are you and Jacob still seeing each other?" I asked.

"Yes, I am. As a matter of fact, he has asked me to marry him," Melanie said.

"Oh, how wonderful! Did you say yes?"

Melanie giggled. "Yes, I accepted. We're talking about marrying in October."

"I'm so happy for you!" I gave her a hug. "You'll let me know when the date is, won't you?"

"Yes, I will most definitely," she replied.

"Thank you for all your help, Melanie. I know it's much appreciated." I said.

I went to check on Mrs. Chesterfield and then went to look for Michael. All the family members had been found, so all we had to do now was help clean up. The children were all taken care of and being supervised. *Now where is Michael?*

After looking around for several minutes, I found Michael. He was talking to Mr. Chesterfield. I wasn't going to disturb them. I went over to the house and began to help clean up the mess. It was going to take some time for them to rebuild. We had to help them find a house.

A short time later, Michael joined me in the cleanup. It was going fairly fast with so many of us helping. It wouldn't take much time at all to get it done. Then Deputy Roy rode up.

"Well, sheriff, we have a real good town. The hotel manager said business was going so well that he decided to help out the Chesterfields. He's giving them two adjoining rooms for a few weeks at no charge to give them time to rebuild," Roy said as he dismounted his horse.

"That's wonderful news!" I exclaimed.

"Yes, I'd say we have a great town. People willing to help others makes for a great community," Michael said.

Just before Roy took the Chesterfields to the hotel, I hugged Mrs. Chesterfield and told her not to hesitate to ask if she needed anything. We finished cleaning up the Chesterfield's house and headed for home.

"It's a real shame they lost their little girl," Michael said.

"I know, I don't know what I'd do if we ever lost Lucy. My heart goes out to them," I replied, "I hope they will be able to rebuild soon."

"They will, many of us are going to pitch in and help so they can be back home in no time."

"Oh, Michael, that's wonderful! It's so kind of you and the others to help out!" I said.

The next morning, I woke with the sun shining bright in our room. The air was crisp and cool, but the sun seemed warm. Sally knocked at the door and brought in a tray of food with her. "What's this?" I asked.

"Morning. It's your anniversary breakfast. Happy Anniversary!" she said.

"Well, thank you so much! How sweet of you to do this for me. Where's Michael?"

"He'll be here in a minute with the coffee," Sally said. Just then, Michael came in with the coffee.

"I guess you plan on having breakfast with me?" I teased Michael. There was plenty of food for both of us. He sat on the bed next to me, and we shared a lovely breakfast together. How romantic this was.

"What are we going to do today besides having supper at the restaurant?" I asked Michael.

"Well, I thought we'd go for a picnic at the other end of town by the river. Sally is going to tend to Lucy all day for us. You only need to feed her before our picnic and after."

"That sounds wonderful, my love."

We went down the river to a nice secluded spot to set up our picnic. After we unloaded the carriage, we went for a swim. It was a bit chilly, but we warmed to it quickly enough. It was beautiful here. There were trees all around us with the river flowing between them. Several types of wildflowers were around some of the sunny spots near the river. There were pink, purple, blue, yellow, and white flowers with such lovely fragrances, making the air smell sweet.

While we were swimming, Michael held me in his arms and began to kiss me with such passion that it set me on fire. One thing was certain: this man of mine knew how to love a woman. He was gentle, playful, charming, strong, and protective. He would give his life for me as I would him. He held me as if he never wanted to let go. He caressed me gently yet with hunger. He was a man that I never imagined I would have. I loved him so deeply it was amazing. Our love making was incredible. He sure made a woman feel special. He claimed me as his own, as if it were our first time. He was remarkable. He carried me to the blanket.

After we made love, we had our dinner. We picked up a dinner from the café since it would be quicker than making it ourselves. We had chicken and dumplings, rice, and apple pie. It was fantastic! We talked as we ate and took our time, so we could enjoy our private time together before we would have to go home and then go to supper. This was turning out to be a wonderful anniversary!

A couple of hours later, it was time to go home to feed Lucy, and we were sorry to see our picnic end so soon. Just before feeding Lucy, we gave each other our anniversary gifts. Michael loved his hat and he gave me a beautiful gold bracelet. "How did you ever manage to get this?" I asked.

"George had to order it, so I made two installments, one when I ordered it and the other when it arrived," he explained.

"Thank you. I love it."

"Thank you for my new hat too. I really needed one and it fits perfectly."

"I measured your old one while you slept one night. I wanted to be sure it would fit."

"Good thinking." He then leaned down to kiss me.

When Lucy was finished eating, Michael and I decided to go horseback riding. It felt wonderful to have the wind on my face and blowing through my hair. I knew it would make it hard to brush later, but still, it felt good. We didn't have to go through town to ride. We just started riding southwest toward El Dorado. We rode for a little while then stopped to rest for a short time. Then we rode back. It was so much fun just to ride.

By the time we got back, it was time to get ready for supper. It had been a very special day so far. We went to the café and just as we sat down, several of our friends came in and yelled simultaneously "Happy Anniversary!" Michael and I were very surprised. We both said our thanks to everyone.

After we ate supper, Rainie brought out a cake. "Happy anniversary! This is a gift from all of us to you. This cake and your supper have been paid for." It was a huge cake, so after we took ours, everyone here also got a piece. Sally just walked in when the cake was brought out. *So she was a part of this plan.* I giggled. It was really a wonderful surprise.

"We thank you all very much, it's so thoughtful!" I said.

"Yes, thank you. It's kind of all of you to think of us," Michael said. We all visited for a little while before we decided it was time to go. We thanked everyone again and we left.

As I got ready for bed, Michael came in with Lucy. She was hungry so I needed to feed her before going to bed. After such a busy day, I was very tired and wanted to go to bed early, so I got comfortable and took Lucy from Michael. "We had a wonderful anniversary celebration, didn't we?" I said.

"Yes, we did, but it isn't over yet," he said with a sly grin.

"Oh, you are such a rascal."

CHAPTER 31

As I held Lucy to my chest, I paced the floor trying to figure out why Lucy was so warm and would not eat. I patted her bottom to try to console my crying baby. I was surprised she hadn't awakened her daddy or Sally, though she wasn't crying really loudly. Whatever was wrong with my sweet babe, I hoped it wasn't serious.

The sun rose with bright rays coming through the windows, as if making a big announcement of its entry. After pacing for quite a while, I went into the kitchen to put water on the stove. Lucy was in need of a bath since she soiled herself clean through. As I put Lucy in the tub, I held her and gently washed her down. Michael came in then and asked, "Is everything all right?"

"No, Lucy is sick. She's very warm with a fever. She won't eat, she's so irritable and seems to be in pain, although I can't tell you where she hurts," I said.

"Should you be washing her in a bath if she is so sick?" he asked.

"Probably not, but she needed it. She soiled clean through, so I didn't have much of a choice."

When we sat down to breakfast, Lucy was still crying, but she didn't seem as warm now. "We need to get Doc Kiley over here," Michael said.

"I agree, my love. She's still acting as if she were in pain."

"I think it would be a good idea too. Poor little thing crying for so long, I'm surprised she hasn't cried herself to sleep by now," Sally said.

"All right, after breakfast I will go get him," Michael said as he took another bite of his food. It was difficult to eat while you had a crying baby to your bodice, but I did my best, nevertheless.

"Morning," Doctor Kiley said as he entered through the door. "I understand that your little one is having some trouble."

"Yes, Doctor, she is. She has been crying mildly since the wee hours and she won't eat or sleep. She seems to be in pain, but I have no idea as to where she may be hurting," I said.

"Well, shall we go into her room so I can examine her," Doctor Kiley said as he stretched out his arm as if to lead me in first.

I laid Lucy down onto the bed and stepped aside. Doctor Kiley examined her all over. He felt her belly and checked her head, ears, nose, and mouth. "Has she been coughing?"

"Yes, a little."

Lucy's crying seemed to be quieting. The poor thing must be exhausted. "Since Lucy doesn't have pain anywhere else, I would say she has a headache. That could explain the mild crying. It would hurt more if she cried hard. Has she been around the Ellsworth children?" Doctor Kiley asked.

"Not since we were there a couple of weeks ago."

"Well, we will need to keep a close eye on her. She still has a fever, and with the other symptoms she just might have contracted the chickenpox from the Ellsworth children."

"Oh, no, isn't she too young? Could that be serious?"

"We'll just have to watch her and try to keep her warm and keep her fever down. In the next two days, she should develop the rash, little bumps over her body. So let's just stay focused, all right?"

"All right, Doc, we will. Right, honey?" Michael said as he stood leaning in the doorway.

"Yes, darling, I will do my best," I replied with hesitation.

Doctor Kiley left, but not before he told us what to do for Lucy. I couldn't help but worry about Lucy getting the chickenpox. She was too young! I knew the doctor said it was rare in an infant so young to have the chickenpox, but it just happened.

Lucy finally fell asleep. After I got myself a glass of lemonade, I went back to our room to sponge Lucy, as the doctor had ordered.

She moaned a little in her sleep but didn't wake up. Maybe she would eat when she woke up.

We managed to keep her fever from getting too high, but she still would not eat. "Michael, I'm worried. She hasn't eaten in two days." Michael came over to me and held me.

"It's all right. The doctor said it was normal. She'll eat soon. Have you checked her for the rash yet?"

"No, not yet. I didn't notice any when I changed her this morning."

"Maybe it isn't the chickenpox, after all."

"Let's hope so," I said.

Doctor Kiley came knocking at the door then. "Afternoon, Doc," Michael said as he let the doctor in.

"Afternoon, Michael. How's our little one doing?" he asked.

"At her last change, she still didn't have any spots," Michael explained.

"Well, let's take a look." Michael followed the doctor to the bedroom.

"Hello, Doctor Kiley," I said.

"Hello, Cheyenne, how's our little one?"

"She's doing all right, considering. I didn't see any spots when I last changed her a couple of hours ago. Maybe she doesn't have the chickenpox after all."

"Let's take a look," Doctor Kiley said.

CHAPTER 32

I picked Lucy up from her cradle and laid her on our bed. The doctor looked in her mouth, under her arms, and on her belly. Then he said, "Spots are now forming on Lucy. It's the chickenpox. She made it through the worst part with the fever. Now she will begin to itch. You need to prevent her from scratching or she will spread them and end up with scars. Her fever is low, and it should go away now. Has she eaten yet?"

"No, not yet," I said sadly.

"Don't worry so much, this is normal. Just keep trying to feed her, she will eat soon."

"I will, thank you, Doctor Kiley." After he was done checking on Lucy, he left.

Sally made a wonderful dinner today. A stew with dumplings and biscuits that tasted heavenly. Lucy was restless but she slept, so I put her in her cradle. "How long do you think Lucy will have the chickenpox?" I asked no one in general while we were having our dinner.

"I don't know. The doctor didn't mention it. Hopefully it won't be too long," Michael said.

"I hope she gets better real soon," Sally said.

"Me too, Sally," I said.

"She must be exhausted after all the crying that poor baby did," she said.

"She is, but hopefully she will sleep enough to build her strength up," Michael said.

I checked on Lucy and although she slept, she began to scratch. I didn't know what to do to prevent her from scratching. Sally came in then to see how Lucy was. "I don't know how to keep her from scratching," I told Sally. Lucy woke up then and started to cry. I picked her up and decided I would try to see if she would eat. I sat on the bed and allowed Lucy a chance to eat, and she did.

"You may want to wrap her tight in her blanket to prevent her from scratching," Sally said.

"That's an idea. I'll try that."

Lucy ate very little, but it was better than nothing. I took a lightweight blanket and wrapped Lucy carefully in it, keeping her hands at her sides immobile. As I wrapped her up, I noticed the spots were multiplying on Lucy's skin. They seemed to be coming in all over her body. Oh, how my heart went out to her. I just hope and pray she gets better quickly. She didn't like being confined very much, but it was for her own good. So I just sat and held her until she settled down.

I went into the kitchen as I held Lucy. Sally was busy making biscuits for supper. "How is she?" she asked.

"She hates being wrapped up like this, but hopefully she'll get used to it by bedtime. Otherwise it's going to be another long night," I said.

"If that happens, just wake me up and I'll tend to her so you can sleep."

"Are you sure? You'll lose sleep too then."

"Yes, but I can always take a nap in the afternoon."

"Oh, how a nap would have been so great. Well, if you're so willing, I wouldn't mind going to sleep early tonight, and you could tend to her for a while. When you're ready to go to sleep, you can just wake me up to take over."

"That's fine with me," Sally said.

That was exactly what we did. Sally let me sleep for a couple of hours while she took care of Lucy in her room. Then it was my turn to take care of Lucy. She didn't seem to mind our arrangement. Thank goodness Lucy wasn't such a Momma's girl yet. At dawn, Michael woke and told me to go back to bed for a while, and that he too would tend to Lucy. I didn't know what I'd do without these two people.

I woke to the smell of bacon being cooked and bread baked. I stretched and wondered how long I had slept. I felt very rested, even better than I had felt in days. I put my robe on and went to the kitchen. "Morning," I said.

"Afternoon," Michael said, smiling.

I quickly looked at him and said, "Afternoon! It's afternoon already? Why did you let me sleep so long?" Michael and Sally laughed.

"You needed your rest after the last several days and you looked so peaceful I didn't have the heart to wake you," Michael said.

"Don't worry yourself, we had everything under control," Sally said. "Are you ready to eat?"

"Yes, I'm very hungry. Thank you both." I gave them a smile.

I noticed Michael brought the cradle into the kitchen, and Lucy was sleeping soundly. "How is our baby today?" I asked as I took the chair to my husband's right.

"She's doing pretty well. She seems to be adapting to being bundled up, she isn't fighting it so much. We need to hold her more while she's awake, however."

"I don't think that's a bad idea, my love. She needs to be preoccupied, so she'll not scratch herself." I then turned to Sally. "Dinner is excellent, Sally."

She smiled and said, "Thank you."

"Thank you for helping with Lucy, Sally. She was good for you this morning?" I asked.

"Yes, she was as good as could be, considering her circumstances," Sally replied. "I tried to give her some applesauce too, but she wouldn't take it."

"She must be hungry by now then. When she wakes, I'll try to feed her again."

As we ate, I realized that it was raining outside. It was funny how storms would just move in on a beautiful sunshiny morning.

I heard thunder in the distance. Since the storm just started, there would probably be more thunder.

"Sounds like we're going to get a nice storm," Michael said.

"It does, but hopefully not a real bad one," I said. Sally began to clear away our dinner dishes, and I sat back with a cup of coffee.

"I need to check in with the office, but I won't be gone long," Michael announced as he stood up.

"All right, Michael." He then leaned down to kiss me.

"See you soon," he said.

Suddenly, Lucy woke up crying. I picked her up and moved to the bedroom. I tried to get Lucy to eat, but she didn't want to. So I took her in the kitchen and grabbed the applesauce Sally tried feeding Lucy this morning. To my surprise, she began to eat it. I was so relieved. "She loves this applesauce," I told Sally.

Sally grabbed a cup of coffee and sat down and said, "I see that."

"I hope the doctor comes by today. I want to know how long this will take."

"I heard it could last more than a week."

"Lucy seems to be feeling some better since she's eating. Hopefully she won't be sick for too long."

"I agree, Cheyenne. It's a good sign that she's eating now. More coffee?"

"No, I think I'll wait for a little while yet, thank you."

"The storm is really kicking up, isn't it?" Sally said.

"Yes, it is. I hope Michael makes it home all right. It sounds so mean out there," I said as I looked out the window.

When I finished feeding Lucy, I changed her and wrapped her in a clean blanket. Oh, I wished it wasn't raining, so I could wash these things. About then, Michael came home. I met up with him in the hallway. He was soaked clean through.

"It's really pouring out there," he said.

I giggled. "I see. And the thunder sounds mean too." Michael took off his coat then took Lucy from me, and together we went to the kitchen.

"How is she?" he asked.

"She's better. She ate some applesauce."

"That's great. She's a trooper."

Sally and I started to make supper and bread to go with it. Michael took care of Lucy while the storm outside raged. The rain on the roof had a calming effect, and though there was thunder, it became a mild rumble. We all just listened to the rain for a bit. Even Lucy was quiet as if listening to the rain with us. After we put the bread in to bake and supper was cooking, Michael handed Lucy to me.

"I'll be back in a few minutes. I want to check on the horses. This much rain could flood the barn," he said.

"All right."

Lucy was getting a little restless now, but I put her in the cradle to start a fire in the bathing room. It was cooling off very quickly even with the stove going. I didn't want Lucy getting any sicker than she already was. Besides, Michael would probably appreciate it when he came back inside.

Once the fire was going, I went back to Lucy. She wasn't fussing yet, but I was hoping to avoid that. When Michael came in, he was pleased with the warmth of the house. I went to get him a clean pair of pants and a shirt. He could change in the wash room. After he was changed, he came into the kitchen and sat at the table.

"The barn floor is a little flooded, but it isn't too bad. The ground is soaking it up some, so hopefully it won't get too much worse. The horses are fine now," Michael said.

"That's good, my love. I know how they hate storms," then I said, "are you warm now, Michael?"

"Yes, I'm getting there. A cup of coffee would help." He was looking at Sally with a pleading face. Sally laughed and brought Michael a cup of coffee. We talked a little more until supper was ready. Then I handed Lucy to Michael, and Sally and I put supper on the table.

Doctor Kiley came over while we were eating supper. The rain had stopped, allowing for the doctor to make his rounds to the homes who had chickenpox. We invited him to join us. When we finished eating, he checked on Lucy. "She's doing better?" he asked.

"Yes, she ate some applesauce earlier and should be ready to eat again soon. Unfortunately, however, she didn't want my milk," I replied.

"Don't worry so much, Cheyenne. Her appetite is coming back, and that's what matters, so just give her more applesauce." When he finished examining Lucy, he explained what was to come next. First would be the blisters then they would crust up and go away. He was very pleased that Lucy wasn't throwing up, and that she was eating.

"This is all good. It could have been worse especially considering her age," he said. I just looked at Michael, and he too looked at me. We thanked Doctor Kiley and then he left.

Lucy started to fuss, so I thought I would try to feed her. I was pleased when she ate. She was definitely getting better. I thought her headache was gone as well. She was no longer as fussy as she was before.

"What do you think he meant, my love?" I asked.

"I don't know, but I'm glad it wasn't worse. He did say it was rare for an infant to get chickenpox, so I guess we got lucky, honey," Michael replied. "Any fever is bad for all of us, but I'm sure it's worse for an infant. Let's not worry about what might have been and just be grateful we didn't have to experience it."

"You're right, my love. I'll stay focused on the present and the future instead of the past."

The next several days passed by without incident. Lucy's blisters were crusting and she got no more new spots, just like what the doctor spoke of. We still kept her wrapped in her blanket though, so she wouldn't break open the blisters. But the good thing was that she was eating really well now. She liked to have her milk as well as mashed fruit. I was so happy it was coming to an end for her. What happened to her really scared me, especially in the beginning. Luckily at that time, I didn't know that it could have been worse. I didn't know if I would have kept focused on what to do for Lucy. She was a strong baby, and I was grateful she would be all right now, and I hoped I would never have to have that kind of fear again. Although if we were to have more children who would ever come down with this illness, at least I would already know what to do and what the risks were.

CHAPTER 33

S ally and I cleaned up the kitchen from breakfast and Michael was tending to Lucy. "It's a lovely day for a wedding, don't you think?" I asked.

"Yes, it is," Sally said.

"It makes me think back to our wedding, Michael," I said.

"I'm not surprised, honey," he responded.

"As soon as I'm done here, I'll give Lucy a bath and get her ready to go. Sally, will you put some supplies together for Lucy please?" I asked.

"Of course."

"Thank you, Sally."

As she was entering the bathroom, she also asked, "What was your wedding like, Cheyenne?"

"Oh, it was wonderful! It was a glorious day, just beautiful. It was the most perfect day for a wedding. I wore a gorgeous white gown, and Michael was so handsome in his black suit. The ceremony was perfect. The reception lasted the whole day and into the night, even after we left," I narrated with excitement. "There was so much food too, of all kinds. Luckily there was so much because almost the whole town came. It gave folks a good way to visit and have fun at the same time. The dance floor was packed most of the time. It was a wonderful day! I will never forget it!"

"It sounds wonderful, Cheyenne. I wish I could have seen it. Mine was just a few people. But it was beautiful too. After we married, we moved here. I'm looking forward to going to this wedding. I'm sure it will be fun," Sally said.

"Me too," I replied.

With everything that was needed packed into the carriage, Michael, Sally, and I headed to the wedding. Hopefully we wouldn't get any sudden rain showers.

As we approached the house, there were dozens of folks who had already arrived. Everyone was mingling while waiting for the ceremony to begin. It was nice to see so many people attend. This was going to be a very nice wedding.

The ceremony was short but beautiful. Melanie was a gorgeous bride. She was wearing a white satin gown. Jacob looked so nervous, more so than the bride if you could imagine. Everyone now was sitting down to eat. There was as much food here as there was in my wedding. Sally went to sit with Dean while Michael and I took seats near Gerri and Mac. Mitch didn't come. I guessed he was still struggling badly with the loss of his wife Sandy. No one could blame him. I missed Sandy very much too.

As we ate, Gerri and I talked about the wedding and just to catch up with each other, since we hadn't seen each other for quite a while. The food was delicious too. Mrs. Taylor was right; food tasted better when you didn't have to cook it.

When everyone was done eating, the dancing began. Everyone looked so nice. The announcer had a special bridal dance, and Melanie and Jacob looked quite good together. Then the bridal party went on to the dance floor. After that dance, there was a dance where everyone would dance with the bride and groom for either a penny or a food gift. What an unusual type of dance. The rewards would help the bride and groom start their new life though.

In between dances, they stopped so the bride and groom could cut the cake and throw the bouquet. While the dancing started back up, the bride and groom left. Everyone continued to eat and dance until dusk. This had been a fantastic, fun day. It was time for us to head home now.

"Wasn't it a wonderful day, my love?" I asked Michael.

"Yes, it was, honey. It reminded me of our own wedding day," he replied with a smile.

"Yes, it did for me too. Sally, did you enjoy yourself?"

"Oh, yes, it was lovely! Dean was a perfect gentleman, and we had a wonderful time," Sally said.

"Lucy is very tired. You would have thought she too was out dancing to be so tired." We all laughed at that.

"She was a very good girl today," Michael said, looking at Lucy and then at me.

Once we got home, I put Lucy to bed, and then Michael, Sally, and I decided to sit on the front porch awhile. The evening sky was so beautiful, and the stars were coming out to brighten up the sky. The moon was also shining brilliantly down on us like a beacon. It was a little chilly, but I figured it was nice to relax out here before going to bed.

CHAPTER 34

"The spring air smelled so lovely, crisp and clean. The sun is showing off its bright rays. It's going to be a beautiful day. The birds are singing soothing songs, which are music to my ears," I said.

"Yes, it does, honey. Shall we go?" Michael said.

Hand in hand, Michael and I walked to the barn. Then we saddled our horses to go for a morning ride.

We rode the southern pasture and enjoyed the wind in our faces. "Michael, are you certain we should do this?"

"Yes, I've thought about this for some time now. I want to be around to watch my children grow up. After this past winter, it would be a better life I think. Don't you?"

"I guess you're right. It would be a better life. How do you feel today?"

"Better, at least I can ride again."

"When will you get the horses?"

"In the next couple of days."

"When will you see Doctor Kiley again?"

"At noon, but I really don't think it's necessary."

"It's necessary because you're getting better. It's because of Doctor Kiley that you're improving," I said.

Although Michael was still recovering from a bullet wound to his leg he received this past winter in a gunfight, his spirits have lifted. He seemed happier in the last few days than he had in the past two months. Being able to ride and deciding to start a new life was what did it. It was possible that Michael's leg would not improve much more. He still had a limp with pain, but at least he had improved better than we first thought he would. He is walking.

As we rode, I thought about this past winter. It went so fast this year for some reason, but I was grateful it did. After having a lovely Christmas—Lucy's first—everything changed. Michael had gone after some rustlers who stole some of Dean Ranson's cattle. When the posse caught up with them, they had a big gunfight. Some were killed and some injured, including Michael. Three of the rustlers went to jail, one was injured, and the other three were killed. A bullet went into Michael's thigh and into the bone. After much effort, Doctor Kiley finally got the bullet out. Michael got an infection, and we almost lost him. After that, Michael was very depressed knowing his leg may never heal completely and that he would have a limp for the rest of his life. It was a very bad time, but the days went by quickly for me.

A week and a half ago, Michael discussed with me his plans of becoming a horse rancher like his father. With much discussion, we finalized the decision that Michael would give up being a sheriff and start a horse ranch. This brought him out of his depression. His mood improved more each day. He was becoming the man I married.

Lucy and I were ready to go visit Grandpa. I was very nervous. I'd never met him. He was ill when we married, so he couldn't come to the wedding. Michael came in to get our bags, and we walked to the wagon. It was fully loaded with food to last the whole trip. Michael hired a cowboy who was great with horses yesterday, and he would be driving the wagon. Michael took the baby and helped me get up onto the seat of the wagon. Then he handed Lucy back to me.

The cowboy's name was Shane. He was a fine-looking young man with black hair and brown eyes. He wasn't as tall as Michael, but he was tall nonetheless. He too grew up with horses and had a real talent for them. He was going to be a great help indeed.

Michael would be purchasing some horses up near his father's ranch as well since he wouldn't be getting too many of his father's. His father also offered to help us financially to get started and said that we could just repay him when we were able to sell our second herd. But Michael and I would not take the money since we really didn't need it.

Our trip went smoothly, and it had taken us only three days to get there. As we pulled up into the yard, we could see all the beautiful horses in the corrals. There were so many of them! More than I had ever seen. They were all thoroughbreds with several colors like, roan, black, and silver. They were Morgans, Michael had told me.

As Michael helped me out of the wagon, his father came out. He looked very pleased to see us. He was very tall and lean, and had hair that was as black as coal and eyes that were a brilliant dark blue, which sparkled with excitement. He was a very good-looking man.

Once I was down from the wagon, Henry came over to take the baby. "So there's my first grandbaby! She's beautiful," he said as he leaned over to kiss my cheek. "And how is my lovely daughter-in-law?"

I giggled. "Just fine, thank you. How are you?"

"Never better. Come let's go inside the house, shall we?"

Michael grabbed a few of our bags and had Shane carry the rest. As soon as we entered, I saw a huge room with a very high ceiling and rugs on the floor. This room was the sitting room with all kinds of furniture, from the settee and chairs to the tables and the piano. It was a lovely room and very well-decorated.

"Would you like to go to your rooms and freshen up first?"

"Oh, yes, that sounds wonderful," I said.

Henry showed us our room, including Shane. The rooms were decorated with lovely wallpaper in soft pastel colors. The bed was large and sat between two windows with tables on either side. There were two chairs by the fireplace on the right and a changing area on the left. It was a very nice room, indeed.

After I cleaned and dressed Lucy up, I worked on myself then. Then Michael had his turn. We took our dirty clothes downstairs for Henry's housekeeper to clean. When we came to the kitchen, I immediately saw that it was huge, bigger than ours. Janey, the housekeeper, offered us some coffee and told us to sit and she would fix us something to eat.

About then, Shane and Henry came into the room. "So, I see everyone is settled," Henry said as he and Shane sat down.

"Yes and the room is lovely," I said.

"Thank you, Cheyenne. My wife decorated the whole house. I think she did an excellent job."

"Yes, she did."

Janey gave Henry and Shane coffee and then prepared to serve dinner. "Everything looks grand," I said to Janey.

"Thank you," she said.

"So, how many horses can you spare?" Michael asked his father.

"I'm going to give you two hundred. That should be a good start for you, especially since you said you were going to buy Arabians to breed with," Henry replied.

"Thanks, Pa. I appreciate all you're doing to help us out. We can't thank you enough, but we don't need the money, we have plenty," Michael said.

"No need to worry about that. I know how you feel. As for the money, I want to help. All I'm doing is saving it anyway." Then Henry said, "How long are you staying?"

"Just three days. We have a lot to do. I already have the corral set up for them, but there are also other things we need to do. I still need to go to Kentucky to get the Arabians," Michael replied.

"That's understandable. So let's make the best of our three days together. We can go into town tomorrow. I need to go to the bank anyway."

"All right. That would be just fine, Pa."

After we finished eating, we went out to look at the horses. They were all just magnificent. Some seemed a little skittish, but most of them were friendly. Some were even showing off a little, which made us laugh. The horses would be chosen the day before we would leave. It would take time to go through all of them, but I was sure Henry would have most of them separated already.

As we watched the horses, I let Lucy down to play. With her walking now, she got around quickly. She liked the horses but she would rather play in the dirt. "Well, it looks like someone is going to need a bath this evening," I said as I giggled.

"Yes, I see that. You may want to put her in her bath clothes and all," Michael said. Then we were all laughing.

"Well, she can bathe in our bathing room just before supper. She will love the tub," Henry said.

"I'm sure she will. She swims like a fish in ours." I giggled.

It was getting late, so we needed to get into the house for supper. I had to bathe Lucy first, and then we could eat. Lucy wasn't too happy to leave the dirt, but when I told her it was bath time, she ran to the house.

At the supper table in the dining room, we talked about the horses, the ranch we would have, and more of our plans for tomorrow. Henry also asked me questions about my past. We didn't go into my beatings, but instead just talked about the rest with Momma and Daddy, and Aunt Janet, the wedding, and such things. Henry told us some stories too of Michael as a boy. Like when he was four, he'd put his hands on his hips, tilt his head when his daddy didn't understand him and he would say "Pay attention, Papa." We were enjoying ourselves immensely.

The next day came, and Michael and his father would be going to pick out the horses, with Shane's help. As soon as they left, I played with Lucy, visited with Janey, and rested while Lucy napped. I thought about our day yesterday. We had a lot of fun.

After the men took care of the bank and arrived a while later, we went to dinner at a nice, big restaurant. I had never seen one so big. The food was fantastic too. We did a little shopping. I bought a dress for Lucy and myself, and Michael bought a full outfit as well. We bought a few extra things that were not really necessary, but we wanted.

Independence was bustling with people. There were so many that we had difficulty walking around. We saw trains and wagons as far as we could see. Mostly they were all headed west. Some of them were very friendly, and even told us about their plans. It was quite interesting.

I must have fallen asleep thinking about our day because the next thing I knew, Michael was standing over me with Lucy in his arms. "Time to wake up, honey," he said.

"Oh, I didn't realize that I fell asleep," I said.

"Well, it's suppertime. Are you ready to eat?"

"Yes, I'm hungry."

So we went to supper. It was grand. We talked of our plans for our ranch, and after Henry's invitation, we agreed to stay one more day.

CHAPTER 35

Today was the day we would be heading home. We already had all the two hundred horses, and as we left, Michael went to buy fifty more from a neighbor. Yesterday, he hired five men to help take the horses back home.

When we said our goodbyes, Henry held me so tight that I cried. He also hugged Lucy just as long and tight. Instead of her struggling to get down, she hugged him back, and that made all of us feel good. He said he would come visit us after he sold some of his horses to the army next spring. There was too much to do come this season, which we understood.

On the way home, we thought of the two hundred and fifty horses that we now had, and the six men guiding them, including Michael. We needed to pack extra to accommodate the new hands. It would only take three to four days to get home if all would go well.

The days were long, but at least we were on schedule so far. At noon, we decided to stop so we could rest and eat. We made camp just before dark. I made good meals almost as if we were home. The men took shifts by pair in looking out for the horses. All went well until later at night, when one of the hands came up to Michael to tell him that we were being followed.

"Are you sure?" Michael asked.

"Yes, sir, there are four of them," the man called Hank said.

"All right, I want you and Gregg to go watch them undercover. You must not let them see you. Then report to me what you find out as soon as possible," Michael said.

Hank put his hand to his hat in a salute and said, "Will do, boss."

"Why would someone be following us?" I asked.

"I don't know, but I don't want you to worry," Michael said.

"Will they hurt us?"

"If they're going to do anything, they'd steal some of the horses and leave. They usually don't want us to know who they are. If there's trouble, you and Lucy get into the wagon immediately."

"All right." I was a little nervous and I certainly didn't want anything to happen to Lucy.

After we finished eating, we were ready for bed. I put Lucy down in her bed and after she fell asleep, then I went to sleep myself. Michael and I slept peacefully.

When morning came, everything was as it should be. No horses were taken, Lucy was still sleeping, and all was well. I started to make breakfast, and as I did, the men also started waking up. It was a chilly morning, and everything was covered in dew. Hopefully it would be a nice day. Hank and Gregg, who were sent by Michael to spy on our followers, rode in just as everyone was finishing breakfast.

"Well, boss, they have plans of stealing some of the horses tonight. We overheard their conversation," Hank told Michael.

"Really now? Well then, I guess we better be ready for them," Michael said.

As the men began forming a plan to stop the rustlers, I cleaned up.

"I say we hit them now," Hank said.

"No, they have to be in the process of stealing the horses or it would be murder. We have to ambush them when they come for the horses," Michael said.

"Three of us can take care of the herd, while the rest of you hide in the areas closest to us without letting the rustlers see you," Gregg said.

"Good, when they sneak up on you, we will sneak up on them," Hank said.

"We just have to be careful so none of us gets hurt," Shane, one of the other men, said.

"One of us will watch for the rustlers. As they come in, he will give us a bird whistle to warn us," Gregg said.

"Who's best at the bird songs?" Michael asked.

"I'm pretty good," Shane replied then gave a sample.

"Yes, you're very good. You'll be the lookout. We have our plan."

I didn't hear the rest of the details of the plan since I was washing up the dishes. When I was finished, Michael called me over. "Yes, Michael?"

"We already have our plan, and I want you to have a rifle."

"Oh, no, I can't."

"Yes, you can and you will," Michael insisted.

"All right."

"Now, when you get into the wagon, if you see anyone strange or hear unusual sounds, fire one into the air and I will be here within seconds. Then point the gun at the intruder and say it was just a warning shot. This way he'll believe you know how to shoot real well and wouldn't miss shooting him. If he points a gun at you, then you'll need to shoot him first. Don't show fear," he said.

"All right, I understand and will do as you say."

"Good, make sure Lucy is lying down." Michael then loaded the gun and said, "Keep it at your side while riding on the wagon, just in case trouble comes before we can initiate our plan."

"All right," I said.

As the day went on, nothing happened. Maybe Hank and Gregg didn't hear the rustlers right. Maybe they weren't going to bother us at all. But I knew I couldn't think that way right now. I had to be prepared for whatever might happen tonight. The rustlers would strike at night to make it hard for anyone to see them coming. Usually, that would work well. This time however, the rustlers would hopefully be the ones to get surprised.

Evening fell so we stopped for the night as usual. It wasn't dark yet, so we ate supper and talked until it got dark. Then three men went to watch the horses while the rest went to their hiding spots between the horses and the rustlers.

After cleaning up, I took Lucy into the wagon with me. Sitting in the middle of the wagon on one side, I started watching both entrances and Lucy as well. I put her to sleep as soon as I could. I thought I heard a shot, but it was only once so I didn't think it was anything. But I was already curious then.

A few hours later, Michael came riding in followed by the men and their captives. There were only two of the captives I saw, however, so I asked Michael, "Where are the other two?"

"Dead, I'm afraid. One was shot when he turned on Hank, so Hank had to shoot him. The other, well, he was hit on the head way too hard," Michael said.

"None of you were hurt?" I asked.

"No, not one."

"Where are we going to drop off our unwanted guests?"

"We're very near to Topeka. In the morning, we'll stop there to turn them over to the sheriff."

"I guess your plan worked out very well."

"Yes, it did," Michael said as he chuckled.

"I'm looking forward to being home," I said.

"We'll be there tomorrow," Michael replied.

Hank and Shane tied the men to the trees for the night. They laid them down and tied their feet tight and their hands around the tree. That way they could sleep but couldn't get lose. One of the men would guard them while everyone else went to sleep, although the rest of the men had their guns by their sides ready in case something happened. Michael had me sleep in the wagon with Lucy, while he slept at the entrance.

After leaving those two rustlers with the sheriff, we went to dinner. The men thanked us for the special surprise dinner. They enjoyed it very much. We took two boxed dinners to the men watching the horses so they could eat too. Then we headed home.

We arrived home just before suppertime. Sally was so happy to see us that she hugged us all.

"When's supper?" Michael asked.

"You can't possibly be starving, love," I said giggling.

"Not starving, just hungry," he said.

Sally laughed and said, "In about an hour."

"I'm going to give Lucy and myself a bath."

"Good idea." Michael laughed and winked.

"Oh, you," I replied, waving the comment away.

Once the tub was filled, Lucy and I took a bath. Then Sally yelled that supper was ready, so we dried and dressed and hurried to the kitchen. As we ate, we told Sally of our adventure. She got worried when we told her about the rustlers.

"You could have been killed!" she said.

"Yes, well, luckily that didn't happen. We're all fine so stop worrying," Michael said.

"I'll try, but it's scary to think about what could have happened to Cheyenne and the baby. Oh, I can't think about it."

"No, don't think about it. We're safe and so there's no need to worry," I said. "How were things here while we were away?"

"Quiet and boring, really," she said.

"What do you mean boring?" I asked.

"It was lonely, and no one to cook and clean for. So there was nothing to do."

"Well, I guess I can understand why you were bored," I said.

"After supper, I need to find out if any of the hands want to stay. We can only hire one more, so hopefully they all don't want to stay," Michael said.

"When do you plan to go down to get the Arabians?"

"Next week, I want to get things settled here first."

"Will you be gone longer than this trip took us?"

"Yes, it will be a lot longer. I may be gone for a month and a half or so," he replied.

"Oh, goodness, that long?"

"I'm afraid so, honey."

After supper, Michael went to talk to the hands while I put Lucy to bed. I went to the kitchen then to have some coffee before bed. A short time later, Michael came back in.

"So how did it go?" I asked.

"Hank and two other hands are staying here, and the rest of them will wait until I telegraph them that I'll be off the train on a certain day and time. Then they will meet me there to bring the horses home."

"We can't afford to pay them that long," I said.

"They're going to wait here for a small flat fee, and we give them room and board," Michael said. "They won't be working unless they choose to, but the fee won't change. They might help build a bunkhouse while they wait. For that I will pay them a little extra later."

"Sally, I guess we will need to increase how much food we make," I said.

"At least, I won't be bored," she replied.

CHAPTER 36

I got off the train in Lexington, Kentucky. It was a nice-looking town. The green grass almost looked blue. It was a beautiful color, none of which I had ever seen. It was a bright and shiny day, making it easier to see.

I grabbed my bag and my saddle bags and went inside the train station. I asked the man in charge if he could give me directions to the Franklin Farm in Fayette County, Kentucky. Fortunately, he knew of the place, so he gave me directions. It turned out that it was not too far from here.

I got my horse saddled up. As I rode, I saw more blue grass, lots of trees, and flowers. *A beautiful place indeed*, I thought.

After riding a while, I finally arrived at the Franklin Farm. It was just a small horse ranch. The three-hundred-fifty-acre land was filled with lush grass encircled by fences that were sectioned off, and the horses were beautiful too. There were several different colors—black, bay, chestnut, roan, and gray.

I went to the door and asked to speak to the owner. A lady asked me to wait.

"Morning, I'm Michael Hallowell and I would like to buy seven horses from you."

"I'm Leo Drake." He showed me around and I saw the Arabians up close. Other than their high speed, they were also strong and had good endurance.

We stopped by the corral to look at the horses. "Well, Mr. Hallowell, I have some real nice horses. However, I will need to choose the horses because there are certain ones I will not sell. The horses are high-spirited, strongly alert, and quick to learn. They get along great with people. They will not tolerate being mistreated in any way. They're very friendly for the most part," he said.

"Thank you for the information. Be assured however, that they will never be mistreated on my ranch," I said.

"Shall we go get you some horses?"

We went through and picked out the horses. They certainly were beautiful. I got three stallions and four mares. They were friendly horses and took to me quite easily.

"I will send two hands to help you get them on the train. When will you be leaving?" Mr. Drake asked.

"Eleven o'clock sharp tomorrow morning," I replied.

"Very good, I hope you're happy with the horses."

"Yes, I am. Thank you very much. Good day, sir."

"You're welcome, good day to you."

The next morning I was aboard the train and on my way home. I had to make special arrangements with the train office to get the horses home. It wasn't any problem, but I had to pay extra fare.

I telegraphed Cheyenne when I would be in Jefferson City, Missouri, so the men should be there when I got there.

> > > < < <

"Sally, would you be so kind as to make some tea?" I asked.

"Sure, Cheyenne, a cup of tea sounds good to me too," Sally said.

"I sure miss Michael, and he hasn't even been gone that long really. Just three weeks. It just seems longer."

"He'll be back soon. The time will fly by." Just then someone knocked at the door. "Who is it?" Sally asked.

"It's Deputy Roy, ma'am," the voice said.

Sally then let him in. "Morning, Roy, would you like some tea or coffee?"

"No, not today, thank you. Just checking in on you. If you need anything, just ask," Roy said. "How are you today, Miss Cheyenne?"

"I'm fine, thank you. How has your morning been so far?"

"Everything's going smoothly so far. I only hope it stays that way."

"How is it going with the new deputy?"

"Just fine, Zack is a good man." After a while, he said, "Well, I should go. I have a lot to do today."

"All right, have a good day," I said.

"See you later, Roy," Sally said.

It was getting to be dinnertime, so both Sally and I made dinner. Then I had to get Lucy so she could eat. I chased her around the house to catch her. She was starting to think it was a game. I finally trapped her in her room and brought her to the kitchen.

Laughing, Sally said, "She just loves making you chase after her, doesn't she?"

"Yes, she does. She wears me out," I said, giggling. "After dinner, while Lucy is napping, I'm going to go for a ride."

"You're going to take someone with you?" she asked.

"No, that's not necessary, I'll be fine. There's nothing to worry about."

"Yes, but—"

"Stop worrying. Nothing is going to happen to me, so I don't need a guard," I interrupted before she could finish saying what she was about to say.

It was a lovely afternoon to go for a ride. The sun was warming the air so nicely and there wasn't much of a breeze. The wind in my face was refreshingly cool and gave me a feeling of being alive. I so loved the way I felt when I ride. I never thought I'd be doing this, so I was very happy that I could.

As I rode, I noticed I was being followed. So I turned around to head back to town. The rider ducked into the trees and was out of sight, but when I passed him, he came out and followed me again. I rode to the sheriff's office to let Don and Roy know. When I came out, the man was gone.

When I got home, I told Sally about being followed.

"What are they going to do about it?" she asked.

"There isn't much they can do. They're going to look for any clues, but Sheriff Don just isn't sure there will be anything out of the ordinary," I said.

"Oh, sorry, Cheyenne, maybe you shouldn't go out alone until Michael gets back. Do you want some lemonade?" Sally said.

"Yes please. And I agree with you. Going out alone could prove to be a dreadful mistake. Now let me go and check on Lucy first."

I then went to check on Lucy. She was sleeping soundly, so I went back to the kitchen for my lemonade.

As I was sipping my lemonade, I suddenly thought about what happened two days ago. I went to the mercantile then to get some supplies when I strongly felt as if I were being watched. I remembered it was such an eerie feeling. At first I thought I was just being silly. But now, after being followed so obviously, I was beginning to wonder who was so interested in me and why.

So far, everything was running smoothly while Michael was away, but I missed him beyond belief. It was lonely here without him. I knew Lucy missed him a lot too, she was always asking for him. How could I explain to her why her daddy was gone? I kept telling her that he would be back. So far, that seemed to suffice.

It had been five weeks since Michael left, and I was getting anxious waiting for him to come home. It shouldn't be much longer, one or two more weeks he should be here.

I still felt like I was being watched, so I didn't go out alone anymore. I didn't see anyone following us yesterday though when I went for a ride with Hank.

Hank was a good man, a bit rough around the edges, but a good man nonetheless. He was kind to me and protective. He looked quite capable too. He was tall like Michael and big-boned, which made him look very strong in the chest, shoulders, and arms. He had a rugged look. His hair reminded me of the beach and his eyes sparkled like the night sky.

Michael would be pleased that Hank took such good care of Sally and me. He came in daily to check on us, but never at the same time, however. He watched the grounds looking out for strangers, even while he tended to the horses. He seemed very devoted. Shane too was devoted and protective.

I went for a ride again today. It was such a beautiful day. As we rode, I kept thinking about Michael. He had never been away this long, not even early on in our relationship. *Oh, I can't wait until he gets home.*

Hank pulled closer to me and said, "Get down. We're going to ride fast so hang on."

"Why? what's wrong?" I asked.

All he said was "rider". Suddenly we were going as fast as the horses would go. We were chasing the rider! With the rider so far ahead, we couldn't catch him. He even rode through town at a fast rate of speed. Hank slowed then and said, "If the Arabians were here, we would catch him for sure. Are you all right?"

"Yes, I'm fine," I said.

Before going home, we stopped off at the sheriff's office to tell them we were followed again. They asked if we saw the rider's face, but we didn't so we couldn't help them further in that. Hank described the man's coat and hat, but that was all we had seen of him. Hank described the horse the man was on, however.

"The next time you go for a ride, stop by here first so we can keep watch. Do you ride on a regular basis?"

"No, my riding is not a daily thing. There's no set time. I just go when I feel the need to ride," I replied.

"Let's plan for the same time tomorrow," Hank said.

"What I'd like to know is how he knows when I go for a ride? It's not the same each time," I asked.

"He must be watching you from somewhere," Don said.

"I keep a close eye on the ranch and Miss Cheyenne. So far nobody has come on the property. I suppose he could be hiding in the trees around there somewhere. I'm just going to have to look in there," Hank replied.

"I'll have Roy and Zack help out. Even if we don't find him, we may find clues," Don said.

"So we have a plan?" I asked.

"We have a plan," Don said.

CHAPTER 37

Driving the horses home wasn't too bad. We traveled a good distance each day, better than I thought even. So far, we hadn't had any trouble either. The horses were cooperating nicely. We brushed them down each evening before going to bed. They seemed to like that. Anytime we spotted water, we stopped so the horses could drink. We didn't need to stop long since they all drank at once.

The weather cooperated too until today. It was raining, not a heavy rain, but a steady rain. So we kept moving. We had no shelter so stopping didn't seem to be necessary. We were going to get wet no matter what anyway, so we might as well keep going.

We were probably still a week away from home when one night, we were surprised by a pack of coyotes going after the horses. Shane woke us with a gunfire.

"What's going on?" I asked sleepily.

"The horses!" one hand said.

"Coyotes are trying to get to the horses," another hand said as he reached for his gun.

"Let's take care of them," I replied.

I got up immediately and went to Shane who was shooting at the coyotes. As he did, the pack of coyotes scattered and left a few dead behind.

"Were any of the horses injured?" I asked.

"I don't think so, I think I got to them just in time," Shane said.

"Let's check them to be sure," I said.

Shane told the hands, "All right, you heard the boss. Let's check them for injuries."

After inspecting the horses, Shane found one with minor abrasions. He doctored him up and told me about it.

"Will he be able to travel?" I asked.

"Yes sir," Shane said.

"We will have to keep a closer eye on them from here on. Shane, go get some sleep. I'll take the next shift.

>>><<<

Hank and I went for our planned ride, but today, we weren't followed. This was infuriating, why didn't the rider follow? Twice before I went riding, he did it, so why not now? We turned and went back home a short time later. Sheriff Don came by then. "Well, we didn't see anyone follow you," he said.

"Maybe it's because you were out in the open watching."

"Maybe, we must try again. This time we will need to be less conspicuous."

After putting the horses in the corral, Hank came up to the house. I told him what Don said.

"Maybe we should try again tomorrow," Hank said.

"Tomorrow would give us away. We need to wait a day or two longer," Don said.

"All right, in two days at the same time," I said.

The men nodded in agreement. "Try not to worry over this too much, Miss Cheyenne," Hank said.

"I'll try," I replied.

Two days later, we went for our ride only to have the same results. Had Hank not been with me on that one day that I was being followed, I would start to think it was my imagination. I didn't know what we were going to do to find out who was following me and why. Oh, how I wish Michael was here. Since he was a marshal, he might be better at finding this person.

Hank and the two deputies looked all over the ranch, but found nothing. Where was the man hiding? He must be near in order to know when I ride. I wondered if it was someone here in town. Oh, I didn't know what to think.

I went into the kitchen to have some coffee. "Hello, Sally, is the coffee hot?"

"Yes, how did it go today?" she asked.

"Not well, he didn't follow again. This is getting so frustrating."

"Maybe he stopped following you because he left town."

"Oh, I hope so, but it would have been nice to find out why he was following me."

"I understand that," Sally said.

We talked for a while until it was time to make supper. Lucy woke up and was playing quietly. She was becoming very independent, and was getting so big so quickly.

Just then, Hank came to the house. "They are coming."

"Really! How wonderful!" I said with much enthusiasm.

I ran outside to see the horses coming in. It would be several minutes before they arrived. I was so excited to see my husband. I stood on the porch waiting. I left Lucy playing in the house because I didn't want her out here while the horses were being brought in.

I watched the horses as they came in, and they were beautiful, outstanding horses. Their colors were simply gorgeous, and I was sure they would make beautiful offsprings with the Morgans. Then I saw Michael, sitting tall in the saddle. I so loved to see him ride. I started getting goose bumps at the excitement of his arrival. Then I thought of our night tonight. It was going to be a wonderful welcome home.

Instead of riding the herd into the corral with the others, Michael rode over to me. He climbed off his horse and flew into my arms. He then picked me up and twirled me around in circles, kissing me at the same time.

"Oh, honey, I missed you," he said.

"I missed you so much too, my love." I giggled.

After several minutes, Shane came over to Michael and took his horse to the barn. Michael and I walked into the house. He was anxious to see his daughter, and Lucy was so happy to see him too. I almost cried at the site.

I told Michael all about the man following me and all that happened. He didn't want me to go anywhere alone, not even to the mercantile. He was worried about it but tried not to let on, although, I could tell he was.

Once the horses were settled and Michael paid the hands, most of them left. Hank and Gregg stayed on. They were good and hardworking men and took great care of the horses. Michael and I rode two of the Arabians and I found they were so easy to handle. It was as if they had known us their whole lives. We always rode them so they would stay in shape, and they loved it. They were really fast. I almost didn't think I'd be able to stay on, but I did. I went out often for Michael to show me how to help take care of them, especially the Arabians that needed special attention. And that was fine with me.

A couple of mares were ready to be mated, so they were set aside with a stallion so they could breed. The stallions seemed to be very happy at this. It shouldn't take long for the mares to conceive.

By late spring, we had many mares that were expecting. They'd be born around eleven months or so. We needed to watch the mares closely so they would have healthy deliveries. Therefore, for the last three months of their pregnancy, the mares needed to have extra food and be exercised daily, but not ridden. Once the colt or filly was weaned, they needed to be alone in a stall until it was ready to be with the rest of the horses.

One evening, while we were riding on our land, we saw smoke. Michael and I rode to investigate. Once we came closer to the smoke, we saw a small group of people. When we got close enough, Michael spoke to the group. "This is private property, what are you doing here?"

"This is our land, it's paid for all legal like," one man said.

"Then you were duped," Michael said.

"What do you mean? We have the deed and bill of sale," the man replied.

"I'm sorry, sir, but this land belongs to me and has been mine for two years now."

The man reached into a bag, pulled out the deed and bill of sale and showed them to Michael.

"Mister, this deed is fake. My deed is from the bank. Who sold this deed to you?"

"It's Thomas, William Thomas, a man up in Kansas City," he said.

"Well, Mr. Thomas, I will allow you to stay a day or two. By then, you will have to clear out. I'd appreciate it if you don't mess around with any of my horses in the meantime," Michael said.

With that, we turned and rode home. As we rode, I asked Michael, "How did they get onto the land with it all fenced off?"

"The fencing isn't finished this far out yet. It will be done by October at the latest," he replied.

"How can you prove his title is a fake?"

"My title is witnessed by the bank, his wasn't. A copy of our deed is on file in the state capital's courthouse. Then I need to find who is selling off my land and get him to the sheriff."

"Why don't you have your marshal friends find him? After all, you're a rancher now."

"You're right, of course. I don't want to be away that long, anyway."

"Good, I agree with that," I said with a giggle.

"As soon as we get home, I'll go to the bank and get the manager's help to get confirmation that my deed is filed in Topeka. Then I can show that to the squatters," Michael said.

"Why can't you let them stay for a little longer until they can find somewhere to go?"

"We'll see how cooperative they are first," he said.

So Michael went to the bank and was told that the information he needed would be telegraphed from the state capital. A letter would be forthcoming.

Two days later, the banker came by with a letter from Topeka. The letter was hand-delivered by someone. Michael took the letter and showed it to the squatters. The people were very nice about it and accepted the information. Michael agreed to let them stay a little while longer until they could find other accommodations. Michael also requested their fake deed, so he could give it to the marshals, and they gave it to him. The rest was up to the marshals now.

CHAPTER 38

What started to be a good April day turned sad. We received a letter today telling us that Michael's father passed away a month ago. This news hit us pretty hard. It was so unexpected.

The letter stated that Michael needed to come and take care of his father's affairs. Michael inherited the house and his horses since he didn't have any siblings.

"I want to leave here in two days. I want you to go with me, but I would like to leave Lucy at home with Sally," Michael said to me.

"All right, my love, I will ask her now."

I went into the kitchen and talked to Sally. I explained the letter and that we would like to leave the baby home with her. She said it would be fine.

Michael left to telegram the lawyer who wrote the letter, letting him know when we should arrive. Then he went to talk with the men and told them that he would need them to handle things at the ranch.

After all the plans were made, Michael and I left for Independence. We would have to have his father's men help us to bring the horses to the ranch. It was a solemn ride to Independence, and neither of us were in a very talkative mood. My heart went out to my husband. This hit him hard. I understood how he felt. I too lost my parents so unexpectedly.

It took us three days to arrive. Once there, we went straight to the lawyer's office. "Mr. and Mrs. Hallowel, I'm happy to meet you, though sorry it's under these circumstances. Please come in," Mr. Curtis said. "As I have said in my letter, you have inherited your father's property. Now, I understand you have your own ranch. May I offer that I sell his house for you and send you the money when it sells minus a small fee? I will have the money hand-delivered, of course."

I looked at Michael and he looked at me, then he said, "I think that would be fine. I can't be away very long, and it will take about four days to get the horses back home."

"Very well. I'll just need you to sign these papers. Also, your father left you a great deal of money. We will need to go to the bank to withdraw it. Then you will need to sign those papers as well. What do you want to do with your father's furniture?" Mr.Curtis said.

"There are a few pieces I would like to keep. I'll hire someone to take the furniture I want to Auburn. The rest can be sold with the house. There are some personal things I want too. Can you do something about those as well?"

"Yes, all right. Why don't you do that while I get all the papers together for you," the attorney said.

"All right, thank you for all your help," Michael said.

We then left. We went to Henry's house and looked around. It took some time before Michael started going through Henry's papers and putting it all in a bag to take with us. Then he picked whatever furniture he wanted and put a piece of paper on each piece. After that, Michael went out to talk to the hands. When he came in, we went back to the Mr. Curtis' office before we looked through any more of Henry's belongings.

Once there, we signed papers and then Mr Curtis took us to the bank. A very large sum of money was withdrawn and given to Michael. Then Michael asked if he knew of anyone willing to take the furniture to Auburn. The man said yes, so we went to see that man next. The man said yes, and Michael paid him right there.

Back at Henry's house, we took our bags to our room to unpack. We would be here only a couple of days but we wanted our things put up. There was still daylight left, and we wanted to go through the parlor. Tomorrow we would work on the rest of the house. We had also decided to give some of the things to Janey. She worked for Henry for so long, and she deserved some things.

As we looked through the parlor, we noticed things we had not seen before, like a sketch of Lucy. "How did he do this?" I asked Michael.

"I don't know, but he had a great memory it seems, such detail," he said.

We saw his mother's basket of yarn. His father had kept it all this time. It showed how much he really loved her. There was a beautiful china set, and the rugs would go with us as well. It would be nice to have them as a reminder of his parents.

"You know, we're going to need more room at home, so I was thinking that I should add on to the side of the house. Make a larger bedroom for us and a spare room," Michael said.

"That would be wonderful," I replied.

"I'll start that as soon as we get home."

"Are you all right, my love?"

"Yes, I'm fine. Why?"

"Because you seem to be avoiding the fact that your daddy died. You need to mourn." Michael said nothing, just went back to work.

"Oh, my love, if you need to talk, I'm here," I said.

I was starting to worry about him. He wasn't even thinking of what had happened. He was avoiding the subject altogether. Maybe when we got home he'd feel more comfortable talking about it. I stopped thinking and started to work.

We sat down to supper and talked with Janey. I asked her what happened. "I don't rightly know, he just fell over on his desk. At first I thought he fell asleep, but when I couldn't wake him, I knew something was wrong."

"It happened very quickly then," I said.

"Yes, I brought him some coffee not too long before. It was still sitting on his desk almost full when I found him," she said.

"Then maybe it was painless. That's a good thing."

Later when we went to our room, Michael wasn't even slightly frisky. I knew he was in pain, but I wished he would talk to me.

"My love, won't you please talk to me about it?"

"What do you want me to say? He's gone and not coming back. I have a lot to take care of so I need to stay focused," he said. He didn't exactly snap at me, but close.

"All right, love," I said solemnly.

"Oh, I'm sorry, honey, forgive me. I just have a lot to do in a short amount of time," he said as he came to hug me.

"I know you do. Get some rest," I replied. "I love you."

"I love you too, honey."

We managed to get the horses home. We had five of Henry's hands to help. The man hauling the wagon with all the furniture and things we brought back with us was right behind us. I rode in the chuck wagon and prepared the meals.

Janey stayed at the house. She didn't want anything to happen to the place before we could sell it. Then she would go back home to Kansas City, she said.

The trip itself was pretty much uneventful. We had beautiful weather, no rain. Nobody bothered the horses. One night however, a man came into our camp. He seemed real nice, but Michael was suspicious of him. I gave him his coffee and a plate of food, for which he was grateful for. He and Michael talked for a little while then the man left.

Later I asked, "What's wrong, Michael?"

"Something doesn't fit right with me about that man," he said.

"What do you mean?"

"It's like I have seen him before but I haven't. I have a bad feeling about him."

"Why? He seemed real nice."

"I have a sixth sense of such things, which was why I made such a good marshal. I could sense things about people and that man is not what he seems," Michael said.

"What are you going to do about it?"

"I don't know yet, but I'll keep my eyes and ears open and ask the men to do the same."

The good thing was we never saw the man again. All the men seemed to be extra watchful and cautious. They knew that trouble could happen any minute.

But Michael was still bothered by that man. He kept thinking he had seen him before, yet he knew he didn't. Somehow, I found that strange, but then again, Michael was a US Marshal and a sheriff for a while. From the stories he had told me, he was usually a good judge of character. For as much as this bothered him, his feelings just might be right.

"I want you to never go out alone, or answer the door without finding out who it is. Keep the doors locked. I want you to be extra careful," he told me.

"All right, Michael, I will. Are you all right?" I said.

"Yes, I'm fine. I'm just puzzled about that visitor. If he shows up here, don't let him in unless I'm here. Understand?"

"Yes, my love." I changed the subject then. "Do we have enough room to sustain these many horses?"

"For a short time, we do, but I need to buy a little more land, which I intend to do first thing tomorrow," Michael said.

"Oh, that will help, won't it?" I said.

"Yes, it will," he said chuckling.

Four days had passed and Michael had started building the new addition. He helped with the horses early in the morning and spent the rest of the day building. And he had also found help. When some neighbors found out what he was doing, they came by to help. The addition would be done in no time with this much help. They worked until they couldn't see anymore in the night. Some of them came in to supper while a few chose to go home. I hadn't even gone riding since they were all so busy. The hands had their hands full with all the new horses.

That evening after supper, I gave Michael a surprise. "My love, we're going to have another baby," I said.

That news lifted his spirits. He grabbed me and hugged me so tight I thought I'd burst. We both laughed with excitement. Lucy started laughing too, bless her heart.

"When is he or she due to be born?" Michael asked.

"In mid to late October," I replied.

"That soon! Why didn't you tell me sooner?"

"With everything going on, this was my first chance to see the doctor."

"That means you were expecting while we were at Pa's."

"Yes, love, but I didn't know then."

"Well, all right, at least you're both well. We will celebrate tomorrow. I'm taking you to supper."

"That would be lovely," I said with a smile.

Michael finished the new addition just in time for the delivery of our baby. Doctor Kiley figured two more weeks before I would finally deliver. The bedroom that we would be moving into had a separate bathing room, so we could have privacy. We gave Sally the option to have the same room or move into a new room. She chose to stay in her room.

We put his father's bed in our new room, along with a few pieces of the furniture we brought home. We furnished the other bedrooms with the extra wardrobes. We put his parents' beautiful wash basin and pitcher in our new room too. We also added a few new pieces of furniture in the parlor, and put the bath sheets in our room. We also had things to put in the kitchen, like the china set. The house and our new room looked fantastic with all the new things added. We had the rugs in the parlor, in Sally's room, and in our room. Tonight would be our first night in our new room. I loved this room, it was so big. I'd never had a room like this.

Michael was able to get the government contracts that his father had, so he sold the two hundred horses to them. Next year, he would be able to do the same. Now we really could afford to hire two more hands to help out. Michael asked Hank to see if he could find some hands in town to hire.

After two days, Hank found two new hands who wanted to work. They were going to work out fine, we thought. They were very good at answering the questions Michael had. Their names were Ben and Patrick.

A while later, nightfall was upon us, so Michael and I went to bed early. We made long passionate love in our new room. Michael seemed to be making love as if it would be our last time. It was gentle, sensual, intense, and passionate love. Afterward, we held each other close and went to sleep.

CHAPTER 39

The birth of our son, Joshua, arrived on October 9, 1855. He was a big baby boy and a hungry one at that. The birth was not as bad as Lucy's. In fact, I had very little morning sickness with him too. He had black hair, and his eyes were a dark blue, like the night sky. He looked so much like his father.

Lucy just loved Joshua. She wanted to play with him, but she didn't understand that he was too young to play her games. Right now, he just needed a little cuddling, so Lucy was sitting by me and holding him, looking so cute.

Doctor Kiley wanted me to rest for a few days to gain my strength back, which was good because Mrs. Taylor was coming to town for a visit next week. She would be so happy to see Joshua and Lucy. I thought she planned this visit so she could be here for his birthday, but Joshua came early. I should have had her plan it in late September.

"Oh, Mrs. Taylor, do come in. It's so good to see you," Michael said.

"Hello Mrs. Taylor. It's been too long," I said.

"Hello, Michael, Cheyenne, it's about time you called me Anna, don't you think?" she said as she hugged me. "Oh, I've missed the delivery. I'm so sorry I really wanted to be here."

Then Lucy ran into the kitchen. Mrs. Taylor—Anna—got a big smile and snatched Lucy up hugging her like there was no tomorrow. Anna talked to Lucy for a few minutes until Lucy wanted to play. Then Anna asked, "Where's the baby? Is it a she or he?"

"He's sleeping. You can take a peak, if you like," I said.

"No, I'll just wait until he wakes up. How are you, my dear?"

"Oh, I'm fine. It was a much easier delivery."

"I'm so happy to hear it. So how are things?" she said looking at both of us.

Michael looked at me and nodded. So I explained everything to her, about meeting Michael's father and his passing away a year later, the horse drives, and the new addition to the house, which I showed to her after we had our coffee. And just as I thought, she adored the furniture and rugs.

Anna told us all about everyone in El Dorado. Carol was expecting a baby. Deputy Jackson and his wife had two children now and they built a house just outside of town. There were also some new people who moved into town, and according to Anna, they were very nice too. She also shared about a fire that burned down a saloon. Everyone else got out safely, except for one who was killed in the incident. We talked even through dinner because there was just so much she was telling us. So much had changed since I left there. It was so amazing when you thought about it.

"So was it Max's place? Who died?" I asked.

"A saloon girl. It was so sad, really. Yes, he couldn't afford to rebuild by himself so he put an advertisement in the paper in Wichita. He got a response back from a woman. She showed up in town one day and went straight to Max and told him she would be his new partner," Anna shared. "At first, Max fought the idea, being in partnership with a woman was completely unheard of. Well, she told him that if he wants his saloon built he'd better take her offer. With much argument, he finally gave in."

"Really? What's she like?" I asked.

"Well, she's a good-looking woman. She's rather tall though. She has red hair and a nice personality. She has a full figure with a trim waist, with eyes the color of a stormed ripped sea. She's one who will not tolerate being ordered around like some slave, she says." Anna giggled. "And she'll take no guff from anyone either."

"She sounds like a woman I'd like to meet," I said excitedly.

"When they were rebuilding, she was right there the whole time making sure they were doing the job right. The men complained, but when she heard about it, she gave them what for. Believe me when I say they didn't complain again. At least, not at the site." she laughed. "It's almost finished. They have a few things left to do inside, and it will be done."

"I wonder what a partner she's going to be once it's ready to open."

"I think she's going to make a good go of it. She may end up being the boss of the place at the rate she's going." We both laughed then.

Then Anna changed the subject. "I would like the children to call me Grandmother if it's all right with you," she said.

"Oh, that would be wonderful, thank you," I said as I hugged her and laughed.

She laughed too almost in tears. "You've been like a daughter to me, Cheyenne, so I think it's only proper for your children to know me as their grandmother."

"It would be an honor, Anna," Michael said.

After dinner, Michael went to check on the horses, and Anna and I went to the mercantile. Anna wanted to buy some things there. She went her way and I went mine to get what I needed. When we came home, she showed me what she bought. She bought me a handbag and a matching dress, outfits for both children, and a new shirt for Michael.

"You didn't need to do that, Anna," I said.

"Yes, I did, and I enjoyed it immensely," she replied.

Later, before supper, I wanted to go for a ride. I asked Anna to watch the babies while Michael and I went for our ride.

It was cold, but I needed to ride. It had been way too long since I rode. Luckily there's no snow. It was a lovely evening to ride. As we came closer to town, I had the feeling that someone was watching us. I didn't see anyone though. "My love, it seems like we're being watched," I told him.

He looked around but saw nothing. There were only trees. "I don't see anyone. Are you sure about this?"

"Yes, it's a very eerie feeling. Let's get home."

"All right," Michael said, so we went home.

"We've actually tried to find him so many times and couldn't, but I know someone's there, my love," I said.

"I believe you, honey, don't worry about that. If only we had snow we could see tracks better. All we will find in the trees will be broken branches. The tracks will be hard to follow, but we will check, anyway," he replied.

As soon as we got back home, Anna noticed our mood. "What's wrong dear?" she asked.

"Well, someone's been following me a couple of times, but we couldn't catch him. We don't know who he is. I also feel like I'm being watched. It's happened many times," I said.

"Are you sure?"

"Yes, this has never happened before, and I've never had these feelings before."

Anna just looked at Michael and me.

"I'm going to take a couple of men out to the trees first thing in the morning and see if we can find anything that would tell us who this is," Michael said.

"Good, look hard," Anna said.

The next afternoon, Michael came home from the search. "We followed tracks but lost them in the river. Do you recognize this?"

He showed me a scarf. "Oh, no, that's not possible."

"You recognize it?"

"Yes, but it can't be his, he's in jail," I said almost in a panic.

"Calm down, honey. Are you talking about Finch?"

"Yes."

"I should have told you this a long time ago. It's almost positive that Finch broke out of prison," he said.

"What? How long have you known this?" I asked.

"A long time, I'm afraid. I didn't want you to worry yourself sick. I did what I thought was best."

"You should have told me."

"You know now so you need to stay calm but alert. Take all the precautions I have told you and just stay calm, that's very important. I'll be near too," Michael said.

"You mean to say, that criminal that almost killed Cheyenne could be on the loose?" Anna asked.

"Yes, I'm afraid so," Michael replied.

"Oh, my dear, I'm so sorry," Anna said as she grabbed my hand.

I didn't know if I should be angry with Michael or not. I was hurt that he didn't tell me. How did he think I'd react? He should have told me. I couldn't let him keep secrets from me, especially secrets such as this. My life and the lives of my children were at risk. How dare he keep that from me!

"That's probably who has been watching and following me," I said in a near panic.

"It's a good possibility, honey. I'm sorry, I should have told you," he replied. "I think I should have Don hire two single deputies to keep an eye on the house and on you if you go out. I'd feel better knowing you'll be safe when I'm not close."

"Well, I think that would be a very good idea," Anna agreed.

That's just what he did. Now there was a deputy at the front door and one at the back door. The men also helped watch the house and check on me.

"I think you're over doing it a bit. I don't need deputies guarding my doors. I'm perfectly safe in my own home," I told Michael one time.

"You remember one time that you weren't safe in your own home? I don't want anything to happen to you, so you will have deputies posted at the doors," he said strongly.

"All right, Michael," I just replied. Arguing about it wouldn't change his mind.

"I'll feel better knowing you're being protected after I've gone back home."

"I know."

Nothing more was said on the subject. I just had to accept that. I still couldn't believe he was out of jail. How did he escape? That was a question that may never be answered. He had been out of jail for a while now, and he hadn't bothered me for a long time since, so why would he want to come now? He should be glad to be rid of me. And what if he was the man who had been watching and following me? It couldn't be, it just couldn't. He hated me, and I would think he'd want nothing to do with me. But what if he hated me so much more after I became responsible for putting him in jail in the first place? I needed to stop thinking about this so I didn't get all worked up.

"Are you all right, dear?" Anna asked.

"Oh, yes, I'm fine. I was just thinking."

"If you're thinking about that man, don't. He isn't worth your time. Stay focused on your husband and children. Speaking of children, are the babies up yet?"

"I'll go check, be right back."

Anna stayed for a few more days before she went back home just a little shy away from the first snowfall. She came late in the year only to be with me when I gave birth. We had been lucky so far that we hadn't had any snow. Sometimes it snowed in late October here, so hopefully it wouldn't snow until after she got home. I thought of how much I was going to miss her.

I really enjoyed her visit. It was too bad she couldn't stay longer. That was the only problem with living here, she was too far away. I was lucky if I got to see her twice a year. She even wanted to be a grandmother to my children. How sweet was that? We wouldn't get to see her often, but she' would make a good grandmother, anyway.

CHAPTER 40

The next morning, we woke to a very cold day. At least it was warm in the kitchen. While we drank coffee and waited for breakfast, I asked Michael, "What are you going to do today?"

"Well, we have to put up a new barn for the extra horses and we need to get it done quickly. If we could only hold off the addition to the house, we would have had done it by now. Luckily, it won't take as long as the addition did," he said.

"So you'll start that today?"

"Yes, I sent Shane to buy the wood needed yesterday. I already asked our neighbors for help when they were helping with the addition."

"Good, then it should get done quickly."

Later in the afternoon, long after they were done working, Michael came in to get everyone something to drink, so I put some lemonade in the pitcher and sent out cups. I thought he just wanted to come in to see me because he kissed me several times before he left.

The men all worked so hard and spent whole days building the barn. I had never seen men work so hard and fast. I took out food and just watched them for a time. It was a sight to see.

The barn went up so quickly I couldn't believe it. It was truly unfortunate that it did just right about then because a snow storm was already rolling in. The snow came down in big flakes hard and fast. The harder it snowed, the more worried Michael was getting about the horses. We couldn't lose any of the horses. It was only the middle of October, so the snow came early.

Before the snow built up too bad, Michael bought feed for the horses since they may not be able to get to the grass. He did everything he could to try to protect them. The Arabians were in the barns, along with most of the Morgans. Some of them didn't want to be inside.

The snow kept coming and coming. It was a bad storm—no, a blizzard described it best. I just hoped we were stocked up enough on supplies.

"Sally, how are we doing on supplies?" I asked.

"We're good for now, but I don't know how long it will last if we're snowed in too long."

"Get a list ready quickly," I said.

I went out to get Michael, and found him in the first barn. I told him we needed some supplies before we got snowed in too badly. He said he needed to take twenty horses to the livery anyway because we couldn't stable them all. So he and Shane went for the supplies taking the horses with them. I'd given him the list Sally made. They had to hurry because the snow was getting a little deep. At this rate, it wouldn't be much longer before we would be snowed in.

A while later I was still waiting for Michael and Shane to get home. I was becoming worried by the minute. "Sally, I'm getting worried. Michael should have been back by now. There wasn't that much on the list."

"Yes, I know," Sally said as she put a fresh pot of coffee on the stove. "You know, the bunkhouse probably needs supplies as well."

"You're right and if they did, it would be hard to carry all that stuff home. Normally, they would use the buckboard, but with this much snow they had to walk. Oh, I should never have sent him to the mercantile. We should have made the supplies stretch. If anything happens to either one of them, I'll never forgive myself." I couldn't help saying.

"Now don't go thinking that way, Cheyenne. Nothing is going to happen to them, it's just taking a while longer without the buckboard," Sally said in hopes of consoling me. Just then, we heard a cry.

"Oh, Joshua is up. I need to go feed him. I will be back soon." Somehow, I was thankful for the distraction, however short-lived. As I fed Joshua, I kept worrying about Michael and Shane. I didn't think about the fact that they wouldn't be able to use the buckboard. I looked out the window and saw the snow was so heavy now that I couldn't see anything out of the window except the snow. I hoped that they would be home soon. I remembered they had to take the horses too.

When I was finished feeding Joshua, I went to the kitchen for some coffee. Still, Michael wasn't home. Now I was really worried. I looked out the door, expecting to see them walking in, but all I could see was the plain block of white, unmoving.

Suddenly, Hank came bursting in to the house, shivering and a little out of breath. "The tool shed roof collapsed, and Ben is in there," he said.

"We have to get him out right away," I said.

"We're doing that now, ma'am, he may need doctoring."

"If we can, we need to bring him here to the house so we can take care of him," Sally said.

Hank brought Ben to the house. He was hurt pretty bad. He was hit in the head, his ribs were hurt too, as well as his arm. "Ben, I think your arm is broken," I said.

Ben moaned and said, "Can you set it?"

"I don't know, I've never done this before."

"Well, I suppose you should learn on me," Ben said, in an attempt to lighten up the mood.

With Hank's help, I straightened Ben's arm. We made a splint using some leftover wood from the barn we built. Hank went to get it and found one almost the perfect size that he just had to break it down only a little. Then, I made a sling out of the spare material left in my sewing. Once the makeshift splint was done, we carefully wrapped it around Ben's broken arm.

"Are you all right now?" I asked.

"It hurts, but I'll be fine."

"I'll bet you do. As soon as we can, we'll get the doctor over here for you. In the meantime, you just rest and Sally will bring something for you to eat," I said.

"Thank you, ma'am," he said.

I sat down to drink some coffee when suddenly someone beat on the door. I answered it and saw Shane carrying Michael!

"What happened?" I quickly asked.

"We were on our way back when the cold snow injured his bad leg. He fell in the snow, and I had to get the supplies that fell out and put them aside. I brought him as soon as I could," Shane said.

"Here, bring him to our room."

He laid Michael on the bed. "We had to get some for the bunkhouse as well as your list. Then it was hard walking back with all that stuff. That's what took us so long," Shane explained. "I must get out there and get the supplies now, ma'am, before the snow destroys them."

"It's all right, thank you. Be careful out there, Shane." And then I turned to Michael. "Michael, are you all right?"

"I'm afraid that I'm in a great deal of pain. I can't walk right now so I'm a little bit upset," he replied.

"Let me get you out of your wet clothes so I can put a hot bath sheet on your leg. Get under the blanket."

He did as I asked, and when I came back in with the bath sheet, he was ready for me.

"How's that?" I asked him as I finished putting the bath sheet on his leg.

"It feels nice. I guess I'm going to have to be careful from now on when it's cold outside."

"I guess so. Do I need to get Dr. Kiley? You had me worried sick. I'm so sorry you're hurting, but I'm happy it's not as bad as it could have been."

"I'm sorry too. No, I don't think I need the doctor."

"Well, you might still see him, anyway." I told him about the shed and that we had Ben taken care of in a spare room. Michael was upset and wanted to see Ben, but knew that he couldn't do that yet. He could deal with the toolshed needing a new roof, but he was having a hard time about Ben.

"My love, he's all right. As soon as the weather lets up, we'll get out and go get the doctor for him. You need to rest so you can be up and around as soon as tomorrow. Then you can see Ben. All right?"

"You're right, honey. Take good care of him as I know you will," he said, smiling.

"Let me know when the towel cools. Maybe later if you can stand up and lean on me to walk, you can soak in a hot tub." I gave him a kiss then.

"Maybe, we'll see," he said.

A short time later, Shane came back with the supplies. He had his hands full with all that stuff. After he gave me ours, he took the rest to the bunkhouse. Gregg knew how to cook, so he would be the one to provide the meal for the men.

We were only snowed in for four days. It stopped snowing just as quickly as it started. The sun came out the next day and started melting the snow. It was cold but not too bad. Then it really warmed up, as warm as late spring, which melted the snow quickly.

Having a blizzard in October was unusual. We had had snow before, but not like this. But we just kept ourselves busy since there was also a lot to do. We played with the children, cleaned extra special, and went out helping with the horses. The roof of the shed was being fixed now that the snow was gone. Michael was limping badly, but at the very least, he was already up and moving around. It was rough for him, but he managed quite well, I thought.

CHAPTER 41

It was a beautiful morning with a gentle cool breeze blowing, and the warm sun shining brightly. It wasn't too cloudy either, and the birds were singing cheerfully. It was hard to believe that we had a blizzard just eight days ago.

"Breakfast is almost ready," Sally called out.

"Thank you, Sally." I put the baby in the cradle and went to join Michael and Sally in the kitchen.

"It's such a beautiful day, and I'm thinking of taking Lucy and Joshua for a walk after breakfast," I said as I entered the kitchen.

"Morning, Cheyenne. That sounds like fun, but I have to run over to the mercantile to get some things. Do you need anything?" Sally asked.

"We need some coffee," I told her.

"It's already on the list," Sally replied.

"Good, thank you."

"Don't stay out in the sun too long, honey, all right?" Michael said. Then he added, "I think someone should go with you."

"All right, Michael, I'll go get Melanie."

After we finished cleaning the kitchen, we got ready for the walk. Just as Sally opened the door, I remembered I left my bonnet in the bedroom. So I ran to get it and told Sally to wait for me. When I came back into the kitchen, I gasped in shock and saw Sally lying on the floor. I hurried toward her. "Oh, Sally!" Then I looked up, and gasped again at what I saw, but this time in horror. I couldn't believe it! "What are you doing here? How did you find me? What did you do to Sally?"

By the time I got the words out of my mouth, he was on top of me! Before I knew it, my hands were tied and he put a filthy cloth into my mouth. All I could think about was Joshua and Lucy. *Oh, please leave my babies alone*, I prayed.

He picked me up off the floor, threw me over his shoulder, and went down the hall to the back door. There was a horse waiting outside. He threw me over the horse on my belly, tossed a blanket over me, and rode as fast as he could away from town. My hopes were shattering the farther we got away from town. My ribs were hurting at the uncomfortable position I was in, and all I could think of as I was taken farther and farther away from home was, *Michael where are you? How did the hands not see me?*

>>><<<

Sally burst into the sheriff's office, shouting and rambling so fast that I couldn't make out what she said. "Whoa, hold on there. Take a breath Sally and calmly tell me what is wrong. Is it Cheyenne? Or the children? Are they all right?" I said.

"He took her Michael, he took her! I can't believe this is happening! Why would anyone want to take her? I hope that man won't hurt her," she said hysterically.

Right away I was up and at her side. I took hold of her shoulders and asked, "Who took her, Sally? Is it Cheyenne? The baby and Lucy? What happened?" I asked.

Sally was hysterical so it took several minutes for her to calm down enough to speak. At the same time, my heart was pounding outside of my chest and my hands clenched in tight fists.

Sally spoke as she started to cry. "He took Cheyenne! The baby and Lucy are with Gerri and they're fine. We were getting ready to leave for the walk. I opened the door as Cheyenne went back to get her bonnet. Before I could close the door again, he burst right in shoving me back. Then he hit me. That's all I remember until I woke up on the floor and found Cheyenne was gone."

"Who took her?" I asked holding Sally's shoulders again almost in a panic.

"I don't know who it was," she said, crying.

"What did he look like?"

"He wasn't quite as tall as you, but close. He had dark hair and dark eyes. He was big in the shoulders, I think. He's a big man, but that's all I can remember. I didn't get to look at him long enough. I'm sorry, I hope nothing will happen to her. Maybe they just want a ransom or something like that," she said.

"It's all right. Try to calm down. I want you to go take care of Lucy and Joshua for me, all right? Do you think you can do that?"

"Yes."

"Good, we'll find her," I said, then turning to Sheriff Don, "Don, get Roy and gather up some men. We have to move fast if we want to track him down to see where he took Cheyenne." I grabbed a rifle and a few extra bullets. And then once again, I turned to Sally. "Go to Gerri's and stay there with the babies. I'm going to the house to look for clues."

>>><<<

We rode several hours before we finally stopped. We were at an old abandoned cabin deep inside the woods. He pulled off and pulled me into the cabin. It was cold and dark. He pushed me onto a bed and lit the lantern. Then he lit the stove. Right away I thought Michael could find me as long as there was a fire going. He left me sitting there for a while before he even looked at me. He made himself some coffee and something to eat.

After he finished eating, he came over to me and took the cloth out of my mouth. "You're going to explain to me why you left!" he boomed.

"Why do you want me around so badly when all you do is hit me?" I asked calmly.

"That's my business!" he shouted. Then he backhanded me. "I'm the one asking the questions!"

I screamed at him then, "That's why! You always hit me! You hate me, but I don't know why! I've always done what you have told me to do, but still you manage to find a reason to hit me! Please, once and for all tell me why you hate me so much! What did I ever do to you for you to hate me? How did you find me? What happened to the deputy?"

"He's dead. You made the mistake of writing to the boarding house woman. I got it outta her real easy."

"I hope you didn't hurt her," I said.

"Nah. Not much." He sneered. "As for hitting you, the way I see it, you owe me so I aim to collect in any way I want too. Do you get that?" he yelled.

"How do I owe you?" He hit me again.

"Don't sass me girl!" I didn't respond, and he threw me onto my belly. *Oh, no,* I thought. He then began to beat my backside. "This is a reminder of what will happen to you if you try to escape again, and I'm just getting warmed up," he said.

>>><<<

I looked around inside the house. On the kitchen floor was Cheyenne's bonnet. I looked around until I saw that the back door was open. I went into the yard. Horse tracks! They were easy to spot since no horses went through here very often, especially this close to the house. I looked around the yard but found nothing else, so I went back to the sheriff's office to see if Don was back with the men.

Don and Roy were waiting for me at the office. "We have eight men for the posse and six more to stay behind to keep an eye on the town," Don said.

"Good, I went to my house and found horse tracks. We can follow the tracks and maybe find them quickly. Let's mount up, boys!" We all mounted up, and I said, "Let's ride!"

>>><<<

He sat at the table quietly for a little while. I stayed in the same position since I hurt so much. I hoped Michael found us soon and beat the living daylights out of this evil man!

Then David came to me and untied me. "Clean up this cabin. I have some friends coming," he said.

"Friends?"

"Yes, friends. Now get to work before I tan your backside again."

Oh, no, he has friends coming? What's going to happen to me? Oh, I hope they won't hurt me too. I got up and looked around. It was a mess. I looked for things to clean with, and I found a torn-up bath sheet and a pail. There was no soap at all here. "I need to get some water," I said.

He grabbed me and answered, "If you try to escape, I'll kill you! Do you understand me?"

"Yes," I replied as I grabbed the pail to get some water. All the while, I just kept hoping Michael would find me soon. But I also knew that the head start we had would make it very difficult.

It took me a couple of hours to clean this nasty-looking cabin. When I finished, he made me make him something to eat. He had this place stocked up as if he planned on being here for a very long time. It had been more than two years since I had last suffered from this man. *I thought it was over! I am happily married and have children of my own now! Oh, my little Lucy and Joshua. I hope they're all right. How are they going to feed Joshua while I'm gone? Oh, Joshua and Lucy, momma's so sorry.*

>>><<<

We followed the tracks until we came up on several tracks. "Well, boys, we have several horse tracks now," I said. "There may be more than just one who have Cheyenne. They have a pretty good lead on us, but hopefully we will find them quickly." Then I jumped off my horse to look. I checked several of the tracks, and then climbed in the saddle. "This way has the freshest tracks." Then the men followed as we rode away.

"Mike, we don't know how long Sally was out before she realized that Cheyenne was missing," Don said.

"No, we don't, Don, but it wasn't that long since I left the house. I figure they have maybe three or four hours on us."

We were riding slower than they might be because we had to track them. Hopefully we weren't going too slowly. *I'll kill him if he hurt her! Huh, look who I'm thinking about, he's a dead man!*

"Mike, we'll find her. She'll be all right, I'm sure of it," Roy said.

"Yes, we will. Thanks, Roy."

We had been traveling for about three hours now and there was still no sign of them. We were losing the trail. Multiple horses came through here recently, so it was going to be hard to find her now. Oh, how I hoped she wasn't being held by more than just Finch. I didn't think she could handle being brutalized by several men.

"Hey, Michael, there are so many tracks now. How are we going to find her?" Don asked, suddenly bringing me out of my thoughts.

"I don't know, but we can't give up. She may be in more danger than we think," I said.

"How do you mean?" Roy asked.

"What are you talking about, Mike?" Don said at the same time that Roy spoke.

"Well, since there are so many tracks, there may be more than one man holding her. The prison break, there were eight of them, remember?" Everyone just looked at each other. No one spoke.

>>><<<

"Bring me some coffee and put some food on for my friends. I'm sure they will be hungry when they get here," David told me.

As I was bringing the cup to him, I stumbled and the coffee went flying. Although it barely touched him, he hit me so hard I fell to the floor.

He was on me in a minute. He flipped me onto my back, pinning me there. "You're damned lucky you didn't burn me! You want to know why I hate you? First, let me tell you a story. Your parent's death was no accident!"

"What? What do you mean?" He slapped me and told me to shut up.

"I planted that snake there and rigged the wagon," he said it with such venom that it made me shiver in fear.

"No," I said sadly.

He continued. "Your mother wasn't supposed to be there! She wasn't supposed to die! It's because of him she's dead! Your father stole my land and my woman! It was all his fault and I hated him!" he shouted viciously.

I couldn't believe what I was hearing. He had to be lying. He went on screaming at me then. "You don't believe me, do you? You think I'm lying. Well, he took my land from my father during a poker game! Then he took my girl and built up my land! I only married your aunt because I knew when I killed your father, your aunt would inherit the land and I would then be able to get it from her. Turns out that she didn't inherit the land, you did! Before I could get it from you, you left and got married! Now your husband will get my land!" he bellowed. By this time, I had never seen him so angry.

"If you want the land, you can have it. Anything, just let me go," I said.

"Nah, I don't want just my land back now, I want more and I aim to get it! Your man will come for you and I will be ready." He sneered.

>>><<<

As we rode, I could only think of Cheyenne and those who took her. I couldn't believe someone had the nerve to burst into my house and take my wife. How was it that no one saw a thing, not even the ranch hands? One deputy was dead, but where was the other? If he or they lay one hand on her, I would kill them. There wouldn't be any prisoners.

Before I met Cheyenne, I had a good life. I worked steady as a US Marshal. I had everything I needed. I was a happy man, or so I thought. Then I saw her in town. My heart desired her immediately. I hadn't actually even met her, I just saw her and she right away stole my heart. This had never happened before. I met a lot of women, but none ever made me feel like this. What was confusing was that I had not even met the girl.

Next thing I knew, I was investigating her life and situation. When I found out she was being abused, my heart ached for her. All I would have liked to do was kill Finch. How could he have claimed he was her family? Now I wished I had. But then I thought if I had, I would have gone to prison for murder and would not be married to Cheyenne now. Evil was a minor word to use in describing Finch. Any man who beat a woman deserved the same treatment.

After meeting Cheyenne and talking with her, my heart ached to have her. Not only was she beautiful, but she was also a strong, brave, and caring person, which was why I fell in love with her, my beautiful, loving wife. I had thought I'd have her away from her past when I married her. Now, my heart was breaking. I couldn't find her, and I was scared to death.

Oh, Cheyenne, where are you? I hope they aren't hurting you.

Chapter 42

O*h, where are you, Cheyenne? I need you, honey. Stay strong for me and for our babies, honey. You are my life, without you I'd be lost. Please help me find you, Cheyenne.* Just thinking of what they could be doing to her set me on fire with rage. No woman in the world deserved this kind of thing. Oh, how I hoped they didn't rape her. She was a very strong woman, but I didn't know if she could handle that.

"Michael, look!" Roy shouted as he pointed. I looked over into the trees. I saw some smoke. It was a good distance away and appeared to be in the woods.

"There's a little bit of smoke," Don said.

"Maybe it's not them," Daniel chimed in.

"It's got to be them, unless we went the wrong way altogether," Roy said.

"We better not have, considering the distance we just rode," I said. "Let's go, boys!"

My heart was racing. There didn't seem to be an abnormal amount of smoke for just a campfire. If this wasn't her, how in the world was I going to ever find her? Worse yet, it may not be just David that had her. There could be eight of them. Oh, I couldn't think this way. I couldn't believe this.

We were riding pretty hard now and were coming up onto the woods. We stopped just short to look for the smoke. It was going to be hard to find where the smoke was coming from by the look of these woods. "All right, boys, keep your eyes open. It's going to be hard to track the smoke from here," I told them.

Shortly after entering the woods, I couldn't see the smoke. "Does anyone see the smoke?" I asked.

"No, I don't," Don said.

"No, don't see it," Roy replied. None of the others saw the smoke either.

"All right, let's spread out a little, stay within earshot so we can go in together once we find out where the smoke is coming from," I said.

Everyone took a slightly different direction. With the woods being so thick, we had to move slower. The longer it took to find her, the more harm would come to her. We had to find her soon!

Don came over then and said, "We have a campfire."

We rode over to the fire pit to examine it. It was still warm.

"We must be close," Roy said.

"I don't know, something doesn't feel right," I replied.

"How do you mean?" Daniel asked.

"There was too much smoke before we entered the trees to have been this little fire," Don said.

"Exactly," I said. To make matters worse, it was also getting close to nightfall, which made it almost impossible to see inside these woods.

>>><<<

As the food cooked on the stove, someone banged on the door. David looked out through a little hole to see who was there. Then he opened the door. Three men walked in. They took one look at me, and I could see their drool coming out of their mouths. Right away I started to panic but said nothing. I stirred the soup just to look busy so David wouldn't hit me.

"Come on, boys, have a seat," David said as he looked at me grinning from ear to ear.

The men sat down and they were staring at me. I felt this cold rush go through me and I could have just fainted right there. But I held it together so they wouldn't come rushing to me. Just like David, they were all filthy and smelled bad. I didn't want them touching me.

"Listen, boys, you will have some after I get done, so be patient," David said.

"Where did you find her?" one man said, nodding at me.

"Yeah, she's fine, all right," another said.

"She's my wife's niece. She's a handful, but she will obey me." David said.

I was beginning to panic. My heart was racing, I could feel the strong beat coming through my chest and I was getting sweaty.

"Let's go with the food already. These boys are hungry," David snapped at me as he smacked my behind. The men laughed.

Yes, but hungry for what? I thought. I began serving up the soup, and one of them grabbed my behind and squeezed. I jerked away. When I did, David jumped up and looked like he would kill me.

"If you spill any of that soup, I will tear you apart," he said. "Now finish serving the soup!"

I did as I was told. After serving them, I sat down on the bed with my head down so I didn't have to look at them. As they ate, they made snide remarks about me and laughed, including David. Oh, how my heart was sinking. *Where are you, Michael?*

I hoped he had lots of men so they could get me away from these men and soon. *Michael, he's going to kill you. I wish I could warn you somehow.* He would be walking into a trap. If he didn't come soon, these men were going to hurt me. But he would be in danger if he came.

"Get this mess cleaned up now!" David shouted bringing me out of my thoughts, He backhanded me again. I was too deep in thought, I had to be careful not to do that again. "You need to listen and do as I say! Now get busy!" he shouted.

I did as he said. As I gathered the dishes, the men kept grabbing me. No sooner did I jump back from one, another grabbed me. Then they all started laughing.

"All right, boys, you've eaten and seen the merchandise so now I want you to go back to the camp, stay there and wait for me."

"Aww, we're just starting to have some fun," one man said.

"Yeah, we're just starting," another man whined.

"Who are you to tell us what to do?" the third man said. He looked meaner than any of them.

"The merchandise is mine, which I'm willing to share, but not until I have my fill. Now get going. Remember, stay until I get there," David said. I began to panic. I was washing up the dishes while they spoke, but I didn't know that I could finish. *Oh, Michael, where are you? Please hurry and come for me.*

The men got up, grabbing their gear and left the cabin. David looked at me. "You're not finished yet? Hurry up. I can't wait all day!"

I finished as fast as I could. Then I turned around and said, "I'm finished. What are you planning to do with me? You can't give me to those men," I said quietly.

David got in my face then. "I will do as I want with you. You belong to me! Your precious husband can't help you now. If he tries, he's a dead man!" He threw me toward the bed and then hit me so hard I fell on the bed. I didn't move. "As for those men, I owe them for breaking me out of prison and I pay my debts! If you give them any grief, I'll kill you! I can't have them angry at me and want to kill me." Then he was on top of me.

While holding me down with his body and one arm, he tore up my dress, then he ripped off my under garments. I started struggling then, and he backhanded me. I hoped he wasn't going to go through with this. I even begged him, "Please, please don't do this! You're my uncle, for Pete's sake!"

"I'm not your uncle! Now shut up and lie still!" he yelled as he backhanded me again. He looked so strange, like he wasn't all there. He then rose up enough to undo his pants. He spread my legs out with his leg and leaned down. He wasn't paying any attention to me.

Just as he was entering me, I remembered something. I reached into my bodice and pulled out the forty-four derringer Michael gave me during my target practice.

CHAPTER 43

We rode longer, I was getting so frustrated. We couldn't see the smoke because the trees were so thick and we didn't know how many we would be dealing with. We had been riding for hours. I would think that they would have to stop somewhere since it was getting dark. I hoped by following the smoke we were headed in the right direction. Hiding out in these woods was a good idea if you wanted to slow down a posse. It was hard enough to see in these woods as it was, but with nightfall quickly approaching, it was becoming very difficult.

We looked at the trees to see if there were any signs of them coming through here, but we hadn't seen anything. I hoped we were going the right way. When I did find them and got my hands on him, I would tear him apart with my bare hands!

"Mike, hold up," Mac said, coming up to me. "I've seen some men over there riding away from here. Should we check them out?"

"Yes, let's go." I turned to tell the men what was going on. They all turned to follow Mac.

We ended up back at the fire pit we found earlier. Slowly, they crept up to where the men sat.

"I don't see, Cheyenne," I whispered.

"I don't either, Mike," Mac said.

"There's only three. We need one alive to see if he knows where Cheyenne is. They may not even be a part of this kidnapping, but we won't know until we talk to them. That one looks familiar though," I said.

We spread out then and slowly walked up behind them as quietly as possible with our guns drawn. Then I said, "Put your hands up and don't move. There are many of us and only three of you. We're looking for information and that's all."

The men did as they were told. "What do you want?" one man asked.

"We are looking for a missing woman can you help us?"

"No, no," they all said simultaneously.

"I don't believe you. So let's have it," I said.

Then they hit the ground pulling out their guns and started to fire. However, we were just a little bit quicker. They were all hit. We went up to them and took their guns. Then I asked again, "Where is she? Where is my wife?" At closer look at them, they matched some of the descriptions of the men who broke out of jail. This one was the man who came to our camp when we brought my father's horses home.

"Fine, but take me to a doctor," one of them said.

"After you speak," Michael answered.

"She's in a cabin in the woods," he said. But that was all he would say.

"I have seen you before, you were in my camp a while back. You were following us, weren't you?" I asked.

"So what of it?" the man replied.

"Have four men stay here and take the prisoners to jail in the nearest town, if they live that long," Don said.

We rode away then. They wouldn't live long anyway, considering how badly they were hit. They were no threat to us anymore.

>>><<<

As soon as I pulled the gun out of my bodice, I put the gun to his chest and fired. He didn't even have a chance to react. I didn't move. David fell on top of me and wasn't moving, but was he dead? After several minutes, I started to push him off me. Dead or alive I had to get him out of the cabin. Once I got him off, and got to my feet, I was shaking, but I was all right. I grabbed his legs and dragged him. He was such a big man that pulling him was very difficult. I had to get him out of here!

After what seemed to be an eternity, I finally managed to get him out the door enough so I could close it. I grabbed what wood I could carry and bolted the door. I hoped those other men didn't show up again. If they did, I didn't know what they would do to me, especially if I killed David. Hopefully they wouldn't be able to break in here. Luckily there was only one door.

I decided that I needed to make a bigger fire. I knew Michael was looking for me, so he needed to see the smoke to help find me. If I ran out of wood, I would burn the chairs and anything else I had to. He must find me, especially if David was still alive.

I needed to eat something at least for the baby. I hadn't eaten since breakfast this morning. So I cooked some bacon and eggs. I ate all of it. It tasted so good. I drank some coffee and I would just sit and wait for Michael to come, which I hoped would be soon.

All the target practice Michael made me do paid off, but it didn't prepare me for how I would feel after taking a man's life. I tried to convince myself that he deserved it, but that wasn't up to me. He deserved to spend the rest of his life in jail. How was I going to deal with this guilt? I knew I shouldn't feel guilty because I was just trying to protect myself. I had never taken a life before. Maybe it would get better as time went on. He may not even be dead. Maybe he was just unconscious. But what if he was dead?

"Listen to yourself, Cheyenne. You did what you had to do." I said out loud. I wasn't proud of it, but I was glad it was finally over and maybe forever. Well, except for those other men. *Oh, Michael I hope you show up first before those men come looking for David. If they show up first and find him dead...* Oh, I couldn't think about it.

I just had to think about what I had in my life and realize how lucky I was. Maybe then I could put it all behind me. Oh, I just hoped Michael showed up soon. It was getting dark out there. I hoped he could see the smoke in the dark.

>>><<<

"Mike!" Roy called out. "Look, I see the smoke! It's coming from over here." All the men gathered together.

"All right, is everyone ready? Remember, it could just be David or five of them. Be on your guard," I told them.

About fifteen minutes later, we came closer. We went very slowly so we could watch for anyone on guard. Then I saw it. I saw the smoke as it appeared through the trees just a little. And there was a cabin! It was just a small cabin, and it was difficult to see, but it was there. My heart started pounding very hard and my breathing increased. I pulled out my riffle. "Can you see anyone?" I asked quietly.

"No, not a soul," Daniel and Roy said.

"All right, Mike, are you ready?" Don asked.

"Let's do this!" I said.

The cabin was in plain sight now, but we saw no one around. Then we saw him, a big man, just lying on the ground outside the door. Why would he be sleeping in front of the door? Guarding the door was the only explanation. We rode up on him. I jumped from my horse and, holding my rifle, went up to him. I pulled him up.

"He's dead!" I said. "Don and Roy, could you dispose of this buzzard meat, anywhere will do." Then I tried the cabin door but couldn't open it. Something was in the way of the door.

>>><<<

That was Michael I heard! I unbolted the door and opened it, and I saw that it was Michael. "Michael!" I yelled and flew into his arms. I began to cry out of pure joy and relief. Michael held me tight.

"Now that's what I call a warm embrace, Cheyenne," he said. I just squeezed him harder. "How did you know it was me and not someone else?" he said.

"I heard you ride up so I put my head to the door so I could hear. Then I heard you tell the boys that David was dead. I'd know your voice anywhere."

He then put me down and looked at me. He was furious at what he saw. "Are you all right? He hurt you pretty badly. Is there anyone else around here?"

"Yes, I'm fine. No, no one at all. Well, at least not now. There were three earlier. I was so scared they would show up here before you did. If they had and saw David, I don't know what would have happened."

"Don't worry about them, we took care of them. It's too dark in these woods to head home tonight. Would you be comfortable staying here for tonight?" he asked.

"I will be fine as long as you're with me," I replied.

"The boys can camp outside."

"All right," I said, "are you hungry? I can fix you some supper."

"Yes, we all are. It's been a long ride to find you," he said. "Are you sure you will be all right staying in the cabin?"

"Yes, you're here and there are men all around to protect me," I said with a giggle.

As I cooked them all something to eat, I told Michael about David. He was pleased that I wasn't harmed worse and that by practicing shooting a gun may have saved my life.

CHAPTER 44

By the time we got into town, it was almost dinnertime. Michael decided we would eat at the café before picking up Sally, Joshua, and Lucy. Everyone was so happy to see me safe. I was bruised, had cuts on my face, and my ribs were killing me, but otherwise I was fine. Rainie was so happy to see me safe that she gave me a free supper. I had asked Roy to go get Sally and the children for me. I missed my babies so much and thought I may never see them again. I just had to hold them.

When Sally, Joshua and Lucy walked in, I ran to hug them, even though it was painful. Then I took Lucy and just cuddled her and then I cuddled Joshua. I gave Joshua to his father. We sat down to eat. "You haven't eaten dinner yet, have you?" Michael asked Sally.

"Yes, but I will have dessert and coffee," she replied. I held Lucy while I ate. Michael had Joshua and I kissed him again.

"How did you feed Joshua while I was gone?" I asked.

"Rainie was still nursing her son, so she offered to feed Joshua as well," she said.

"Wonderful! I'm going to have to thank her!"

As soon as we finished eating, and I thanked Rainie for the dinner and for feeding my baby and told her that I couldn't be more grateful to her. She then hugged me and said that it was her pleasure.

After we got home, Michael went for the doctor. He said that he wanted my ribs looked at. After feeding Joshua, I put him to bed. I came into the kitchen and made coffee. By then, Michael was back with the doctor. "Sorry it took so long but the doctor was busy with Johnny, Billy and Kathryn's son," Michael said.

"It's all right, it gave me time to feed Joshua and put him and Lucy to bed," I said.

After the examination, Doctor Kiley said I probably had two broken ribs. He wrapped them and told me that he wanted me on bed rest for a few days to give them time to heal. We sat in the kitchen with Sally for a little while, drinking coffee and talking. I briefly told her of my kidnapping and how I killed David.

"I'm so glad it wasn't worse. With David dead, you won't have to worry about him anymore," Sally said.

"And with his brother Denny being hanged to death and his friend Damian dead too, we don't have to worry about them harming you again either. The other three are either on their way to the nearest jail or dead as well. Either way, they can't hurt you now," Michael said.

"Yes, but I killed a man. I feel terrible about that," I said solemnly.

"Honey, you did what you had to do to survive. It will get better, I promise you. So don't worry so much over it now, all right? It's getting late. I think we should say good night. You've had a rough two days, Cheyenne. Besides, the doctor said you are to be in bed," Michael replied.

"Yes, love. Goodnight, Sally, and thank you," I said.

"Good night to you both." With that, Michael and I left for our room.

I walked over to check on the children. They were sleeping peacefully. I changed into my nightgown and climbed into bed. Michael was waiting for me with his arms open. I cuddled up next to him and put my head on his chest. He folded his arms around me. There was nothing more precious than this and the lives of those we loved. I was grateful to be alive to count all my blessings. "Good night, my love. I love you!" I said.

"Good night, honey. I love you!" he replied.

Yes, I was truly blessed, indeed.

EPILOGUE

I woke to a beautiful, warm, sunny morning. What a wonderful day we had yesterday. I couldn't believe we had been married ten years already. It seemed like we just got married. The years had just flown by so quickly.

Michael and I shared gifts. He got me a gorgeous pale green dress with a matching shawl. I made him a new light blue shirt and dark blue vest to go with it and bought him a new bolo tie, which he loved.

We celebrated even into the early morning hours. Our sweet passion exploded in positively sheer ecstasy. It was a splendid night indeed!

"Good morning, honey!" Michael said.

"Good morning, my love!"

"How do you feel today, honey?" he asked.

"I feel wonderful. How are you?" I replied.

"The same, the children are up except for the babies."

"They'll be up soon enough. Is breakfast over?"

"No, it's just now ready. I was about to come wake you to eat. The children are overly anxious to eat this morning for some reason," he said, chuckling.

"Oh, Michael, can you believe it's been ten years already?"

He sat on the bed and put his loving arms around me. "No, honey, I can't believe it either," he said. "What a wonderful ten years though. Let's go eat before it gets cold."

We went into the kitchen and there was Sarah, our housekeeper for the past eight years, setting the table. Sally married Dean, who was Melanie's cousin. Three of our six children were already sitting at the table: Lucy, nine years old with black hair and brilliant blue eyes, Joshua, eight years old with black hair and dark blue eyes, Dominic, six years old with strawberry blonde hair and dark blue eyes. Marlene, three years old with blonde hair and light blue eyes, was running around so Michael had to catch her. Our babies, who were only three months old and identical twins, were Josiah and Jolene, both of them with blonde hair and brilliant blue eyes. As I was holding Jolene, Josiah was sleeping in his cradle. What a handful we had.

"Our Anniversary party is at one. We'll be eating dinner there and supper as well. So eat well now so you have full bellies until one o'clock. Sarah, are all the pies ready?" I asked.

"Yes, they're all packed up now. I hope eight pies will be enough. Almost the whole town is coming, so I hope there's enough food," Sarah replied.

"I need to pack up extra outfits for the children after breakfast," I said.

"I'll help with that," she said.

"Good, then I can get my bath quicker and soak a while."

After breakfast and after the kids were cleaned up and the clothes packed, I finally got into a hot tub. Michael would keep the children occupied so I had some peace. As I leaned back to relax, I thought about how much had changed. I went from a horrible abusive life to one of great joy and peace. It was most definitely a dream come true, and one that I never thought would come true for me.

I had a wonderful, loving husband, six beautiful children, and a nice house. Lucy and Marlene had a big bedroom, the one that used to be ours. The two boys were sharing the big room across the hall from the girls. Sarah had the same room as Sally, and the two bedrooms in front of our room, were Josiah's and Jolene's rooms.

We sold my parents house and land. It was good to know that I inherited it, and because I married Michael, we got the deed to sell it. I missed that house, but I loved my home. We gave Aunt Janet some of the money from the sale.

Whisper, my first mustang, died five years ago. Michael had given me one of the new breed of horses. Her name was Willow, and she was such a beauty. Michael named his new crossbreed Dusty, and both of them were such fast and beautiful horses. It still amazed me how they bred so well, Morgans and Arabians.

"Hey, honey, if you want to make the party in time, you might want to hurry," Michael said.

"Oh, is it that late already?"

"Just about."

"All right, I'm coming."

We were on the way to the party now, and I couldn't help but notice what a beautiful day it was. Hopefully it wouldn't rain today. It was a bit warm, but not too hot, with a cool west wind, and not a cloud in the sky.

Michael looked so handsome today. He was wearing his new vest, shirt, and tie with a deep, dark, blue pair of pants that I bought for him. I was wearing a glamorous, cherry red satin gown and matching shawl, which we had especially ordered and made. The children were all in their Sunday best.

"Oh, Gerri, it's an outstanding anniversary party!" I said.

"Yes, it turned out fantastic. Everyone is here. Plus we have a surprise for you. Now, if you'll just be good enough to sit down over here and close your eyes." So I did as she requested. "All right, open your eyes," Gerri said.

When I did, I saw Mrs. Anna Taylor, Sheriff Mason, and Tami Marcus. I jumped up to hug them all. "How wonderful, you're here! I've missed you! Thank you for coming to see us, it's been too long," I said with tears in my eyes. I looked at Gerri and thanked her for making this possible.

"It's great to see you too, dear. We're all happy to be here for such a splendid occasion," Anna replied.

Tami walked over to me and, I noticed, with a man on her side. "Cheyenne and Michael, I'd like you to meet my husband, Jordan Swanson. He's a rancher back home," Tami said.

"How do you do, Mr. Swanson," I said. Michael shook hands with him and they nodded to each other.

"Please call me, Jordan," he told us.

"Sure thing," Michael replied.

"It's so terrific that you got married, Tami. How long have you been married?" I asked.

"Five years now," she said.

"Congratulations to both of you! I'm so happy for you, Tami!" And then we sat and talked for a little while. "Do you have children?"

"Yes, we have two, Jacob and Emily."

"So then, where are the children?"

"They're over there playing with Jordan's sister's children. I'll bring them over soon."

"That would be fun for my children to meet them."

"I can't believe it's been that long already, ten years! I remember your wedding as if it were only yesterday."

"Yes, I can't either. Time has just slipped away," I said as I looked around the barn. "Isn't it beautiful here?"

"Yes, it is. The decorations are splendid."

The big barn that we used for socials and town meetings was decorated splendidly, as always. There were streamers, ribbons and bows, a banner, and flowers. There was a ton of food too. There was just almost everything you could think of. There were only six other pies there so I didn't know if they would be enough. Then again, there was the cake. Music sweetened the air, and I could see people eating, talking, and dancing. It was a spectacular day.

Michael then came to me and asked me to dance. We danced and danced until we were both feeling giddy.

After the third dance, someone came over to me. And to my surprise, it was my Aunt Janet! I couldn't believe my eyes. She came with Derrick, her youngest son. Aunt Janet remarried and this time, to a wonderful, honest, and kind man. His name was Robert. Oh, how great it was that they came.

"Oh, Aunt Janet, I'm so happy to see you," I said.

"Oh, honey, it's good to see you too. Happy Anniversary! The children are growing fast. Let me see that baby." She took the baby from my arms and held him up so she could take a good look at him. "My, but he is handsome! He'll grow up to be as big as his daddy. He's still so little, but he's broad-shouldered already. He has his features as well. Where's his twin sister?"

"Thank you, and yes, he is. Melanie has her," I said. "How is Kerri? I wish she were here."

"She's fine. She's too far along in her pregnancy to come, but she sends her love and will come see you next summer. She asked me to give you this letter." We sat and talked for about an hour before Michael whisked me away again.

"Oh, Michael, I couldn't ask for a better day!" I said. He chuckled and swung me around the dance floor.

"Thank you for becoming my wife, Cheyenne," he said.

"Thank you for rescuing me so I could marry you." I laughed as I spoke. Michael swirled me around as we continued our dance.

I had everything I could possibly want The only good thing that came out of my past horrible life was the fact that I learned how to appreciate all that I had and to love them with all sincerity, kindness, and unconditionally!